Striking Gold

Romancing the Californian Cowboys

Book 2

S M SPENCER

Cover design by BookPOD

Cover images by iStockphoto

eISBN: 978-1-922270-29-0

ISBN: 978-1-922270-69-6 (pbk)

Related books in the Copperhead Creek Australian Romance series:

A Chance to Come True

A Chance to Get it Right

A Chance to Let Go

A Chance to Belong

A Chance for Snow

Related books in the Copperhead Creek Mystery series:

Murder at the Creek

Related books in the Romancing the Californian Cowboys series:

Discovering Gold

PROLOGUE

Early November – Masons Flat, California, base of the Sierra Nevada Mountain Range

Nick Gold sat perched on the arena's top rail, watching as his cousin Denver worked a young horse. Although interested in the progress being made with the gelding, Nick was also thinking about the offer he'd had a few weeks earlier. His good friend, Patrick, would be spending all of December and January in Ireland with family and had suggested Nick join him for at least part of the time. Nick had been itching to visit England to see where his ancestors were from, and now after listening to Patrick's tales about Ireland, the time seemed right for an overseas trip to both places. After all, he'd always figured he be married by the time he turned thirty, and starting a family shortly after, so wouldn't now the perfect time for a trip like that—before he had those commitments?

He glanced up at the threatening clouds overhead. The weatherman hadn't predicted a thunderstorm, but one certainly looked to be brewing. He started to shout to Denver to say they should call it a day when a sudden flash of lightning, followed by the loudest thunderclap he could remember hearing, nearly launched him off the rail. Grabbing the rail with both hands to regain his balance, he looked over his shoulder as his mind grappled with just how close it must have been. Now, turning back toward Denver, panic swept through him.

Denver was no longer riding across the arena at a casual trot. Instead, he lay sprawled on the ground, holding his leg by the knee. The horse stood a short distance away, covered with mud on one side, shaking, its eyes wide with terror.

Nick jumped off the rail and raced toward his cousin. 'Are you okay?'

Kneeling beside him, he could see the tormented look on Denver's face.

'My ankle ... I think it might be broken,' Denver said, looking at him with fear in his eyes. 'I heard this terrible cracking sound, and it hurts like a son-of-a-gun.'

Nick pulled out his phone and rang Travis, Denver's older brother, who had only a few minutes earlier gone inside the barn to tend to the horses they'd finished working.

Travis appeared in moments, and quickly assessed the situation. 'Help me get him into my car ... it'll be quicker for me to get him to the emergency room than to wait for an ambulance.'

~~*~~

After tending to the horses, Nick made the fifteen minute drive to the hospital in Sonora in his own car. Alex, Travis' girlfriend, arrived shortly after him, and now the three of them sat waiting to hear from the doctor to find out how bad Denver's break was.

They'd been lucky—there was an orthopaedic doctor on duty when Travis arrived at the emergency room with Denver—but the fact that Denver had been behind closed doors for over two hours didn't bode well.

Nick had never seen Travis look as worried as he did right now. He was certain that Travis, being the more responsible of the two brothers, would somehow try to take the blame for the accident even though they'd all known it was not the best day to be working those young horses with the wet ground and threatening weather.

Nick stood and gestured toward a coffee machine down the hall. 'How about I go grab us another cup of coffee?'

Alex stood, too. 'I need to find the ladies', so how about I get them on my way back?'

Travis blinked slowly, nodding his head almost imperceptibly. 'Yeah, okay.' He let out a long, slow sigh before continuing. 'I sure wish I'd insisted Denver finish up when I took the other horses in.'

Nick sat down again as Alex walked off. 'Denver knew what he was doing ... or at least he thought he did. It was just bad luck. That's life.'

Travis turned to Nick, shaking his head slowly. 'Maybe, but I still should have made him come in.'

There was no point arguing with Travis. He'd get over it in his own time. Nick tried a new subject. 'How do you think you'll do ... getting those youngsters ready to take to the penning event?'

'On my own? Assuming Denver's out of action? Not a chance.'

'And it's important, that you take them?'

Travis nodded, looking exhausted. Or was it defeat that made him look older? In a low voice he answered. 'Well, it won't be the end of the world, but it's my best chance of selling them this year. If I don't sell them, it means feeding them through winter, crossing our fingers that none of them injure themselves, and then gearing up again to sell them in spring as rising four year-olds.'

Nick frowned. He knew the reason Travis had gotten behind with the horses. Travis' daughter, Annie, had spent the summer with him, and that had taken up a lot of his time.

But it wasn't only Annie who had distracted Travis. Travis had met Alex Mason, the beautiful Australian woman who'd arrived in town a few months earlier to claim her inheritance. Alex wasn't just any woman, she was *the* woman, and between Alex and Annie, Travis hadn't focussed on the young horses anywhere near as much as he normally would have. He had started working them steadily as soon as Annie had gone back to her mother's, but by then he was running out of time.

Nick had come up for the past few weekends to give them a hand, but Nick knew they still weren't at the stage Travis wanted them—where they'd fetch top dollar. Now, with Denver out of action, Travis would have to do everything himself around the property and that wouldn't leave much time for further training. Of course, there was one solution, and Nick had been mulling it over the whole time they'd been sitting there.

Nick started to make a suggestion when a doctor walked up. He wasn't frowning, so maybe it wasn't completely bad news.

Travis stood; his face stern.

'Travis?' the doctor asked as he walked up.

'Yes, I'm Travis Gold. How is he?'

The doctor shrugged slightly, a serious look on his face. 'He's sustained a spiral fracture to his fibula. Luckily, the break is stable, but he'll be out of action for several weeks.'

'But it'll heal, right?' Travis asked, his voice full of anxiety.

The doctor's face pinched up a bit. 'Of course. He's a young man, and in good physical shape, so it shouldn't cause him long-term problems.'

'Does that mean he can come home with us now?'

'Yes. He's in a splint. And he's not to put any weight on it until I see him next week—or sooner if there are any problems. I'll probably put a cast on it when I see him, and we'll assess it further at that time.'

'Okay, doctor, I'm sure we can keep him off it,' Travis answered unconvincingly.

The doctor squinted slightly. 'Please do.'

'And once he's got the cast on it?' Travis asked.

The doctor blinked a few times before answering. 'With this type of injury it's generally about six weeks before we want the patient putting much weight on the leg. After that he can gradually commence light exercise, but I wouldn't call riding young horses light exercise. Another fall could put him right back to square one.'

Nick had stayed silent the whole time, but when Travis didn't comment he turned to the doctor. 'Thanks doc, for looking after him.'

The doctor turned to Nick and raised a brow. 'Nurse Stevens will bring him out shortly. We'll be sending him home with some crutches and a prescription for some pain medication. Here's my card. Make an appointment with my office. And please, keep him off horses.'

Alex returned a moment later without the coffee. When Travis sat back down with a thud, she sat next to him and took his hand.

Nick let Travis take a few deep breaths, and then turned to him. 'You know, I'm wrapping up the project I've been working on for the last eighteen months, and I've been seriously considering taking some time off to travel overseas. If you want me to, I could come up and stay with you guys—give you a hand with the horses or whatever else needs doing around the place until Denver's able to get back to work. I can go overseas after that.'

Alex peeked around Travis and met Nick's gaze, a warm smile removing some of the worry from her face.

When Travis turned to him, his deep frown started to ease for the first time in hours. 'Seriously? You'd do that?'

The relief in Travis' voice settled it. 'Of course I would. It'll be great being a ranch hand once again. Besides, it'll give me a chance to work out an itinerary and organise visas—you know, all the travel stuff. In fact, the more I think about it, the more I'm looking forward to it.'

When Nick winked, Travis finally cracked a smile.

'That's so much more than I could ever ask you to do.'

'You aren't asking. I'm offering.'

Travis sat up, threw his arm around Alex's shoulders, and let out a long sigh. 'You wouldn't believe what sort of load that takes off my mind.'

Alex gave Nick a look that said *'thank you'*, then turned toward Travis, her smile giving away how much she loved him. 'And if you think it'll help, I can come over to stay until Denver's a bit more mobile ... so you won't have to pop into the house checking on him all the time.'

Nick could feel the smile creeping onto his own face. He'd speak to his boss about the situation on Monday and, one way or another, he was sure he could be out of there by the end of the week.

CHAPTER 1

Late November – Over the Pacific Ocean

Casey Mason turned to her twin, Taylor, watching as she softly snored in the seat beside her. She envied her sister's ability to have slept for most of the flight, while she had watched something like a dozen movies. Physically they were quite similar—in fact, she shared similar physical features with both her sisters; all tall, with auburn hair and green eyes flecked with gold—although Casey had chopped off her own locks years earlier. But Taylor's ability to sleep through just about any disturbance was something Casey definitely envied.

She returned to looking out the window as the plane began its descent into San Francisco International Airport. It was only a few days before Thanksgiving, technically winter, so they'd expected a rough flight, yet the whole way across the Pacific from Australia the flight had been perfect. Now, approaching California, the sun shone brightly in a cloudless blue sky.

'I can't believe we're actually here,' Taylor said in Casey's ear, startling her.

Casey turned, bumping into her sister's head, not realising Taylor had leant across to look out the window.

'Good morning; again,' Casey said with a wink as she rubbed her head.

Taylor smiled, straightening up and doing a huge stretch. 'Did I nod off again after breakfast?'

'Clearly,' Casey said with a touch of envy in her voice. 'Can you believe it's been almost eighteen years since we were here? And yet, somehow, I'm sure I remember this exact same view when we landed last time.'

'It's so exciting ... and to think we're having five whole weeks here. That's the longest I've ever been away from work.' Taylor practically shivered with anticipation.

'It is going to be so much fun; you, me and Alex—together, just like old times,' Casey said, pulling her bag out from under the seat in front of her. She clutched the bag to her chest and supressed a yawn. She wasn't going to allow herself to be tired. Not today. Today she would embrace every minute, because something told her that life as she'd known it was about to change.

~~*~~

The sun had already disappeared behind a large cluster of trees when nearly three hours later Casey watched as Alex pulled the Range Rover off the main highway, driving past a sign that read *Welcome to Masons Flat*.

She remembered Alex telling them about the town being small, but Casey hadn't expected it to be quite this small. The main street had maybe a dozen businesses on each side, and there were only a few cars parked along the street. As Alex pulled up in front of a two-storey wooden structure, painted cream and dark green, with a verandah running all across the front of the upstairs, the word quaint came to Casey's mind.

Alex turned to her sisters. 'I thought you might like a quick walk around town before we go home—just to orient yourselves.'

Casey felt a brow rise before she had a chance to stop it. 'Yeah, quick being the operative word. There isn't much here, is there?'

Alex shrugged. 'I told you what it was like. Remember?'

The three got out and stretched their legs, breathing in the fresh mountain air.

'Smells like Christmas—must be all the pine trees,' Casey said as a waft of nostalgia washed over her as she recalled the Christmas they'd spent with their father in California when they were young teens.

'Yes, I sometimes think that, too,' Alex said, a warm smile spreading across her face. She pointed to the building they'd parked in front of. 'So, this is our hotel. We'll have dinner here tonight, if that's okay with you?'

Casey and Taylor both nodded and spoke in unison. 'Sure.'

'Great. We can have a good look at all the shops tomorrow, but for now I just wanted you to see a little bit of the town while there is still some daylight. Do you want to go for a quick walk?'

As they began to make their way down the street, Alex continued. 'These next five shops along here are ours—the antique store, the lolly shop, my little fruit & veggie shop, the western-wear shop, and the most recent addition, the salon. They do both hair and nails there, if you're interested.'

As they slowly made their way along the wooden walkway, it was as if they'd stepped back in time—reminding Casey of walking down the streets of Sovereign Hill, the open-air gold mining museum back home.

When they got to the end of the shops, they crossed the street and made their way back toward the car.

'And on this side of the street, we've got our saloon,' Alex said as they approached the front door and had a peek inside. 'Don't suppose either of you fancy a drink?'

Casey shook her head as she looked at Taylor, who answered for both of them. 'Not right now, but maybe tomorrow night. It looks like a fun place.'

Alex called out to the woman behind the bar. 'Darleen, these are my sisters, Casey and Taylor. They've just arrived from Australia.'

The woman smiled, and waved. 'Welcome to Masons Flat—come on in, the drinks will be on the house.'

Casey and Taylor both said hello, then Alex continued. 'We might give drinks a miss tonight thanks, Darleen, but we'll come down later in the week. They'll be here for a few weeks.'

Taylor beamed as she called back. 'I'd love a game of pool and a pot of ale.'

Alex's face mirrored Casey's own surprise, so she playfully jabbed Taylor in the side with her elbow. 'A game of pool and a pot of ale?'

'What's wrong with that?' Taylor replied defensively.

'Nothing. It ... just doesn't sound like something you'd do.'

'Can't a girl do something out of the ordinary from time to time? It's something I'd *like* to do.'

Casey and Alex exchanged barely concealed smirks. 'Yeah, okay then,' Casey replied as they crossed the street and made their way back to the car.

A few minutes later they pulled up in front of the house they'd inherited from their great uncle—the house that Alex had been living in for a little over six months now.

She'd seen bits of the house via FaceTime calls with Alex, but it hadn't prepared Casey for how nice it was. Modern, and constructed from a combination of corrugated metal and masonry walls, it made the old cream-brick-veneer unit she lived in at home look dilapidated by comparison. And whereas her unit's garden was barely a postage stamp, this house had a lovely garden out the front which Casey immediately imagined herself pottering in.

As they followed Alex in through the front door, a shiver of excitement ran down Casey's spine. This wasn't just a house; it was a home. She smiled and drew in a long breath, relishing the scent of fresh lavender.

'This is my room,' Alex said, pointing to the first door on their left. 'I've been staying over with Travis and Denver while Denver recuperates, but I still want this room. You two can fight over the other two bedrooms. I swear, Uncle Steven must have had us in mind when he built this house as all three bedrooms are almost the same size, and each has a walk-in-wardrobe and en-suite.'

Casey walked ahead of her sisters, and poked her head into the next two bedrooms. They were massive compared to her bedroom at home.

'I'll take the last one, if that's okay with you Taylor,' she said looking back over her shoulder. The last bedroom, a tad smaller due to its layout, had the added benefit of windows on two sides. Casey knew she would love the natural light, and the view out to the gardens. 'The last one is definitely the right one for me.'

Alex flashed a smile when Casey turned back to her. 'So, if I come back here at ten to six will that be enough time for you to shower and get ready for dinner?'

Casey turned to Taylor, who shrugged her shoulders in agreement. 'Sounds great, Alex. Will Travis be joining us?'

'I didn't ask him this time. I thought you might both be pretty tired and just want a light meal and an early night, but I can bring him along if you want me to?'

Casey pulled a face for a moment, thinking about Travis and the description she'd heard of his younger brother, Denver. She'd certainly been looking forward to meeting Denver, but if Travis came Denver probably would too, and she'd prefer to save meeting him for when she was at her best. 'Nah, you're probably right. I wouldn't want my future brother-in-law, or his good looking brother, to see me dropping off into my soup bowl.'

Alex grinned. 'No worries. I'll see you soon.'

~~*~~

Casey recognised Travis the moment they walked into the dining room. She'd met him four months earlier, when he'd arrived in Melbourne to chase down her recalcitrant sister. She nudged Alex. 'Thought you said he wasn't invited?'

Alex grinned, shaking her head slowly. 'I didn't invite him. It's either a coincidence or he worked out that we'd be likely to come here.'

Casey watched as Travis cleared the distance between them in a few long strides, threw his arm around Alex and pulled her in close to kiss her cheek. Then he turned to address Casey and Taylor.

'Welcome to Masons Flat! I figured you'd end up here tonight, so I thought we'd eat here on the chance we might get to be an unofficial welcoming committee. Why don't you join us? We'll pull another table up.'

'Is that okay with you guys?' Alex asked, smiling at Casey. 'I know you're pretty tired.'

Although Casey was weary, Taylor's expression suggested she was pleased with the situation, so Casey nodded. 'Sure, that'll be nice.'

Travis led them to the other side of the room, and as they reached the table one of the two men stood and came around to greet them. The other just gave them an apologetic grin. Even if it weren't for the fact that he didn't stand, she'd have known Denver—with his dark hair and eyes, there was no mistaking him as Travis' brother. The other man she didn't know. Fair, with straw-coloured hair and cobalt-blue eyes, he didn't look to be related. He was dressed in jeans, a western belt, a long-sleeved-checked cotton shirt and boots, all of which suggested he was a cowboy. She raised an eyebrow questioningly as he approached, remembering how excited she'd been at the prospect of meeting some cowboys. She hoped it was just her exhaustion tempering that enthusiasm.

Travis swept his hand across in front of him, pointing toward the seated man. 'Over there, that's my brother, Denver. And this other good looking bloke here is my cousin, Nick, who's come up from Sacramento to give us a hand. These are Alex's sisters, Casey and Taylor.'

Casey turned to Travis in surprise. 'Alex teaching you to speak like an Aussie, is she?'

Travis flashed a crooked smile. 'What do you mean?'

'Bloke?'

He winked toward Alex, and then flashed another crooked smile. 'Guess I'm picking up the odd expression here and there.'

Casey grinned at Travis. She liked him a lot, and looked forward to calling him her brother-in-law. As for his brother and cousin, they would have to prove themselves before she decided.

Travis and Nick pulled another table up, and Casey took the seat nearest to Alex and Denver, while Taylor sat at the other end across from Travis and closer to Nick.

They chatted as they looked through the menus, and then, as the dining room was quite warm, Casey took off her jacket and hung it on the back of her chair. As she turned back to the table she caught a glimpse of Nick's face. She'd seen that look before when people spotted her tatts for the first time—a mixture of barely concealed disgust and irritation. She cocked her head, and glared, daring him to say something as she prepared herself with an appropriately clipped reply.

Alex must have noticed the silent exchange as she quickly jumped in. 'Taylor is Australia's best baker, in my humble opinion, and if you're lucky, guys, maybe she'll even give me some pointers while she's here. And Casey—Casey knows more about flowers than anyone I've ever met. She's a florist. It wasn't long after she started working in the industry she began getting these gorgeous tattoos. Aren't they lovely? Each one has a story, and although there are far too many to hear about all of them tonight, maybe Casey could tell us about this flower on her forearm?'

Casey flashed Alex a smile as she turned her right arm so that they could all see it. 'Funny you'd pick that one to start—it's one of my favourites.'

She stared at Nick as she turned her arm his way. 'It's the oleander flower. The name oleander comes from the fact that it resembles the olive—olea—but it's nothing like the olive. In fact, ingesting the leaf or berries can be toxic. Delicate, isn't it? But its literal meaning is caution, given the plant's toxicity. I chose it as a reminder that although I may appear delicate, I'm also strong and can be rather unforgiving. It serves as a warning that people shouldn't betray me.'

Nick lifted a brow as he stared right back at Casey. 'Caution, eh? Well, perhaps the caution should have come from the person who did the tattoo—to remind you that tattoos are permanent, and that while you may think they're trendy now you might not think so when you're older.'

Travis shook his head. 'Lighten up, Nick. Lots of people have tattoos these days.'

'Not the people I hang out with,' Nick replied turning to Travis.

'Well, *perhaps* you need to broaden your circle of friends then,' Travis said, his voice warning Nick to shut up.

Nick shook his head, keeping quiet now, but Casey wasn't ready to drop it yet. 'Oh, I won't ever regret my tattoos, but thanks for your *concern*.'

Scooting back in her chair she turned toward Denver. She'd let Taylor chat to Nick. Taylor dealt with idiots all the time, working in retail as she did, so she'd be used to it.

She looked up at Denver and flashed him a warm smile. 'So, how much longer will you be in the cast?'

Everyone at the table seemed to breathe a collective sigh of relief. Or maybe it was just Denver. He gave her what she'd class as a brotherly smile before answering. 'Not long, with a bit of luck. I've got an appointment next week, and if all is well it's coming off soon. Then I can start some physio and hopefully get back to work sooner rather than later. I've been going a bit stir-crazy.'

~~*~~

Nick tried to look interested, but he found it hard to stay focused on Taylor's chatter about food and the Thanksgiving Day parade. Normally the level of excitement she projected would have been contagious, but right now his eyes were continually drawn to Casey at the other end of the table.

At first glance, Taylor was definitely the catch of the two sisters. She was a slightly plumper version of Alex, and he'd always thought Alex a stunner. There was something quite appealing about her mountain of rich rust-coloured hair which fell mid-way down her back, even though he generally went for blondes. And then there was her meticulously applied makeup and her feminine outfit. She was probably not entirely dissimilar to the sort of woman he'd always figured he'd marry someday—one who liked to cook and would probably make a wonderful mother.

And yet, something about Casey intrigued him. He did wonder if it stemmed from his desire to shake some common sense into her—why would anyone want to cover themselves with tattoos?—but suspected there was more to it than that. Everything about her seemed to challenge him—from her short cropped hair, to the multiple earrings on each ear, and to the lack of makeup which made her look as if she'd just stepped out of the shower. And then there was the way she'd cocked her head defiantly, jutting out her jaw even before he'd said anything to her.

Something about Casey brought out the combative side of him—he was certain that was what had compelled him to comment on her tattoos the way he had. Sure, he didn't care for them much, but why should it matter whether she had tattoos or not? He wished she hadn't chosen to sit at the other end of the table, as he would have enjoyed a sparring match with her.

A light touch on his forearm brought his attention back to Taylor.

'I haven't had real American pumpkin pie since we were here for Christmas many years ago. I hope they have it tonight,' Taylor said as her eyes scanned the dessert section of the menu. 'It just says pie of the day. Surely, this time of year, it'd be pumpkin though, wouldn't you think?'

Nick blinked a couple of times as he focused on her question. 'Yeah, I suppose; but then again I really don't know.' He'd chosen his response carefully, because if it had been Denver asking, he'd have said what he really thought—that he didn't care.

'I hope so. What's good here? I might just have an entrée, so I can save room for dessert.'

Nick nodded. 'I usually have a steak and baked potato. They're always good here.'

Taylor dipped her head and looked up at him through her lashes. 'Well, you haven't tried my slow-cooked lamb shanks, smothered in red wine gravy served over mashed sweet potato. Bet I can tempt you with a few things besides steak, but for tonight that does sound good.'

Nick scanned the group, and it seemed everyone had decided what they'd eat. Nervous energy coursed through him so he pushed back his chair and stood. 'I'll go grab Sam to take our order.'

Taylor smiled, and Denver, Travis and Alex all caught his eye and gestured that they were ready. Casey didn't even look up, continuing her conversation with Denver.

The inner teenager in him momentarily considered bumping into Casey's chair as he walked past—just hard enough to cause her to look up and at least acknowledge his presence—but instead, he simply went to get Sam.

~~*~~

As soon as they were safely in Alex's car and out of earshot from the men, Alex swung around in her seat. 'What did you think of Travis' family? They're nice, right?'

Casey decided to let Taylor answer.

'I couldn't imagine you marrying into a nicer family. I barely got to speak to Denver tonight, but Nick is gorgeous ... and such a good listener. And Travis ... he's even nicer than I remembered. You're so lucky, Alex.'

Casey held back the smart comment that crossed her mind. Taylor could talk the ear off a dead man, if truth be told, so who knew if Nick was actually a *good listener*.

'What about you, Casey? Have they passed inspection?' Alex's eyes grew wide in mock fear.

Casey turned to Alex, weighing her words carefully. 'Yeah, of course, they were all really nice. Denver's got a great sense of humour, and so does Travis when you get him going.'

'And what about Nick?'

'Nick? Mister "you're going to regret your tattoos" ... you mean him?'

'Yes, well, I don't know what that was about. I see almost as many tattoos on the girls here as I do at home, but maybe it's not the "done thing" in his circle of friends.'

'Whatever. I'm just glad you seemed to enjoy chatting to him, Taylor, as it kept me from putting my foot in my mouth. I tell you what though, I am tired. Bet I'll sleep well with a full belly and a soft bed.'

Alex grinned and started the car. Within a few minutes, they were home and Casey sat alone in her room. She pulled out her phone and quickly checked her emails, then checked the time in Melbourne. Any wonder she could barely keep her eyes open—it had now been over thirty hours since she'd woken to get ready for the flight. Maybe after a good night's sleep she'd forget about Nick's rude comments, but right now, she struggled to get his smug-looking face off her mind.

CHAPTER 2

Casey was up early and ready to go when Alex arrived to take her and Taylor into town to have a better look around. It was only a few minutes into town, and after a brief drive up and down Main Street, Alex parked in front of her fruit and veggie shop. After a quick look at the produce on offer, Taylor headed next door to the western wear shop, while Casey remained to have a better look at the shop.

Alex had opened the shop less than six months earlier, but it fit in so well with the surrounding shops one would be forgiven for assuming it had always been there.

'I love your shop, Alex. Has it been trading well?'

'Absolutely, but the main thing is I'm having a ball. It's been a great way to get to know everyone in and around town, and for them to get to know me. And with word having spread about my tennis coaching, it gives parents an easy way to find me to have a casual chat about that as well.'

'And I suppose if you get too busy with the coaching you can hire someone to look after it.'

'Oh, I've already done that. I have a part-timer, Paula, who comes in most days. She's more than happy to work whenever I need her—like when I'm coaching—and is hoping to get more hours.'

When a customer came in, Casey wandered to the back of the shop and stood in a large cleared area out of the way until Alex finished serving the woman. Then she called Alex over. 'What's this area for?'

'I thought it would be good to allow room for expansion. And also, when I get a special price on something, I set up temporary tables. Do you think it looks odd having the empty floor space?'

Casey tilted her head in thought. 'Not really—but it does make me wonder about other products that you could sell from the shop.'

Alex shrugged. 'I was thinking that the other day—trying to decide what might compliment the fruit and vegetables. I might speak to some local honey producers, for a start.'

'And of course flowers came to mind straight away, too, right?' Casey said with a cheeky grin.

Alex tilted her head questioningly. 'Flowers? No, it never occurred to me, but I'll give it some thought. I mean, I'm not sure what sort of demand there would be ...'

'Well, perhaps some small pots then? Petunias look lovely in hanging pots, as do impatiens, geraniums, begonias, pansies, sweet alyssum and lots of others. Do you want me to look into sourcing some for you? I bet they'd be popular around Mother's Day and Valentine's Day for instance, and they're always great for birthday presents year round.'

'That's a great idea, Casey.'

They both turned to the door as Taylor flew into the shop. 'Casey, come quickly, you're gonna love these boots they've got. With a pair of skinny jeans and that heavy cable-knit jumper of yours, it would be such a cute outfit.'

'Me? In cowboy boots?'

'Yes, you in cowboy boots. Come on, have a look. I bet you'll love them.'

Alex laughed at the pair, shaking her head. 'Are you both good to wander around town until mid-day? If not, you could always walk back. It isn't that far.'

Casey checked the time—at only quarter past ten she couldn't imagine the town would hold enough interest for her to hang around for almost two more hours. 'Give us your house key. If we aren't here at twelve it'll mean we decided to walk back.'

Alex handed over the key, along with a couple of twenties. 'Why don't you get a couple of copies made over at the hardware store? That way you can both have one while you're here. No reason for us to be joined at the hip the whole time.'

'Great idea, but I don't think they'll cost that much, will they?'

Alex shrugged. 'Probably not, but you might want to check out the ice-cream shop afterwards—my treat.'

Casey laughed, but Taylor's eyes lit up. 'Perfect; boots first, then ice-cream.'

Less than an hour later, Casey had bought not only the boots but also a pair of skinny stretch jeans that were the most comfortable she'd ever tried on. She hoped she wouldn't suffer buyer's remorse when it came to the boots, though.

'Now for ice-creams?' Taylor asked, a smile brightening her face even further.

'Not for me, but you go ahead. I'll go get the keys made and meet you back here afterwards. It shouldn't take too long.'

As Casey headed across the street, her heart began to thump. A man wearing a cowboy hat, and dressed in jeans, a checked cotton shirt and boots, walked into the hardware store. She'd only seen him in profile, and for just a few seconds, but she couldn't help but wonder if it was Nick. She stopped at the front door, took a deep breath, and told herself to grow up. So what if it was him? It wasn't as if she could avoid him for the next five weeks or anything; and besides, so what if he didn't like her tatts. She pushed her sleeves up, exposing both forearms, and went in.

Immediately to her left she spotted the counter with the keys, so she walked over and stood in front of the counter.

'Hi, I'm Beth. How can I help you?'

'Can I get two copies of this key, thanks?'

'Absolutely,' Beth said before turning and starting up the cutting machine.

As she waited for the keys, she glanced around the store. There were a lot of aisles—he could have gone down any of them.

'Excuse me,' Beth said, clearing her throat. 'Your keys? That'll be nine dollars and eighty cents.'

'Oh, thanks. It's a bigger store than I thought,' Casey said as she handed over twenty dollars in exchange for the keys.

The girl shrugged, and took her money. 'You're new here, right? And you have an accent—where are you from?'

Casey grinned with pride. 'Australia. My sister and I are here to visit our older sister.'

The girl nodded slowly as she handed Casey her change. 'Cool. Australia. Kangaroos and koalas. That's all I know about it, but it would be fun to go there some day.'

'You should. It's a nice place. And the exchange rate is in your favour, so it's not expensive other than the airfare.'

'Maybe. If I can save enough money. But that'll mean getting a better job than this part-time one.'

'Yes, I suppose so,' Casey replied, deciding Beth couldn't be much more than sixteen.

With one last glance around, she said goodbye, then left without spotting the man again.

She found Taylor, waiting for her outside the ice-cream shop while finishing her cone. Casey strolled along with her for a few more minutes, but wasn't in the mood to go inside any of the shops.

'Are you ready to walk back with me?' she asked as she handed one of the keys to Taylor.

Taylor scrunched up her face. 'No, I think I'll hang around and wait for Alex. I want to try on a few things I spotted earlier and check out the jewellery store and the saloon too.'

'Okay then. I'll see you guys a bit later.'

Twenty minutes later, Casey sat at the kitchen table drinking a cup of tea. She'd slept well in her new room but wondered if tonight, since it would be dark by five o'clock, she'd drop off just after dinner.

When she finished her tea, she decided to investigate the house. First, she headed to the front for a good look at the formal living room. She loved that it had an open fireplace, and wondered if it would be cold enough to use it while they were there. The furniture had to have been chosen by a man, but the heavy black leather sofa and chairs, and the dark, possibly mahogany, coffee table and side tables, suited the room.

Next, she did a thorough investigation of the combined kitchen, dining and family room. The large open space, delineated only by the placement of the furniture, was not what she'd have designed, but it worked. And it certainly got plenty of sunshine, what with the large windows all down one side.

Lastly, she moved on to the study. Here she found a large desk facing a picture window, affording a lovely view across to parkland—the perfect place for sitting and contemplating life. She sat at the desk and stared out the window, wondering what it must have been like for this great uncle of theirs, rattling around in this huge home, all by himself. Could Alex be right? Had he designed the home with his three great-nieces in mind? Its large study would easily fit at least one, if not two, more desks into the room if, for example, she and or Taylor were to decide to stay.

She chuckled at the thought, knowing full well Taylor wouldn't be leaving Melbourne. Just before they'd left on this trip, Taylor had made an offer to buy a half share in the bakery where she worked. Taylor loved the bakery, loved its location, had built up a dedicated following, and got along with all the staff. While the offer was only verbal at this stage, Casey knew it was genuine.

But it wasn't just Taylor who Casey could never see living in Masons Flat.

She got why Alex liked the small town. Between her tennis coaching and the produce store business she'd set up—not to mention a tall, dark and handsome cowboy who was madly in love with her—there wasn't any wonder why Alex wanted to stay.

But that was Alex, not her. Casey was certain she'd die of boredom in such a small town.

So basically, she was doomed to miss one of her sisters unless she pretended to be like those ultra-rich people, going from summer to summer jetting back and forth between two countries. She could spend summer and autumn here with Alex, and then back in Melbourne for summer and autumn with Taylor. That could solve the problem of missing a sister, but even though she'd inherited a fair amount of money, it wouldn't last long with that sort of behaviour.

Besides, in solving one problem, wouldn't she simply create all kinds of others?

Like, how would she ever find a long-term partner if she was flitting back and forth across the globe every six months? She'd always dreamt of having a loving relationship with the right man, and it was hard enough to find that man staying put. She closed her eyes, remembering the look on Travis' face when he'd spotted Alex walking into the hotel dining room the night before. He'd immediately come over and thrown his arm around Alex's shoulders, adoration clearly written all over his face. He worshiped Alex and didn't mind everyone knowing. Casey had never seen a man direct that look toward her. The likelihood of her finding a man like Travis was slim enough as it was, and would diminish further if she didn't stay put somewhere.

And then there was her job. Maree was the best boss she could imagine, and over the past six months had dropped more than a few hints about Casey becoming more than just an employee. It had started as a part-time job, but wouldn't she like it to become a real career?

Taking time off for a Christmas holiday was one thing, but Maree would have to replace her if she wasn't living in Melbourne full-time.

She drew in a long breath, and let it out slowly. This was way too hard. She'd have to think about it later as this clearly wasn't something she could solve right now. She had to focus on something else.

Like the interesting desk in front of her—their desk.

She opened the various drawers, finding mostly files to do with the house and the businesses, but on the left was a drinks cupboard. Here there were several bottles of whiskey and some glasses. She chuckled at the thought of Alex sitting here sipping whiskey. That was so not Alex. They had to have been her uncle's.

Lastly, she pulled open the small drawer under the writing surface. It held a collection of pens and pencils, a metal box full of paperclips, another full of rubber bands, and a stapler and staple-remover. She rolled one of the pens around in her hand as she gazed out the window again, wondering how often her uncle might have sat here doing the exact same thing.

She put the pen back into the drawer, and that's when it occurred to her that the drawer hadn't pulled all the way out. She ducked her head down and looked inside, wondering if something might be jamming it from pulling out further.

She reached in to feel the back of the drawer, but there was nothing else there. It just wasn't terribly deep. And that led her to wonder, why wouldn't the maker have given that drawer as much depth as possible?

Suddenly she recalled a writing desk she'd seen at an antique market. The shop assistant had revealed a number of secret drawers that the desk concealed, and it made her wonder if that might be the case with this one.

She pushed the drawer back in as far as it would go, then pulled the chair out and climbed under the desk to see if indeed there was a gap behind the back of the drawer and the modesty panel. There wasn't. The wood was solid from the front of the desk to the back. So why wasn't the drawer as deep as the desk?

Her curiosity piqued, she got back into the chair and again pulled the drawer out as far as it would come. Then she lifted it slightly and pulled again, and this time it slid all the way out, revealing a base upon which it had rested.

She set the drawer down on the top of the desk, inspecting it carefully. There was nothing unusual about it. Then she felt around inside the space where the drawer had been. Disappointingly, there were no levers or handles. The desk she'd seen at the market contained thin strips of wood attached to its hidden drawers allowing them to be easily pulled out once discovered. On this desk, she could see nothing of the sort.

Convinced there had to be something there, she reached back as far as she could and ran her hand along the back surface of the space, hoping to discover a small handle, but still, there was nothing there. Trying one last time, she placed her fingertips on the surface, and slowly dragged her hand along from the right to the left. About three-quarters of the way along she felt something—with her index finger she detected a small indentation.

Remembering a flashlight she'd spotted in the pantry, she dashed to the kitchen. Sure enough, the flashlight's beam showed her what she'd felt—a tiny hole in the back panel. Certain this had to be the catch, she tried to put her finger into the hole, but it wasn't even big enough to allow her fingernail, let alone a whole finger, to be inserted. How did that work?

She rubbed her chin, thinking about what she could use to insert into the hole, and the perfect tool came to mind—a crochet hook would do the trick. She knew her uncle wouldn't have any reason to have kept a crochet hook about, but then she remembered the tin filled with paperclips.

Ten minutes later she sat gloating at how clever she was as she stared at the secret compartment now sitting on top of the desk—one filled with stacks of old letters.

CHAPTER 3

Casey's first thought as she stared at the old letters was that their uncle, who'd never married, must have had a secret lover. Why else hide the letters like that? Could his lover have been married to someone else? Was that why he'd never married? Or could his secret lover have been a male? That certainly wouldn't have been acceptable back when he was a young man.

All those theories were quickly squashed as she thumbed through the letters, noting each was addressed to a Mrs Sarah Mason. Surprisingly, there were no sender details on any of the envelopes.

Flicking through the letters more carefully, she noted they were in chronological order, with the oldest being at the bottom of the first stack. It was postmarked in 1918. A quick glance at the last letter showed it was postmarked in 1978. Sixty years of letters—all seemingly to the same woman, and there had to be well over a hundred of them.

Would Sarah Mason have been Uncle Steven's mother, and therefore her own great-grandmother? Could this have been Sarah's desk? And if so, was it possible that Uncle Steven hadn't even known about the secret compartment? Could she have left him the desk when she died, and he'd never discovered the compartment?

Anxious to discover why the letters were hidden, and what secrets they might hold, she opened the oldest of the letters, and began reading. It was slow going, due to the small and at times almost illegible writing, but her curiosity made her persevere.

My darling Sarah,

I am writing to let you know I am safe. I've found a boarding house in San Francisco, and a good job. Can you believe that all those hours I helped Dad with his paperwork are paying off? I've secured a position in office administration and I'll be making enough to pay my room and board, and may even be able to save a little each week.

At this stage, I don't intend returning to Masons Flat. Father may not have told you but he and I had a terrible argument and unfortunately what happened is not something I will ever be able to forgive. He was quite angry with me for standing up to him, and when he discovers that I took some of his secret stash of money, he'll be even angrier. No matter what he might say of me, however, I am not a thief, and I do intend to pay him back, as soon as I can.

Please don't tell him where I am or what I'm doing because I don't want him to come looking for me. I'll leave it up to you to decide if you should say you've heard from me because I have mixed feelings on that. I'm not sure if knowing I'm safe will prevent him searching for me, or if it will make him pressure you for information. I'll let you be the judge of that.

I'll write again soon, but please, if you decide to keep my letters put them somewhere safe—I don't want anyone but you to know where I am. Not even your husband.

Your loving sister,

Daisy

As Casey put the letter back into its envelope and started to pick up the next, she heard the clatter of the front door and the voices of her sisters as they made their way toward the kitchen.

'Hey you guys, you'll never believe what I found,' Casey said, as she joined them.

Taylor looked at her, full of anticipation. 'Did you do more shopping after you left me in Main Street?'

Casey shook her head. 'What? No, not shopping. It's something I've found here, at the house.'

Alex gave her a mischievous smile. 'What—have you done some gardening and stumbled upon a buried treasure?'

'No, not outside—in the study. Come see for yourselves. It's a secret compartment, behind one of the drawers in the desk.'

'Show me,' said Alex, her face suddenly looking serious as she set her handbag down on the table.

Casey led the way back to the study, and showed them the secret compartment filled with the stacks of letters.

'I'd wondered about that drawer; when I was searching for some papers a few months ago I thought it seemed rather shallow, but afterwards I forgot all about it.'

'Cool,' said Taylor, plunking down into the desk's leather chair. 'Maybe they contain maps for some buried treasures.'

Alex lifted an eyebrow. 'Or they might explain why Uncle Steven never married.'

'I thought the same thing, Alex, but the letters began well before our uncle would have been born. I think they belonged to his mother. In fact, I believe this desk may have been hers originally.'

Alex reached for the top letter. 'This is the first?'

'Yes.'

'Sarah Mason. You're right; she was our great-grandmother. Sam showed me a photo of them, Sarah and David, with their two boys, Joseph and Steven. She was definitely Uncle Steven's mother.'

'Letters written to our great-grandmother ... kept in a secret compartment. So there could be a map to buried treasure then, right?' Taylor asked playfully as she gave Alex a wink.

Casey shook her head, rolling her eyes toward Taylor. 'I doubt it. The first is from her sister, Daisy, and since they're all in the same handwriting I guess they're all from her.'

'Daisy? No surname?' asked Alex.

'No, and no return address on any of the envelopes either.'

'Hmmm ... this is interesting. A secret stash of letters ... and you think this is the oldest of them?' Alex asked.

'Yes, they're all postmarked, and this is the earliest. I haven't read any of the others but I did flick through them.'

Taylor turned back to the desk. 'Wow, that's over a hundred years ago. And to think they might have been hidden in there all this time. I wonder if Uncle Steven knew they were in there.'

The sisters looked at each other. Alex eventually answered. 'If he'd found them, wouldn't he have put them somewhere else?'

Casey shrugged. 'Who knows? I mean, I'm sort of inclined to leave them there so maybe he found them and felt the same way.'

'Guess we'll never know for sure, will we?' Alex answered.

Taylor stood up, her interest clearly wanning. 'Let me know when you get to the treasure maps,' she said, 'but for now, I'm hungry, what about you guys? Want me to make some lunch?'

Casey frowned involuntarily. 'Lunch? There isn't anything in the house, is there?'

'We brought provisions. Fresh fruit and veggies, bread and cheese, milk and eggs. I could make us some toasted cheese and tomato sandwiches?'

Casey hadn't realised she was hungry, but the thought of toasted cheese made her mouth water. 'Sure, I'd have one.'

'Me too—sounds great,' replied Alex. 'Now, for tomorrow's lunch, everything is over at the Gold's place. I'll get up early and pop the turkey in the oven, but Taylor, I was hoping I could count on you to make us a couple of pumpkin pies tonight.'

Taylor's eyes lit up. 'Absolutely. Does that mean you bought that pumpkin pie mix, the one in a can?'

Alex smiled. 'Yes, of course. Is that okay with you? I bought everything a few days ago—it's all in the pantry.'

'It's more than okay,' Taylor answered. She got up and headed to the kitchen, saying over her shoulder as she went, 'I wondered why you wanted so many eggs. Did I ever tell you I made a pumpkin pie at home once, but it wasn't the same—the wrong sort of pumpkin I think. I can't wait to make them the proper way.'

Casey chuckled. How funny that Taylor, the chef in the family, would feel making them from a can was the *proper way*.

She sat at the desk again and turned to face Alex. 'Taylor doesn't seem all that interested in these letters, but I think it's intriguing. I can't wait to read through all of them. There must be some intrigue about them for Sarah to keep them secret all those years.'

Alex, still holding the letter she'd picked up, quickly read it. 'Well, it sounds as if that's what Daisy requested. She didn't want her father to find her. It's interesting that she mentions her *father*, but nothing about her *mother*.'

An involuntary frown tightened Casey's forehead. 'You're right. She doesn't say anything about her mother. It's odd, isn't it?'

'Well, maybe her mother wasn't alive. It was probably a lot more common for women to die in childbirth back then than it is now. Or she might have died in some sort of accident. Maybe she'll be mentioned in other letters,' Alex said as she carefully folded the letter and put it back into its envelope.

'I hadn't thought of that. If her mother had died in childbirth, it could explain why her father was so hard on Daisy—maybe he blamed her for his wife's death.'

'You do realise we're making some huge assumptions here, right?' Alex said, lifting a brow. 'Perhaps it's best to just keep reading through the letters rather than us jumping to conclusions. Anyway, I am interested to hear the story, but I've gotta run as soon as we've eaten our lunch, so I might leave the investigative work to you.'

Casey watched as Alex set the letter back on the desk. And suddenly a deep sense of loss enveloped her. These sisters may never have seen each other again. Or even if they had, it would not have been often. Was that what lay in store for her and Alex? Or for her and Taylor? Was distance destined to always be against them?

She turned, letting her gaze follow Alex as she made her way toward the kitchen.

She'd have to think of some way to ensure the type of loneliness that must have defined Sarah's and Daisy's lives didn't overwhelm her own.

CHAPTER 4

As soon as they finished lunch, Alex left to do some errands before her coaching sessions and, with Taylor wanting to get started on the pies, Casey disappeared back into the study eager to continue reading Daisy's letters.

There was one more letter in 1918, followed by a Christmas card, but then the next letter wasn't until March of 1919. It mentioned a flu that had ravaged San Francisco. Many people died, and everyone had to wear a face mask whenever they were in public places. Daisy mentioned how lucky she considered herself to be in managing to stay healthy. She sounded happy with her life, talking all about the city, and how she liked to walk, getting out every day to investigate something new. She'd become particularly taken with the Palace of Fine Arts, near the bay. She explained to her sister about how the building, inspired by Roman and Greek architecture, had housed works of art for the world's fair held in 1915. Daisy said she often walked down there on the weekends, to gaze at the building and watch the activity on the water.

Casey grabbed her iPad and searched until she found the Palace of Fine Arts. It was magnificent; she could immediately see why Daisy had been so taken with it. She imagined Daisy there, sitting on a grassy knoll, or perched on a rock, contemplating her life as she gazed at the lovely building. Was Daisy an artistic type? Had she painted? Or written poetry? Was that something they would have had in common if they could have met? Casey promised herself that at least once during this visit she'd go there so she could gaze at the building as her distant relative had done.

As she continued reading, she wondered if Daisy had been lonely. The letters so far hadn't mentioned any friends. And although she seemed to have a good relationship with the landlady, she mentioned nothing about a love interest. From the sound of things, Daisy kept to herself, enjoying her job and her freedom.

Casey set the sixth letter onto the desk and ran her hand through her short-cropped hair. San Francisco would have seemed a world away from Masons Flat back then. Even now the trip took over two hours by car, and that was mostly via freeway. It could easily have taken several days to make the journey back then and was no doubt expensive. Daisy hadn't mentioned how she'd gotten to San Francisco, and Casey shuddered at the thought of the primitive travel in those days. And then, when Daisy finally arrived, she would have found herself completely isolated from her family; alone, in a big city. As that sunk in, Casey's respect for Daisy grew exponentially. The woman was definitely gutsy, and determined to make things work on her own terms. Would the letters explain why?

A moment later, Taylor walked in. 'The pies are in the oven. I made two regular ones, plus a mini one which we can share as soon as they're done—you know, for a taste test.' Taylor grinned mischievously.

'Sounds good to me,' Casey said, her mouth starting to water at the thought. It had been years since she'd eaten pumpkin pie.

Taylor stopped next to the desk and leaned down to inspect the letters. 'Are you finding anything interesting?'

'Everything about them is interesting, to me anyway. This woman—our relation—was so brave. Can you imagine being several days' travel away from everyone you've ever known, with the only means of communication being by letter? I mean, I suppose some people might have had phones back then, but I doubt they'd have had many up here. And who knows how long it would have taken for a letter to be delivered.'

Taylor ran a finger across the top envelop, but didn't pick it up. 'I hadn't thought of that, but you're right. She must have been brave. Or running away from something terrible.' She straightened up, and crossed her arms in front of her, hugging them to her chest. 'Do you think—I mean this is a horrible thought, but it does happen—do you think her father might have been abusing her?'

'Oh, I hope not ... but I'm not getting the sense of it being anything quite that horrid. Maybe ... I don't know, do you think he could have been trying to pressure her to marry some creepy old friend of his? Or, since it appears she was both clever and brave, maybe she wanted to go to college and he wouldn't let her?'

'I think you might have it with him trying to marry her off—to some old farmer who would force her to milk cows every morning and chop the heads off chickens,' Taylor said, making a chopping gesture with her hand.

Casey cringed, thinking how hard it would be to be pushed into an unwelcome marriage. And at that thought, an image of Nick came to mind.

What if her own father had tried to force her to marry someone like Nick; someone who hated tattoos?

Or worse, what if she'd been forced to marry someone who thought he had the right to forbid her from getting tattoos in the first place?

She swallowed back those thoughts, glad she was living her life in modern times, and not back in the early nineteen-hundreds. 'Maybe she just wanted to get away from this small town and live in a real city. Maybe she said as much, and he threatened to drag her back kicking and screaming if she ever tried to leave?'

Taylor relaxed her arms, then flicked something that looked like flour off her shirt. 'Yeah, that's probably it, but whatever it was, I hope the letters will give you some clues, or even better yet, perhaps she eventually told Sarah the whole sordid story.'

Casey took a deep breath. 'I hope so too.'

Taylor pointed out the window. 'Look, the pies have another forty minutes to go. Want to go for a quick walk with me? I thought maybe we could check out the neighbourhood?'

What Casey really wanted to do was to continue reading, but it would be good to clear her head with some fresh air, and it wasn't all that often that Taylor wanted to do anything physical, so she definitely didn't want to discourage her. 'Sure, let me put these away and grab a jacket.'

The scents of nutmeg, cinnamon and caramelised pumpkin wafted toward them the moment they opened the door on their return.

'It smells like heaven in here—I can't wait to try it,' Casey said as she watched Taylor check her creations.

'They've still got a few minutes to go, and then they'll need to cool. I'll sing out when they're ready to eat.'

Casey made it through one more letter before Taylor called her back to the kitchen. Her mouth watered in anticipation as she watched Taylor cut the small pie, which she'd made in the lid of an ovenproof glass dish, and place the halves onto dessert plates.

‘I think this is going to do for my dinner,’ Taylor said as she handed one plate to Casey. ‘I’m sure I’ll eat enough for three people tomorrow.’

‘Sounds good to me,’ Casey said, a bit surprised that Taylor was showing some restraint, but glad to see it.

After they’d eaten, they made their way to the living room, but when half-way through a movie they both started nodding off, they said goodnight and headed to bed.

The process of washing her face and brushing her teeth had woken Casey up to some extent, but she pulled the comforter up under her chin and closed her eyes, hoping to drop off anyway. Only the moment she closed her eyes, images of the Palace of Fine Arts came to mind and she pictured a young woman sitting on a grassy knoll gazing at the buildings in awe.

And the question that was bothering her all afternoon returned. What could have set Daisy on the path of isolation from her family?

Casey, certain the answers would be revealed in the letters, was anxious to read more of them, and wished tomorrow wasn’t Thanksgiving so she could stay home to continue reading.

CHAPTER 5

Casey stumbled her way into the living room before the sun had even cleared the trees to find Taylor already glued to the telly watching the Thanksgiving Day parade.

'How long have you been up?' Casey asked, rubbing her eyes.

Taylor answered without turning from the screen. 'Maybe an hour? I wanted to see as much of the parade as possible.'

'You're such a kid.'

Taylor turned to her, scowling. 'Hey, it's a tradition. I've seen a couple of clips on the internet, but watching it as it's live is almost like being there.'

'I'm just teasing you. So, what time is Alex coming to get us?'

'Ten-thirty. I'll jump in the shower as soon as the parade finishes. It won't be long now. What are you going to wear?'

'I was thinking those new jeans and boots. It's not like we have to be formal or anything.'

Taylor tapped a freshly manicured nail onto the remote as she thought. 'I might wear the long skirt I bought yesterday—it'll look great with my new sandals. I'm glad I brought them, even if it is winter.'

'Sounds good. Your nails look great, by the way. I meant to mention it last night.'

'They don't look too bad, do they? I thought it would be fun ... while we're on holidays. I got a pedicure to match as well.'

Casey looked down at her own short nails, wondering why Taylor was making such an effort with her appearance. There was the new skirt, the manicure and pedicure. She started to ask, but changed her mind. Maybe Taylor had a crush on someone. Of course, of the three sisters, it had always been Taylor who was the most meticulous with her appearance. She rarely left the house without makeup, for a start, and always wore nice outfits. It was almost a shame she worked in a bakery where she had to wear a uniform. As a florist, there was nothing to stop Casey from wearing whatever she wanted, but it had never occurred to her to get her nails done.

After watching a few minutes of the parade, Casey excused herself and dashed into the shower. As she stood letting the hot water run over her body, Nick's face came to mind. She still couldn't get over his expression when he'd spotted her tatts. She looked down, admiring the images on her arms, calves, shoulders, and hips. She couldn't see the one on her back, but closing her eyes she could picture it—poppies—one of her favourites. She sniffed out a breath. If he'd reacted that way with seeing one tattoo what would he think if he ever saw the rest of her? She knew Travis had a pool—Alex had mentioned swimming over the summer months—but of course that wasn't going to happen this time of year. Just as well; Nick would probably have a seizure or something if he saw the rest of her.

Just before ten-thirty, Travis arrived to collect them.

'Nice outfit, Taylor,' he said as he walked into the kitchen.

Casey was surprised he'd noticed. Perhaps the autumn colours had caught his eye.

Taylor beamed, spinning around so the skirt flared out. 'Thanks—I got it in town at that western wear shop. So, where's Alex?'

'She's a bit busy cooking so she asked me to pick you up. Oh, and she said there's a cool pack in the laundry cupboard that you can put the pies in,' he said.

When they got to Travis' house he showed them through to the kitchen. 'She's banned all of us men from the kitchen this morning—wants to do everything herself. But you two go right ahead.'

Casey gave him a knowing smile as they headed into the bright, open kitchen, to find Alex busy basting the turkey. The aroma of the roasted meat made Casey's mouth water. Later today, when they sat down to eat this scrumptious feast, she would give thanks to the turkey; as today she would set aside her vegetarianism.

'Hey Alex, can we give you a hand with anything?' Taylor asked.

Alex turned to them wiping her hands on an apron before putting the turkey back into the oven. 'Thanks, Taylor, but I've got everything under control. I really wanted to do it all myself. Might be the last time I do it this way, but this time I wanted to do it all. It certainly takes a bit of planning to ensure everything is ready at the same time. I take my hat off to all the American women who do this every year.'

Casey looked at Alex with added respect, feeling only slightly inadequate that she'd never been much of a cook herself.

A moment later, loud male voices moaning with disappointment drifted in from another room. Casey's heart started thumping, just as it had when she'd thought she'd seen Nick at the hardware store.

'Sounds like they're watching football, right?' Taylor asked, turning to Alex.

'Yes, I think it's the Broncos. Or maybe it's the Bears. I don't remember which—seems they've got games on all day—but at least Travis gave me a heads-up on this. Welcome to Thanksgiving Day.'

~~*~~

Nick leaned back from the table and patted his stomach. 'That was a scrumptious meal, Alex. Those sweet potatoes, and the turkey and stuffing—everything was just the way my Mom makes it. I don't remember when I last ate so much at one meal.'

'That'd be last Christmas ... when your sister cooked up a storm,' laughed Travis.

'Or at my birthday barbeque, where I'm sure I saw you refill your plate several times,' Denver added with a crooked smile.

Nick turned to Travis, genuinely happy that he'd met Alex. In fact, they were both lucky to have found each other this second time around. From what he'd heard, they'd both been through pretty rough divorces.

Alex beamed. 'Thanks, Nick; I'm glad you enjoyed it. And I hope your parents are enjoying their cruise, and not regretting missing the holiday with you and your family.'

'Oh, we weren't going to do a big family thing this year.' He looked toward Casey and Taylor and then continued. 'My sister, Stacy, and her husband and daughter, are back east spending Thanksgiving with his family for a change. That's what clinched it for Mom—knowing her granddaughter wasn't going to be around anyway.'

Now Alex turned to Taylor and Casey. 'Stacy and her family live on the property next door. We'd have asked them to join us here if they hadn't already made plans to go back east, but you'll meet them when they get back.'

'That'll be nice,' Taylor said. 'Now, I hope you left room for dessert, as there's pie to come.'

Nick looked around the table, and by the faces staring back at him he was pretty sure everyone would agree they needed a break. 'I couldn't eat another bite ... not right this minute, anyway. A bit later?'

Alex, nodded. 'I agree. I couldn't do it justice right now, Taylor, but maybe in an hour or so?'

'Okay. I'll help you with the dishes then,' Taylor said, her voice clearly demonstrating her disappointment that no one seemed anxious to try her pies.

'I'll give you a hand in the kitchen, too,' Nick said as he pushed his chair back and stood.

Casey turned to Alex. 'I need to walk off this big meal, if that's okay. I'll need to build up an appetite to do Taylor's pie justice. Can the dishes wait a bit?'

Alex shook her head. 'I want to put the food away, so I'd rather do everything in one go. You head out for a walk, that's fine. Taylor, do you want to join her?'

'No, these sandals were made for showing off my new pedicure, not for walking,' Taylor said with a smile. 'I'll stay and help you in the kitchen.'

Denver stood tentatively. 'I'd love to go for a walk—I've overeaten myself—but it'll be a few more weeks before I can do that much moving. Maybe I'll go stretch out on the sofa and watch a bit more football instead.'

Travis stood too. 'Enjoy it while it lasts, Den. Nick, I'll give Alex and Taylor a hand with the clean-up. Why don't you take Casey outside and show her around the property?'

As Nick looked at Travis he could feel his eyes growing wide with disbelief. Had Travis taken no notice of the coolness Casey had shown him all afternoon? He figured it was related to his tattoo comments the other night—not that he regretted anything he'd said. He turned toward Casey, who seemed to be searching for something to say to get out of it, and raised an eyebrow. They were about to become in-laws of sorts—perhaps it would be best if they cleared the air.

He turned back to Travis. 'Sure, okay, I can do that.' Then he turned to see Casey's response.

'Yeah, okay, I suppose it wouldn't do for me to get lost, would it?'

Travis shook his head. 'Oh, I doubt you'd get lost, but you might get zapped by an electric fence, or find yourself face to face with a territorial bull if you wandered into the wrong pasture, so I'd be happier if someone went with you ... until you know your way around.'

Nick grabbed his jacket from the other room, nearly bowling Denver over as he hobbled toward the sofa. For a moment, he envied Denver his broken leg and getting to stay here and watch the football game, but he quickly wiped that thought away. Of course he didn't envy Denver. He couldn't think of much worse than being laid up for several weeks.

Casey was already out on the back porch by the time he got outside. She'd donned a ski-type jacket and with her skinny jeans and boots she looked hot, and he suddenly regretted the way their relationship had started off. He took a deep breath, telling himself to lighten up on her—she was practically part of the family, after all.

He cocked his head toward the barn. 'We'll take this path over to the barn, and then there's a road behind it that heads out to the back pastures.'

'Okay. Is it far?' she asked, jumping off the edge of the porch.

'If we went as far as we could it's probably a couple of miles, but we can turn around whenever you've had enough.'

'We can go as long as you like. My boots are new, but I'll give American boot makers credit, they're the most comfortable things I've ever put on my feet.'

'Glad to hear it,' he said, looking down at his own boots, which had served him well for several years now but might need replacing soon.

They walked along in silence for a time, and every now and again Nick stole a sideways glance at Casey, who was matching his strides almost identically. She reminded him of Alex—from her accent, to her long slender legs, to her colouring and to the way her chin jutted out with attitude. Cut from the same cloth was the expression he sought. He'd seen the similarity with Taylor immediately, but Casey's shorter hair ... and multiple earrings ... and tattoos ... had distracted him at first.

As the word tattoo formed in his mind, he recalled Alex's words. Something about how since she'd been working as a florist she'd starting getting "*these tattoos*". That meant there were others and he couldn't help but wonder how many others, and where they might be.

Then he pulled himself up, and took a deep breath. 'I was out of line the other night, with what I said about your tattoo. It's none of my business if you want ink all over your body.'

Her mouth flew open in surprise, then she scrunched her face, and rolled her eyes dramatically. 'Seriously? So ... what, you're saying you think that as an adult it's okay for me to make my own decisions about what I do or don't put on my body? Gee, thanks.'

The air thickened with something she stopped short from saying.

He chewed on his lip for a moment, regretting his choice of words and wanting to make sure the next ones sounded better. 'I didn't mean it like that. I meant,' he stopped, weighing his words, and then started again. 'Look, I'm trying to apologise for making that comment. I was out of line. I shouldn't have said anything at all. I'm not a fan of tattoos, but it's none of my business.'

Casey's green eyes practically bore holes in him as flashes of gold gave away her inner feelings. She was pissed. But seriously, why? He was trying to apologise, wasn't he?

'You're right, it is none of your business. You shouldn't have said anything the other night. Besides, you didn't need to say anything for me to know you were disgusted. I could see it on your face.'

He took a few more steps as he let her comment soak in. 'Seriously? Am I that transparent?'

'Uh, yeah. You looked like you were about to toss your cookies. You probably would have, if it had been after dinner and not before.'

'Really? I looked like I was about to *toss my cookies,* did I?' He tried to imitate her accent, but he knew it sounded more James Bond than Crocodile Dundee. Then he started laughing, and couldn't stop.

'Geez, you're an idiot.' She shook her head, but a smile began to creep onto her face.

'Look, as I said, it wasn't my place to say anything. I suppose I sometimes talk before my brain is completely engaged—sorry. I was just surprised because Alex ... well, she's so conservative. And, from what I've seen of her so far, I'd say Taylor is too. And then there's you.'

'You're digging that hole deeper now, but you know that, don't you?' she asked, her voice laced with barely controlled laughter.

'Sorry. Can't help myself.' He stopped walking, put on his best grin and extended his hand for a shake. 'Can we start over? Hi, my name is

Nick Gold. I'm staying here in Masons Flat with my cousins, Travis and Denver, and on behalf of all of us, welcome to California.'

She stopped too, let out a loud sigh, and squinted off into the distance. For a moment, he thought she was going to ignore his extended hand.

Then she turned her gaze back to him and reached out.

'Hello, Nick. I'm Casey, Alex's rebellious sister. Thank you for the warm welcome.'

Her hand was warm, and slightly calloused; did that come from working with the floral arrangements? He squeezed it slightly, then looked up at her, noticing how the sun brought out a multitude of shades in her auburn hair. He'd never been particularly attracted to red heads, and couldn't remember ever looking at one in the sun like this.

He released her hand, with surprising reluctance, and they continued walking.

After a few minutes Casey spoke.

'I actually do know what you mean. I sometimes wonder how on earth I can be related to the two of them. I mean, we all look alike, and we're all, like, *really nice people*,' she said with a cute grin, 'but that's definitely where the similarity ends.'

He cocked his head. 'In what ways are you so different? I mean, besides the short hair and, well, you know.'

Her chin jutted out once more. He'd done it again, hadn't he?

'For starters, Alex already knew what she wanted to be when she was about eight years old. She was a tennis star by the time she was seventeen—and then she got married to her first real boyfriend when she was twenty. And as for Taylor, she loved cooking and said she wanted to be a chef ... then later changed to a pastry chef and started working at a bakery as soon as she was old enough to get a job.'

'And is she married?'

'Taylor? No, she's had a few quote unquote *relationships*, but they never worked out, you know?'

He knew exactly. 'Yep.'

'And Alex, she was married for around ten years and hadn't been divorced for terribly long when she met Travis. So that's two relationships.'

He was beginning to get the sense that Casey's list of previous relationships was a lot longer than those of her sisters. He slowed his gait for a moment, about to ask about her relationships, but almost immediately gave himself a mental kick up the butt and sped up again. He was in no position to judge her when it came to multiple relationships. He'd been with plenty of women himself, in his search for the right one. He knew she was out there, and he knew when he found her he'd settle down and start a family. But who knew how many more women he'd have to date before he would find her?

No, he wouldn't question Casey; just let her tell him what she was happy to tell.

'And then there's me. I didn't have a clue what I wanted to do with my life. They have these career guidance people in high school, but nothing they suggested clicked. So I spent two years at university doing an arts degree, but I just couldn't stay motivated so I didn't finish the course.'

'I get that. I thought about dropping out too, until I discovered I had a real knack with computers. I started off doing math and science, but I didn't want to be a teacher, and wasn't sure what else I could do with it ... and then I struck it lucky with a computer science professor who really motivated me.'

Casey frowned slightly, then sighed and continued. 'I guess I was lucky too, in a way. When I dropped out of uni, a friend of mine who was working for the florist got me a part-time job there and the rest is history as they say. I adore working with fresh flowers ... making unique floral arrangements every day; and there's something really special about going to the flower markets. Nothing can compare to the scent of fresh flowers ... roses, in particular. And since the job was enough to pay the bills I stuck with it; although that's not such an issue any more.'

Nick knew about their unexpected inheritance—it was what brought Alex and her sisters to Masons Flat. He also knew that the sisters now owned over a third of Main Street. Travis and Denver owned quite a few properties too, as did his own parents, leaving only a few businesses and shops that had been sold over the years and were no longer owned by the families of the original town founders.

He turned his mind back to what she'd said. 'So ... even if it wasn't a childhood dream, you enjoy being a florist now, I take it?'

She tilted her head, thinking for a moment. 'All those glorious scents and colours—who wouldn't love it? And my boss, Maree, she's the best. I mean, letting me take all this time off for this trip—not a lot of bosses let you take six weeks off. Luckily, we only had two weddings booked for December because I generally work with the brides to do the flower selections and design the arrangements. I'm going to be so busy with weddings when I get back, but I'm looking forward to it, so, yeah, I guess that must mean I love my job.'

He looked at her earnestly. 'It must be wonderful—looking forward to being busy at work.'

'I take it that means you don't wake every morning anxious to get to the office and back in front of your computers?' Casey asked, tilting her head with a slight smirk on her lips as she awaited his reply.

He stared at her for a moment as he thought about how to answer her. He liked his job, but did he love it? He loved the security of it, and the salary that had allowed him to nearly pay off his mortgage. He loved that he felt ready to settle down and raise a family—and that even if his parents lived another forty years and he didn't see a penny of his future inheritance for many years, money wasn't going to be an issue. He'd have no problem sending his kids to good colleges when the time came. 'I like the challenges it presents. And the salary's pretty good now that I'm a project manager. But I envy people who are passionate about what they do for a living—being anxious to get to work each day. I'm not missing my job at the moment, for instance, but I'm not sure how Travis would go having a long break away from this place.'

He stopped—they'd arrived at the gate at the end of the dirt road. 'Want to head back, or keep going to the end of the property?'

'I'm easy,' she said, 'it's not like I'm tired or anything if you want to keep going. I mean, we should probably take advantage of the weather. I suppose it rains a lot this time of year?'

'Yeah, it can rain a lot. It's been good all week, actually, so the track won't be muddy but there is fresh horse manure in there. You might get your new boots messed up.'

Just as he gestured toward the track on the other side of the fence, the horses came running up, putting their brakes on and sliding to a stop right in front of the gate.

~~*~~

Casey jumped back as a group of horses skidded to a stop on the other side of the gate. Milling around and bumping into each other, they sent up dirt and dust everywhere. She half expected them to push the gate right over.

'Crikey, do they always do that?' She cringed as her voice caught—a dead giveaway of her uneasiness around the huge animals.

Nick laughed, but she didn't get the sense he was judging her so much as just amused by her naivety when it came to farm life. 'Oh, you mean stopping on a dime? They're Quarter Horses; it's what they do.'

'Oh, I didn't know, in fact I don't know much about horses.'

He reached over the gate and patted the ones standing at the front. 'They were probably just showing off. Or hoping we were here to feed them; although they're a bit silly as they should know I bring their feed out in The Beast, not on foot.'

Casey frowned, shaking her head. 'The Beast?'

'Oh, yeah, it's actually a rural terrain vehicle, but my cousins refer to it as The Beast. It's like a small dump truck; we use it for a lot of the chores around here.'

When he smiled, she allowed herself to acknowledge his attractiveness—even if he did look more like someone who would be at home on a college rowing team than riding one of those horses. Alex had been quite complimentary about Travis' riding skills, but would Nick be as good, given he lived in the city?

'How often do you ride? I mean, normally, not just now while you're helping out with Denver being laid up.'

'I come up when they're particularly busy, such as in the lead up to an event, or if they've got a lot of young horses coming on at the same time. I'm definitely not here every weekend, but sometimes it can be a couple of weekends in a row.'

She figured he must be pretty good if they counted on him to that extent. 'Do you think while I'm here I might get to go for a ride sometime? I mean, wow, I guess that's pretty pushy, isn't it, but I'd love to try it.'

A slow smile appeared on Nick's face, and his eyes seemed to soften, reflecting the blue of the cloudless sky. 'I can't see why not. Denver's mare, Sally, is as gentle as they come and he's quite happy letting people ride her. I'm sure we could squeeze in a ride while you're here.'

'That'd be great, thanks. So, what else do you do on the weekends, then? I mean, what are your other interests, besides horses? I guess what I'm getting at is I'm pretty sure I remember Travis saying you live in Sacramento, right? So you must have other interests ... things you do in the city.'

He looked into the distance for a moment, as if weighing up his response. 'I play a bit of basketball with some college friends, and I follow a lot of sports. If there's a game on in town, I usually try to go. And there's a group of us that go to clubs to listen to live bands.'

She thought of her own treks to the odd football game, recalling the sort of drunkards who got awfully loud. Looking at Nick, however, she couldn't quite imagine he'd be like that. In fact, something told her she might have been a bit harsh on him the other night and that he was probably quite a nice guy. And since he liked live bands, he mustn't be all bad.

He pointed over the gate to where the road continued on. 'So, what do you think? Go through the pasture and up to the far property line? Or head back? The horses won't bother us if we keep going.' He smiled again, and it seemed genuine.

Maybe she should cut him some slack. After all, he wasn't the first person to criticise her tatts. A lot of people, even a few of her girlfriends, didn't like them. She'd shrugged off haters before; couldn't she simply do it again?

She took a deep breath as she looked at the ground on the other side of the gate. As Nick had said, there was fresh horse manure scattered everywhere, stirred up by the horses as they'd jostled about. She could dodge the larger piles but now that she focused on it the stench was fairly strong—would she want risk getting that on her new boots for the sake of another twenty minutes of walking? 'Come to think of it, it might be best to head back. Taylor will be itching to serve up those pies.'

'Okay, then,' Nick said, then yelled across to the horses as they departed. 'I'll be back with your dinner in a couple of hours.'

As they headed back to the house, Casey kept up with Nick, watching him out of the corner of her eye. When she could see the house coming up in the distance, she was surprised at how quickly they'd gotten back; somehow the trip seemed much quicker in this direction. Possibly because it was slightly downhill—or perhaps due to the fact that she no longer found Nick's company quite as unpleasant as she had earlier.

CHAPTER 6

Casey enjoyed the pie almost as much today as she had the night before, but when Taylor asked if anyone wanted seconds she shook her head. 'I can't believe how good that was, but I seriously couldn't eat another bite. I'm glad I wore my *stretch* jeans today.'

'I'll have hers then,' Denver said, a chuckle punctuating his words.

'I'll have a bit more, too,' Travis said, his eyes bright with anticipation as he stared at Taylor.

'I could probably manage another thin slice since you're offering,' Nick replied with a broad smile directed toward Taylor; a smile that caused a sensation a little too similar to jealousy wash over Casey.

'Coffee, anyone?' Alex asked.

When Alex stood, Casey did as well. Confused by her reaction to Nick smiling at Taylor, she distracted herself by grabbing some of the plates while Taylor took the three that were to be refilled.

Once in the kitchen, Taylor turned to Casey with an inquisitive look on her face. 'Enjoy your walk?'

'It was okay. Too bad you didn't come. You and Nick probably have a lot in common.'

Alex raised an eyebrow inquisitively as she turned to Casey. 'What makes you say that?'

Casey thought about their conversation. 'I got the impression Nick likes women who are somewhat ... shall we say, traditional. Remember the cracks he made about my tattoos the other night?'

'Oh, that,' Alex said, waving a hand across her face, 'I'm sure he was just surprised by them.'

'No, he was disgusted,' Casey replied. She knew that look when she saw it. 'They're definitely not for everyone.'

'True,' Alex replied, slowly. 'It's taken me a while to come to ... admire them. I certainly couldn't imagine ever getting one myself.'

'Me neither,' Taylor chipped in as she cut three more slices of pie.

'Yeah, all right, I get it. I'm the odd one ... I've always known it.' Casey hadn't meant to sound defensive, but she suspected she had.

Taylor smothered the pieces of pie with whipped cream, and then turned to Casey with her hands on her hips. 'You're not odd ... well, maybe a little ... but even if you are we still love you.'

Casey rolled her eyes. 'Yeah, yeah, I know. And I didn't mean to snap at you. I'm probably still not completely caught up on sleep from the flight.'

As Taylor headed back to the dining room, Alex filled a large coffee pot with what smelled like freshly ground coffee. 'You'll have coffee?'

'Absolutely. Smells great.'

Alex nodded. 'It is a nice blend, isn't it? You know, you could do worse than finding yourself a man like Nick. I've gotten to know him while I've been staying here. He's really nice.'

Casey pulled a face. 'He's not what I'm looking for, and you know it.'

'And what are you looking for, Casey? Another footballer like the last guy you dated? Or the one before that ... what, exactly, did he do for a living anyway?'

Casey frowned as she focussed on the kitchen floor. Cooper, the football player, had been a lot of fun, and everyone had liked him—he just couldn't grasp the concept of monogamy. Before him, she'd been with Tom, a jazz musician who at thirty-five still lived with his parents, albeit in a granny-flat out the back of their place. What he lacked in monetary terms he more than made up for in chemistry, but that relationship was doomed from the start, with him working most nights and sleeping most days.

'I know none of my recent relationships have been what you'd call good-catches ... but they had other redeeming qualities. You know I'm never gonna be happy in a nine-to-five job myself, and I can't imagine being happy with any man who has one. Whatever he does, it has to include some sort of creative or athletic endeavour.' She looked up, meeting her older sister's eyes. She, of all people, must get that. Alex had hated it when, after her divorce, she'd taken an office job in an attempt to get her life back on track. She'd dropped that job at the first chance she'd had, so she had to agree with Casey on this, didn't she?

Alex sighed. 'You know, just because a man, or a woman for that matter, has a decent career which requires them to work in an office, it doesn't necessarily define them as a person. Nick has been wonderful, taking extended leave from his job to help Travis. I'm not sure Travis would have coped without him.'

Casey screwed up her face. 'Yeah, okay, it was nice, but Travis could have hired a farm-hand to help out, surely? I mean, the work he's doing around here probably isn't exactly rocket-science.'

Alex tilted her head, then lifting a brow spoke slowly. 'The training that goes into each and every one of Travis' horses is astounding. I've watched Nick ride, and trust me, no a farm-hand would be able to help Travis out the way Nick is doing.'

Casey turned and pulled some mugs from a cupboard, mostly as an excuse to break eye contact and think about her response. 'Look, Alex, I hear what you're saying about me needing to lift my standards a bit when it comes to men, but seriously, you think someone like Nick makes sense for someone like me?'

'I don't see why not. I just think you need to be more open to getting to know different types of men. You might be surprised if you actually judged them on their personality and ... integrity ... rather than relying totally on sexual chemistry and then hoping they've got other worthwhile qualities.'

Casey drew in a long noisy breath. Alex was right—and that was the main problem with Alex, she was almost always right.

~~*~~

Nick was ready to head to the other room to watch football when Travis stood, asking if anyone wanted more to eat and offering to pull the turkey out and slice some for sandwiches.

'You've got to be joking?' Alex said, her brows knitting together.

Nick got up, pushed his chair back under the table and leaned on it from behind. 'No more for me, but thanks anyway, Travis. Everything was delicious, but I couldn't eat another bite.'

Casey rolled her eyes, her face indicating she'd had enough too. 'I think we're all up to pussy's bow,' she said, looking at Travis.

Nick turned to face Casey. 'What did you just say?'

Casey looked at him with the face of innocence. 'Who, me?' she asked, her grin saying she knew full well he didn't understand her comment.

'Up to who's what?' he asked.

Alex shook her head, laughing, indicating her throat. 'It's an old Aussie expression our grandmother used to say a lot—"Full up to pussy's bow"—as in full right up to a bow-tie around a cat's neck. It means not being able to eat another thing.'

Nick nodded slowly. 'Not one I've heard before, but it certainly describes how I feel right now, that's for sure.'

Travis stood too. 'I doubt we'd have bothered if it had just been the three of us men, but it's been great having a real, traditional Thanksgiving feast. Thank you, Alex.'

'Yeah, thanks, Alex ... and Taylor, your pie was wonderful. I haven't eaten so well since Mom died,' Denver said. 'I might have a sandwich or something later, but I think I'll head back out to the sofa for now and watch some more football while I prop up this leg.' He stood, grabbing the crutches beside him and began hobbling his way toward the other room.

'Is football *still* on?' Alex asked, a look of disbelief washing over her—or was it disgust? Nick couldn't quite tell which it was.

Travis flashed a broad smile her way. 'Yep, three games today. Aren't we lucky? Come on, I'll help you clean up whatever is left to be done.' He stacked the cups and saucers as Alex collected the pie plates, and they disappeared into the kitchen.

Nick opened his mouth, planning to excuse himself to join Denver in front of the football, when Taylor spoke.

'Casey used to date a football player. They've all got tattoos these days. It's really quite common in Australia.'

He crossed his arms as he stared, first at Taylor and then at Casey. 'You dated a football player? Anyone I'd know?'

Casey crossed her arms in front of herself too—squeezing them into her chest in a defensive stance. She lifted a brow and glared at him defiantly before turning the same look toward her sister. He suspected she wasn't impressed with Taylor bringing it up.

'Hardly,' she finally replied, glaring at him.

'Try me. I know a lot of the player's names,' he said, trying to put a smile into his voice, hoping to lighten her up a bit.

Casey let out an exasperated sigh. 'Aussie rules, not your football. You wouldn't know him.'

Taylor shook her head. 'Oh, yeah, I should have said that—our football, not gridiron.'

Nick frowned. Gridiron—he'd heard the expression before, and hated it. 'You're right. I wouldn't know any of the Australian football players.'

Again, Casey glared at Taylor, her eyes narrowing dangerously. He would love to be a fly on the wall when those two were next alone together.

'But you have seen Aussie Rules, right?' Taylor continued.

Taylor was clearly ignoring the *shut up* look on Casey's face. She either hadn't picked it, or didn't care.

'Yeah, bits of it, sure.' He was intrigued by where this conversation might be headed.

'And so you know what I mean about the tattoos? Seems most of them have what they call sleeves. It's funny, but I've grown so used to seeing them I hardly notice Casey's tatts any longer. They do grow on you.'

Now he understood what Taylor was up to. She seemed to be trying to justify having brought up the subject.

'A lot of our athletes have them, too,' he said.

Casey turned back to him now. 'Well, Aussie Rules is a much better game than what I've seen so far of your football. Our players don't wear helmets and shoulder pads and all that rubbish. Our players are tough and fast. And they don't stop every few minutes for a rest. They run, constantly, anywhere up to fifteen kilometres during a game. They're fit, not fat.'

Nick wished he knew more about Australian football so he could contradict her, but he was practically defenceless. Practically, but not completely. 'Some of our players are huge, I'll give you that, but only because it's what the position they play calls for. And these guys are tough—don't ever doubt that.'

Casey quirked a brow but didn't answer.

Taylor drew in a noisy breath. 'Maybe I'll go see if Alex and Travis need a hand with anything.' She stood and quickly disappeared into the kitchen.

'And are you into all athletes, or only football players?' Taylor had opened the door to this topic, and now he'd jammed his foot into it to hold it open.

Casey chuffed out a breath. 'Look ... it just so happens I like to hang out at one of the pubs where a few of the football players go. It's an awesome place, full of people who enjoy listening to live bands and having a good time on a Sunday afternoon. I didn't know he was a football player when we met.'

He nodded slowly. 'Taylor bringing it up seemed to bother you a bit, that's all.'

Casey chewed on her bottom lip, making her look really hot again, and making him awfully aware of her lips.

'My sisters ... sometimes they like having a go at me about the men I've dated. In this case, I guess she was just trying to draw a comparison between my tattoos and theirs. Regardless of her intentions though, it's not exactly appropriate dinner table conversation, is it? I mean, I didn't hear you and Denver discussing either of your failed relationships here at the table earlier?'

'Touché,' he replied.

That brought a smile to her lips. 'Thank you.'

'But now that it's out there ... a football player. As in, a rich and famous one?'

She shook her head. 'No—definitely not famous, and as for him being rich, I have no idea. He was generous with paying for dinners and movies and whatnot, but it's not something we ever talked about.'

Good—so money hadn't been much of a factor in her decision to date the football player at least. 'But you like your men a bit on the rough side, I take it?' The moment those words left his mouth he regretted them. He should have gone in to watch football when he'd had the chance.

She tilted her head, squinting. 'Rough? Yeah, well, maybe I do. I've never been attracted to clean-cut-bookworm types if that's what you mean. But why do we keep talking about me and the men I've dated? What about you? How come you aren't married? You must be nearly the same age as Travis.'

He wasn't certain if her crack about clean-cut-bookworm-types was directed toward him, but he decided not to bite at it. 'Me? No, I'm a few years younger than Travis, not that it matters. I suppose I just haven't met the right woman yet.' It wasn't for lack of trying, but he didn't say that as it might make him sound like a player and he'd never thought of himself that way.

'But you've probably had lots of girlfriends? A nice *clean-cut looking* guy like you ... I bet lots of girls would have liked to have called you their Mr Gold.'

So, her comment had been directed at him after all. He'd never had anyone say something so complimentary to him, yet make it sound like such an insult. Did she find him repulsive? Did she think he was too clean-cut for her? And if she did, why on earth would that be digging into his craw like a knife gutting a fish?

He looked down, wishing he hadn't started this conversation. Then he remembered he hadn't. It was Taylor's fault. He stepped back from his chair and looked up at her. 'You're right. This isn't a conversation either of us is particularly happy to have right now, so how about I go see how the football is going, and let you do ... whatever.'

She raised a brow, tilting her head coyly, or perhaps it was smugly. Part of him wanted to say something to wipe that smile off, but instead he tipped his head in parting, and left the room.

CHAPTER 7

Nick looked up when, some time later, Alex ducked her head into the family room to say she would run the girls home. Shortly after, Casey and Taylor looked in to say goodbye as well. He nodded, but stayed sitting next to Denver watching the football game while Travis walked them out. Intent on the game, Nick hadn't even noticed Travis return, but at the next commercial break, Travis made his presence known.

'So, what's going on with you and Casey?' Travis asked, his brows knitted quizzically.

Nick's face tightened at his cousin's question. 'What? Nothing.'

'You sure? The dynamics between you seemed to have changed by the time you came back from your walk.'

Nick hoped Travis was simply trying to stir up trouble, yet Travis wasn't smiling as he normally would when doing that.

'I apologised for my comments about the tattoos. Maybe she hates me a little less than before, but that's about it.'

'Yeah?' Travis said, still staring.

'Uh, yeah, that's it.' He wasn't certain there wasn't something more—wasn't even sure what his own feelings were—but he was certain he didn't want to talk about it.

Denver reached over and slapped his hand on Nick's thigh. 'I thought things seemed different, too. Not that I'd have come out and said it. Way to go, Trav.'

Nick stood and headed toward the kitchen. 'I'm grabbing a beer. Either of you want one?' he called back over his shoulder.

'No thanks, I'm stuffed. How on earth could you drink a beer?' Denver called back.

'I'll pass, thank you,' Travis replied.

Nick stood at the fridge for a moment before opening it. He didn't really want a beer, but he had to get away from that line of conversation. After a few deep breaths, he pulled out a can and popped the top. He took a sip, allowing the soothing liquid to run down his throat. They were just giving him a hard time. It's what they always did, and if he showed it bothered him, they'd do it even more. He had to stay calm, and pretend nothing they'd said had bothered him one bit.

When he returned to the living room, the commercials had finished and Denver and Travis were both glued to the game—perfect timing. But when another commercial came on, Travis started right back into it.

'You know, I get it if there is something going on. Alex is a dream-come-true for me, and her sisters are so much like her, but Casey's going back to Australia, and you're going to be travelling, so it isn't fair to start something with her, and you know it.'

Nick couldn't believe Travis had picked up on whatever chemistry was beginning to simmer under the surface, especially when he was only coming to terms with it himself. 'Trust me, nothing is happening.'

Travis raised an eyebrow and uttered one word in reply. 'Good.'

Denver looked uneasy as he shifted himself on the sofa, then pulled out a cushion and tossed it on the coffee table. 'Give me a hand, will you Nick? I want to rest my leg up on the pillow. I think I've been standing too much today and it's starting to throb.'

He helped Denver and then turned to Travis, not convinced that Travis believed him. 'You do know that I was simply trying to be nicer today to make up for the other night, right?'

Travis smiled. 'Good,' he said, repeating his earlier reaction.

Nick shook his head, sensing that Travis still doubted him. 'Besides, she's nothing like any woman I've ever dated. They've all been more like Kelly, and you know it—petite, blonde, soft-spoken.'

Travis chuffed out a breath. 'Yeah, I know your type—bikini-clad-beach-babes; preferably ones who never contradict a thing you say. But if Kelly was so perfect, why'd you two break up?' Travis clearly was not ready to drop the subject.

Nick's hackles rose slightly. Was that how his cousins had seen Kelly, as someone who constantly agreed with him about everything? And more to the point was it true? Did he purposely date women who were non-confrontational? 'Well, I guess we simply grew apart.' He didn't need to tell them he thought Kelly was too self-centred and materialistic to be a good mother. And that was important to him.

Travis turned to Denver. 'What are your thoughts, little brother?'

Nick's gut twisted. He should have shut up and let the conversation die.

Denver adjusted his leg on the pillow again before looking at Nick. 'Yeah, I liked Kelly, but now that you mention it, she was almost like a clone of a lot of your other past girlfriends. But when it comes to Casey, man is she different. There's definitely something there, though. It was as if she had these little sparklers in her eyes, spitting out bright white sparks of fire. It was the same thing with Alex ... when you first met her, Travis,' he said, nodding toward his older brother. 'You denied anything was going on for the longest time, too.'

Nick shook his head, amazed by Denver's words. 'I don't know about Alex and Travis, but with Casey, I'd be willing to bet those sparks you saw in her eyes were to do with hatred burning in them. She was pretty pissed off about me criticising her tatts the other night. My apology probably didn't cut it.'

Nick looked at each of his cousins, both sporting grins like kids who'd found the secret stash of cookies.

He'd done it.

He'd bitten, just like they'd wanted him to.

They were pleased with themselves, and he hated that he'd allowed them to win.

'Come on, really? You can see me with a woman like her? A woman with her thorny temperament? And all those tatts? Not to mention the earrings. Oh, and who's nearly as tall as me. Casey's like some Amazon woman or something ... and with that short hair of hers she is definitely not my type.'

Travis cocked his head. 'I don't see anything wrong with her appearance; she's the spitting image of Alex after all. Well, with a few exceptions. Maybe you need to reconsider what your *type* is—just not when it comes to Casey.'

'Yep, I hear you. No need to keep harping on about it,' Nick said, beginning to wonder if Travis' concern might be related to the potential for friction if he dated Casey and then it didn't work out. It might have as much to do with Travis protecting his own relationship with Alex, as with protecting Casey.

Through a barely concealed grin, Travis made a gesture of zipping his mouth shut. But it didn't last long. 'One last thing, and then I'll shut up. I've offered your assistance to Casey for a project she's working on.'

Nick closed his eyes and ran his hands across his face, stopping to rub his temples. 'This is giving me a headache. You don't want me to consider dating her, but I should reconsider my type; just not when it comes to her. Yet you want me to work on a project with her. What on earth are you talking about? What project?'

'She found some sort of secret compartment in a desk at their uncle's house, and inside were all these letters written to their great-grandmother. Alex mentioned it, and said neither she nor Taylor has any burning desire to help her with them.'

'And you thought I would?' Nick practically growled out the words.

'Well, not exactly, but I did say that if anyone was capable of looking into old records you would be—what with knowing your way around Sacramento and computer research and whatever else it is you do there. That's why I was *harping on*, as you called it. I told Alex you'd head over there tomorrow afternoon—around three—to see if you could give her a hand with anything. Just tell her what you can and can't do. It's not like you have to hang around all day holding her hand or anything.'

Nick's head jerked toward the sound of a muffled laugh escaping Denver's lips. Then he turned back toward Travis in time to see him doing the mouth zipping thing again as he turned his focus back to the TV.

Nick sighed dramatically but, deep down, a tiny bit of him wondered exactly what both Travis and Denver thought they'd seen.

Would it kill him to offer to give her a hand with this project?

Of course not.

Might it even be interesting?

It might be.

And that was the problem. That he would even contemplate helping her with it confused the daylights out of him.

~~*~~

When Alex, Casey and Taylor arrived back at the house they sat in the driveway chatting, and Casey decided to ask the question that had been on her mind since they'd arrived in California.

'When are you two getting married? It seemed like we were at your house today, not Travis and Denver's. Guess you're spending so much time there it must feel like home to you.'

Alex suddenly looked rather serious. 'It does, actually, but I suppose I just want to give it a bit more time. Don't get me wrong, Travis and I are extremely happy, but neither of us had stellar successes with our first marriages, so I don't want to rush into this. We're together, and we love each other, and that's enough for the moment.'

Casey smiled. Alex was always so rational and logical—sensible, on top of being gorgeous, athletic, and now, thanks to the inheritance they'd all received, quite wealthy. 'But he does want to marry you, right?'

'Yes, and he's anxious to get me an engagement ring. He's also well aware that I'm just not quite ready for that. We'll get there ... in time.'

Casey sighed, thinking how it must be nice to be so sure of a relationship. 'Well, I can't imagine anyone who'd be more suitable for you. The two of you seem to have been made for each other.'

Alex grinned, raising a brow. 'I know, right?'

Taylor chipped in from the back seat. 'I was thinking the same thing; you two seem perfect for each other. I guess that means you'll be staying here forever?'

Alex chewed her lower lip. 'Forever is an awfully long time. I prefer to think that I'll be here for the foreseeable future.'

'Well, I can't speak for Casey but I certainly will miss you at home. Although I suppose it's not like we saw you all that often when you were playing tennis either. And you know, the flight wasn't so bad—we can do this trip again, and you'll come over from time to time to catch up with us and Mum.'

'Of course we'll see each other. It's not like I've moved to some remote jungle that can only be reached by old buses and donkey carts or something. We'll get together regularly.'

Taylor gripped the side of Alex's seat. 'Maybe we can all go on holidays together ... we could meet in Europe? Just perhaps not anywhere that you need to take donkey carts and buses to get to.'

Alex laughed. 'A holiday together sounds great; a beach resort somewhere exotic, like the Greek Islands. Let's work on that. Anyway, I'm going.'

Casey got out of the car and stretched her shoulders back, glad to be standing. She leant over, talking through the open car door. 'I might go for another walk, to get my metabolism working a bit harder. I've got to get back into some sort of routine ... I'm really missing going to the gym.'

'There isn't one here in Masons Flat and I haven't looked further afield as I've been quite happy going for a run most mornings, but I would say there'd definitely be one in Sonora. It isn't far—do you want me to run you over there in the morning?'

Casey shook her head. 'No, but I might take you up on your offer to let us use Uncle Steven's old Buick. You said you'd had it serviced recently, right?'

Alex nodded. 'Yes, I thought you two might want to use it. It's full of fuel, and the keys are in the cutlery drawer—under the plastic tray. Are you certain you're ready to drive on the right?'

Casey laughed. 'It can't be that hard. I mean you've picked it up.' She winked, and looked at Taylor who had gotten out of the back and now stood beside her. Taylor raised her hand and gave her a quick high-five.

Alex rolled her eyes. 'Okay, but remember your body should be near the middle of the road. If it's close to the verge, you're driving on the wrong side of the road.'

Casey squinted as she let Alex's words sink in. 'Yeah, makes sense. Okay, I'll be fine.'

Taylor giggled. 'I might go with you and have a poke around the town while you're working out.'

Alex clapped her hand over her mouth. 'Oh, drat. I just thought of something I was meant to tell you. Nick will be coming over tomorrow, around three, to see if he can give you a hand with those letters.'

Casey could feel the blood rush from her face. 'What?'

'I was telling Travis about the letters, and he suggested Nick should come over in the afternoon to give you a hand.'

'And so you and Travis took it upon yourselves to organise for Nick to come over? What makes you think I need help? I'm perfectly capable of reading the letters on my own.'

Casey looked to Taylor for support, but Taylor just shrugged and pulled a helpless looking face.

'It isn't that you aren't capable of reading the letters, but Nick knows a lot of people in Sacramento—people who work for the state—and Travis reckons he'll know exactly what to do if you need access to any sort of records. You know, driver's licences, birth certificates, those sorts of things.'

Casey let out an exasperated breath as she shook her head slowly.

Alex smiled and winked. 'Besides, as I said earlier, you could do—and have done—a lot worse than spending time with a guy like Nick. It'll be good for your soul.'

'Okay, whatever. He'll probably get bored and leave after half an hour anyway.' She pushed the car door shut, then walked around to the driver's side. When Alex rolled the window down, Casey leaned over and gave her a quick peck on the cheek. As she pulled back she stopped with her face still quite close, staring deeply into her sister's eyes. 'But however it goes, enough with the match-making.'

Alex's mouth flew open in mock exaggeration. 'Match-making? Me? Never.'

CHAPTER 8

Nick pulled up in front of the Mason house shortly before three, and Casey appeared within a few moments of him knocking on the door dressed in sweatpants, an old pullover and flip-flops. He knew straight away that Travis and Denver were right; she was definitely trying to impress him. As if. He started to shake his head and chuff out a laugh, but caught himself, certain she wouldn't know what he was thinking and might think he was being critical of her attire, which he definitely wasn't.

'Hi Casey ... I, uh, Travis said you might need a hand going through some old letters. You were expecting me, right?'

Casey either wasn't as disciplined as he was, or perhaps didn't care what he thought. She drew in a noisy breath, and let it out dramatically as she spoke. 'I'm perfectly capable of reading letters, so I don't actually need any help, but yes, I knew you were coming.'

He stood there, waiting for her to invite him in. When she made no move to do so, he gestured toward his car. 'Well, if you'd rather I left ... I mean, Travis was just trying to be ...' he wanted to say Travis was being interfering, but instead he finished with, 'helpful.'

She glanced back over her shoulder for a moment, then looked at him again and put a weak smile on her lips. 'Sorry, you're right—he thought I needed some help. Come in if you want to. Of course I really won't mind if you'd rather not.'

And there it was—a hall pass. He could leave, tell Travis she hadn't wanted his help, and that would be the end of it. And yet, surprisingly, his feet stayed glued to the spot, and once again confusion washed over him and he no longer knew what he wanted.

When he made no move to leave, she stepped back and swept her arm across in an imitation of a welcoming gesture. He stepped inside and stopped in the hallway.

She shut the door and walked past him, heading down the hallway. 'I was about to make myself a cuppa. Do you want one?'

He'd heard Alex use the expression and knew she meant cup of coffee or tea. 'I could go for a Coke, if you've got one.'

'I think you're pushing your luck, but I'll check.'

She led the way into a large, open-plan kitchen. He'd never been in the Mason's house, and was surprised by its size, given her uncle had lived alone for as long as Nick knew him.

Casey opened the fridge, then went to a pantry and checked there. 'Nope, nothing. I can offer you a coffee or a tea? I'm having tea.'

He nodded. 'Maybe just a glass of water.'

He watched as she made her tea and filled a glass with tap water, then followed her as she led the way to the back of the house and into a study. The room held one large desk and several filing cabinets. On the top of the desk were several stacks of envelopes—he guessed there'd have to be close to a hundred letters, maybe more.

'You sit there, and I'll go get another chair,' Casey said, pointing to the leather desk chair.

'No, that's your seat. I'll grab one from the kitchen.'

When he returned, she looked up from the desk, holding one of the letters.

'So, how do you want to tackle this? I mean, do you want to read these letters I've already read, or should I just fill you in on the general nature of them? Is that what you had in mind?'

'I didn't really have anything in mind, to be honest. Travis just said you might want some help, so whatever you think,' he said as he pulled the chair up to the side of the desk and sat.

She picked up one of the envelopes and showed him the postmark. 'This is the first letter, written in July of 1918 and postmarked in San Francisco.'

When she paused, he wondered if she'd changed her mind about him helping, but then she continued, her voice sounding more agreeable.

'I've only read the first few, but I did flick through all of the envelopes and they're all postmarked the same, addressed the same way and in the same handwriting, so I can only assume they are all from the same person, a woman named Daisy, to her sister, Sarah Mason. In this first letter, Daisy states that she'd been arguing with their father, and that's why she ran off. She'd arrived in San Francisco where she'd found a room in a boarding house and then, shortly thereafter, a job.'

To his surprise, he found it intriguing that she'd come across the letters in the first place, and he watched her handling them with much greater interest than he'd thought he would.

Casey set the first letter on the desk, then counted out several more and held them up.

'These came several months apart and were mostly updates on her job, and places she'd visited as a tourist. Oh, and she mentioned the terrible flu that went through the city and the need to wear masks in public. But there was no mention of a man, so it doesn't seem she ran away to be with anyone. The strangest thing was that there wasn't any sort of return address on any of the letters. My guess is she didn't want to risk anyone finding one of the letters and learning her whereabouts.'

Nick kept staring at the desk the whole time Casey spoke, trying to work out where Casey had found them. 'And all these letters were hidden somewhere in this desk?'

Casey stood, and stepped away from the desk. 'Yes. Do you want to try to find the secret compartment?'

This was more like it—a mystery to solve, albeit one that Casey had already solved. He figured it wouldn't be that hard, given he was forearmed with the knowledge that the secret compartment existed.

He sat at the desk's leather chair, and slowly went through each drawer, running his hands along the sides, tops, bottoms and back walls of each space. He did the same with the whiskey cupboard on the side. When he found nothing, he got on the floor and looked under the desk for any sort of hook or handle. With nothing there, he did one last review of the entire exterior of the desk, inch by inch. Nothing.

'Ok, you're a better detective than I am. I don't see anything.'

Casey smiled. 'You give up?'

He took one more look at all the drawers, then shrugged. 'I guess so.'

Casey grinned. 'Good. I was hoping it wouldn't be obvious. After all, the letters were in there for over a hundred years and, by all appearances, neither Sarah's husband nor father found them. And then our great-uncle had the desk and didn't seem to have found them either. You not finding the drawer, even when you're specifically looking for it, gives me comfort that the letters really were hidden all those years.'

'So, where is it? And how did you find it?'

Casey leaned over him, pulling the top drawer out once again. 'Do you notice anything unusual about this drawer?'

He stared at it for some time, then ran his hand all around the inside of the drawer one more time. 'Nope, nothing.'

'Doesn't it seem rather shallow compared to the drawers on the right side, and the overall depth of the desk?'

Nick pulled out the drawer and then pulled out the top drawer on the right hand side of the desk. It was a good six or seven inches deeper. Why hadn't he noticed that before? 'That's pretty good detective work, Casey. How come you know so much about desks?'

'I had seen one with lots of secret drawers so I knew it was a possibility, but it did take me a while to find it. I just refused to give up.' Her smile held none of the one-upmanship he was pretty sure he'd have on his face if he'd been the one to discover it.

'So how does it open?'

When she showed him the trick, he cocked his head and looked at her with a new level of respect. It was quickly followed by an appreciation that Travis had been right. She might not be his type, necessarily, but she was kinda cute and definitely clever.

Casey grinned. 'Should we read a few more of them and see what mysteries they might hold?'

~~*~~

By quarter past four the room had grown dim so Casey stood and flicked on the overhead light. 'I need another cuppa. What about you?'

'That'd be nice. Whatever you're having is fine.'

Casey made her way into the kitchen, pulled out a mug for Nick, then stood waiting for the jug to boil. Now that they had something to discuss besides tattoos and ex-lovers, she was thoroughly enjoying Nick's company. And surprisingly, he seemed to be enjoying reading through the letters almost as much as she was. She sighed, admitting to herself that she was grateful Travis had thought to enlist him to help her after all. His analytical mind, not to mention his connections when it came to tracking down old records, might prove handy.

Forcing her mind back to the letters, she thought about what they'd learned this afternoon. Daisy mostly talked about places she'd explored, her job at the large oil company, and the few friends she was making at work. Daisy had finally given her sister a return address, and shortly after that there was congratulations offered for the birth of Sarah's first child, a boy named Joseph. That letter had been difficult to read, its ink smeared as though it had gotten wet. Although it could have been from rain, Casey preferred to think Sarah had missed her sister so much she'd shed a few tears while reading it. She'd have wanted to share this new child with Daisy—her only sister—who might as well have been on the other side of the country.

Armed with fresh cups of tea, it wasn't long before their perseverance paid off. Casey held a letter out in front of her and looked up. 'Nick, have a look at this letter. It mentions a child. Daisy's had a son—named Thomas. Did we miss something in an earlier letter? A hint that she was pregnant?'

Nick set his cup down and looked up into Casey's eyes. As he reached for the letter, his fingers grazed her hand and electrical pulses ran through her. The sensation caught her off guard, so she released the letter too quickly and it slipped between them, falling gently back down onto the desk.

'Sorry,' she said, shaking her head as she reached to pick it up. Nick reached at the same time, and again their fingers touched. She pulled back as heat scorched her cheeks.

She didn't look up when he began reading the letter, slowly, out loud.

My darling Sarah,

I have wonderful news. I've had a baby—a beautiful, healthy boy who I've named Thomas.

He's a wonderful baby, truly he is. He hardly cries, and is already sleeping through the night. As for me, I'm fine. It was a relatively easy birth—only a few hours—and I feel fine now.

The other ladies here in the house are quite taken with him, and a few have even offered to sit with him in the evenings from time to time because he is so adorable. And the most wonderful thing is that the landlady here has graciously agreed to look after him during the day so I can go back to work.

It's not that I am in dire straits. On the contrary, the baby's father wishes to provide a generous allowance so that neither Thomas nor I will want for anything. He's tried to encourage me to quit working, but I do enjoy the mental stimulation and I've made a few friends there now. Thomas's father even tried to get me to move to a bigger apartment, which he would gladly pay for, but I am happy where I am, and I feel very much loved here with the other women.

I know it's a lot to ask, but I implore you, please say nothing to anyone. Father doesn't need to know about Thomas, and neither does anyone else. I've given Thomas our family name, as I don't wish to draw attention to his father.

As much as it pains me to say it, I won't be returning to Masons Flat. Please don't worry about me as I feel so blessed here in San Francisco. My biggest regret is that Thomas and Joseph might have grown up knowing each other, becoming close like we are. Perhaps one day, when they are a little older, you can find an excuse to bring Joseph here to see us. I do miss you so very much.

Your loving sister,

Daisy

Nick paused for a minute when he finished the letter. 'She's had a child, sometime in the fall of 1921, and he'd be ... some sort of distant cousin of yours, I guess.'

Casey wasn't sure which emotion was more powerful; excitement about the revelation, or sorrow at the predicament Daisy had been faced with. She met Nick's intense gaze as she spoke.

'The prospect of raising a child on her own, in a strange city, and without any help from her family ... it must have required great courage. Now I see why she wanted the letters kept secret. Daisy didn't want her father to know about his grandson. Maybe she was afraid he'd try to come take him away from her.'

Nick raised an eyebrow, nodding gently. 'It certainly wouldn't have been an easy life for her.' He took a long sip of the tea and set the mug down on the corner of the desk. 'Do you think the cause of the argument will come out in later letters?'

'I hope so—I hope we aren't left just ... wondering.'

'Yeah, uncertainty wears you down,' Nick said, his voice oozing sadness.

Casey was surprised he was taking this so hard. Sure, it would be great to understand what drove Daisy away from her family, but she didn't think it would wear her down if she didn't know. Maybe there was something more to his comment than this letter. 'In what way?'

Nick reached for his cup, but didn't pick it up—just wrapped his hand around it as though warming it. Then he looked up and met her curious gaze.

'I had an aunt that ran off—before I was even born—my Dad's sister. I remember him talking about her occasionally. He was always really sad when he talked about her—mostly because he never knew why she left.'

'Really? And to this day she's never contacted him?'

'No. Not one letter or phone call. It would have put my father's mind to rest if she'd at least told him why she left—it would have put an end to all the speculation. At least Daisy wrote to Sarah. Eve never gave my father that courtesy.'

'Wow, that's really sad. Your poor father.'

'Yeah, well, he hasn't mentioned her in years so I don't ever bring it up, but I doubt he's ever gotten over it.'

Casey took a sip of her tea, using it as a break in the conversation. It must have been terrible for Nick's father; having his sister disappear like that. At least Daisy wrote to Sarah. She tried to imagine what she'd feel like if one of her sister's took off without explanation and didn't contact her, but she couldn't because she knew it would never—could never—happen.

She finished her tea in silence, and then forced her thoughts to return to the current situation. 'At least Daisy seemed to have made some good friends by the time she wrote this letter. And the landlady must have cared deeply about her because an unwed mother back then ... well, I suspect some landladies would not have been so understanding of one of the residents bringing disrepute to the house.'

'You're right ... I hadn't thought of that,' Nick replied, giving her a thoughtful look. 'She says she's given Thomas their family name, but do we know what that is? Do you remember seeing it mentioned in any of the earlier letters?'

Casey took a deep breath, glad to be back onto the mystery of Daisy. 'No. Perhaps that's something you can work out—Sarah's maiden name. Alex said you had access to marriage records, right? And birth certificates? Maybe you could track down Sarah, even if Daisy might have kept below the radar.'

A loud bang from the other end of the house announced Taylor's arrival. A moment later she popped her head into the study. 'Still going at it, are you? Hi Nick, by the way.'

Nick smiled and said hello. Casey answered for them. 'As a matter of fact, the letters have started getting really interesting. And speaking of interesting, where have you been all this time? I figured you'd have rung me to come get you ages ago.'

'I was playing pool and having way too much fun to come back here, until I started to get hungry so checked the time. Alex is expecting us to pop around there for leftovers tonight.'

'So ... how'd you get home?'

'Denver gave me a lift.'

Casey's forehead tightened in a frown. 'Denver's driving?'

'Yes, he can drive an automatic, so he sometimes borrows Travis' Range Rover.'

'Well, well, well. So Denver isn't quite as incapacitated as I thought he was.' She looked at Nick and winked.

Taylor shook her head. 'He only started driving a few days ago, but his cast comes off soon and I bet he'll be back into doing chores shortly afterwards. Wonder if that means Alex will come back here? And what about you, Nick? Are you going to continue to hang around for a while?'

'A bit longer I think,' he answered. 'I had planned to stay through Christmas, but I'll stick around until Travis is sure he can get by without me.'

Casey turned, giving him a sideways look. 'And then I suppose you'll go back to Sacramento—to the same job, or will you do something different?'

Nick cleared his throat before answering. 'No, I won't be going back right away. I'm taking a few months off work to do some travelling. I'm going to England first and then meeting up with a friend in Ireland. And as for going back to my job, it'll depend on what projects they've got lined up, and where they need me. It should be in Sacramento, but there's no guarantee.'

Casey hadn't expected that answer, and the news saddened her. Not that it should—she and Taylor would be leaving soon after Christmas themselves so it made little difference whether he stayed in the area or not. She forced a smile onto her face, and replied with a strong Aussie expression as a way of reminding herself that she'd be back in Australia soon. 'Good on ya. I haven't travelled much myself, and sometimes think I should. Broadens one's horizons, or so they say.'

Taylor's eyes flew open wide. 'Now there's a thought, Casey, we should go on one of those world cruises ... take six months and see everything. It's not as if we can't afford to do it. It's worth thinking about, right?'

Casey smiled at her sister. It was indeed worth some consideration. After all, who knew who you might run into while travelling the world?

CHAPTER 9

Casey hadn't expected dinner to be as elaborate on the day after Thanksgiving, but it was. Alex had made fresh mashed potatoes, sweet potatoes and green beans, had warmed up the turkey, and there was plenty of cranberry sauce left from the previous day's feast as well. She'd even toasted some bread rolls, the aroma of which just about sent Casey to Heaven as they'd walked in the door.

Now Taylor was in the kitchen serving up the last of the pumpkin pie. They'd be smaller slices today, however, given how much they'd eaten the day before.

'I hear the letters are becoming a bit more interesting?' Travis commented, turning his attention to Casey.

'Absolutely. Daisy has had a child, and so has Sarah. Actually, I suppose Sarah's child, Joseph, would be our grandfather, right, Alex?'

Alex looked up. 'Yes, Joseph was our grandfather, and his brother was Uncle Steven.'

'So, who was this child of Daisy's?' Travis asked.

Casey shrugged. 'All we know is his first name—Thomas.'

'I'll go to Sacramento on Monday,' Nick said. 'If we can find Sarah's marriage record, it'll be listed there. Then once we have her maiden name, we might be able to find some records for young Thomas.'

'I take it Daisy's family name hasn't been mentioned in any of the letters?' Alex asked, frowning.

'Not that we've seen so far,' Casey replied. 'Do you think you've seen it on anything? Old letters or files when you were going through Uncle Steven's papers?'

Alex shook her head. 'I can't recall seeing anything with Sarah's maiden name. I suppose there's no real reason there would be.'

'I was just hoping,' Casey said as Taylor set a sliver of pumpkin pie in front of her. 'Thanks Taylor, it looks great.'

Alex raised her hands. 'None for me, thanks,' then turned back to Casey. 'It sounds rather sad, doesn't it? I mean, Daisy having to raise a child on her own, away from all of her family. It wouldn't have been easy. Did she have any other siblings?'

'There's been no mention of any other family members. And I thought exactly the same thing—about how hard it must have been—especially as it does seem Daisy and Sarah were close. Whatever caused the falling out with her father, it doesn't seem that it affected Daisy's feelings about Sarah.'

Alex shrugged. 'You know this is the stuff of sad love songs, don't you? Sisters torn apart by some sort of dispute ... babies growing up not knowing the rest of their families ... and then there's the city by the bay—a country songwriter would have a field day with this.'

Casey cringed, praying Alex wasn't going to mention her own attempts at writing lyrics. It was something Casey did in private, and although she hoped that one day she'd learn to play the piano and turn them into real songs, she didn't want to discuss them right now. She gave Alex a look she hoped said *don't*, and changed the subject. 'This pie is so good, Taylor. I'm glad there was some left for us for tonight.'

Taylor beamed with pride. 'Thanks, Case.'

Travis cocked his head. 'That's a thought, Alex. Nick here is a bit of an amateur songwriter. Plays the guitar and he can sing, too. What do you think, Nick? Can you turn this into a sad country song?'

Casey turned to Nick in disbelief. Nick? Wrote songs? She waited while he gathered his thoughts to answer his cousin.

'I doubt I could do it justice—I mean, I hear what you're saying Alex, but it's not that close to home for me. Besides, I'd hardly call myself a songwriter. I wrote one song when I was in high school, and now Travis thinks I'm the next Blake Shelton or something.'

Alex turned and gave Casey a slight wink before looking at Nick. 'You wrote a song?'

Casey double-downed on the *don't even go there* look, gritting her teeth.

Nick shook his head as he replied under his breath. 'Yeah, I wrote one song ... but it's nothing special.'

'Surely you can let us be the judge of that, right?' Alex said, encouraging him.

'Go on, Nick, grab your guitar and give us a taste of it ... you know you want to.' Travis could barely conceal the laughter in his voice.

Casey wasn't sure why Nick turned and looked at her before answering. Had he noticed the looks she'd flashed Alex?

'Not today, Travis. I ... I'm rusty; haven't played anything for a while. Trust me, ladies, it's not all that good.'

When Alex coughed softly, Nick turned his attention to her. 'Well then, another time for sure,' she said as she stood to clear the plates away. Casey followed Alex into the kitchen.

'Don't you dare say a thing about my songs. You know I've told you about them in the strictest confidence.'

Alex held a finger to her lips. 'Never. Don't worry.'

When they returned to the table, conversation seemed to have hit a dead end.

Taylor looked at Nick, then at Casey, then back at Nick. A smile brightened her face, but then she turned to Casey again, and Casey gave her the same look she'd given Alex. Taylor kept any comments she might have been thinking to herself. Finally, she asked Casey, 'Do you think you'll find anything else of interest in the letters?'

'Hard to say, but I'm anxious to get back to them.' She turned to Nick. 'We could keep working on them tomorrow if you aren't busy, and you never know, maybe I can help you find the inspiration you need to write the song.'

Nick's eyes lit up. 'You want to keep going on them tomorrow?'

Alex jumped in. 'Not tomorrow. The forecast is for sunshine all day, so we're going to take advantage of it and drive down to the city. I want to take Casey and Taylor over to Alcatraz, and then have lunch at Fisherman's Wharf. We might not get too many good days while they're here, so I want to go while we can.'

'Sounds good,' Casey replied. 'And I want to check out the Palace of Fine Arts, where Daisy used to go, if that's okay Alex. I just want to have a look at it.'

Casey turned in time to see Nick's face drop, surprised that he looked disappointed. Maybe he had wanted to get back to the unfolding story as much as she did. Maybe it had affected him more than he'd admitted. Or maybe her offer to help him with another song was part of it. Wouldn't it be funny if he turned out to be happy to give her a hand with some of her own songs, too?

When Alex and Travis headed to the kitchen to clean up, Casey followed. She'd give them a hand, but what she mostly wanted was a chance to think without Nick's eyes burning into her—because she really wanted to get her head around what was going on between them.

~~*~~

When Casey returned from the gym two mornings later, Taylor took the car and headed over to Darleen's house to make some more pies. Alone in the house, Casey was anxious to make a start on the letters, so was pleased when Nick called to say the heavy rain meant he was off the hook for working horses for the rest of the morning.

'How was your day in San Francisco?' he asked as Casey ushered him through the front door an hour later.

'It was great—it was such a perfect day. I feel sorry for anyone trying to do today what we did yesterday—I can't imagine being out on the bay on a day like this.'

'Yeah, it'll be blowing a gale out over the water.'

Casey ushered Nick into the study, where she'd already pulled out the letters. She'd put a rubber band around the stack they'd already been through, and the rest were in neat piles in chronological order.

Deciphering Daisy's handwriting was getting easier now that Casey had become familiar with it, and they quickly scanned the next few letters to find they disclosed nothing new. The two young boys, Joseph and Thomas, were mentioned but only in so far as to say they were both healthy and growing quickly. Daisy had returned to her job and the arrangements she'd made with the landlady at the boarding house seemed to be working well for her. There were undertones of sadness in Daisy's letters, but never anything obvious. Perhaps she simply didn't want her sister to worry about her.

And then another son was born. Ray was born in 1922, a little more than a year after Thomas. Daisy spoke lovingly about her new baby, but made it clear in the letter that she had no intentions of having any further children. She still didn't mention the father's name, nor say anything about where he lived, or what he did for a living. Not even the slightest clue.

Casey set the letter on the desk and took a deep breath. 'It must have been terrible for Sarah ... not being allowed to tell anyone, and not, apparently, being able to visit.'

Nick nodded. 'It's a long trip ... even now, by car. I can't begin to imagine how long it would have taken back then.'

'Would it have been by stagecoach back then? I mean, did they even have cars?'

Nick rubbed his jaws. 'The Ford was invented in 1908, but I doubt there were many around yet in 1922, and even if they were around the roads wouldn't have been terribly good. You could be right—travel was no doubt slow; there could have been trains or boats or as you say, stagecoaches ... but however she travelled it wouldn't have been direct. No wonder there's no indication they ever got together.'

'I need a cuppa. Can I get you one?' Casey asked, standing.

'Sure,' Nick said as he got up and followed her into the kitchen.

As the jug boiled, Casey brought up something she'd been thinking about all morning. 'You know, I really would like to hear that song you wrote.'

Nick smiled. Could he be blushing, or was that her imagination? 'Would you? I could play it for you now, if you like.'

'Seriously? You brought your guitar with you?'

'Not technically. I mean, I didn't bring it here specifically but, since I've been staying at Travis and Denver's place, I haven't felt like playing it. It's still in the car.'

'In that case, I'd love to hear it.'

When Nick returned with the guitar in hand, Casey led him into the family room where they sat on the sofa.

Casey watched as he tuned it, then the fingers of his left hand made the first chord and his right hand strummed the strings slowly.

'This song is called *When You Left,*' Nick said, his voice deeper than normal, his face seemingly transported to another place and time. 'And you've got to remember I was a pimple-faced teenager when I wrote it. Just a kid, you know? So be kind in your criticism.'

When he grinned sheepishly, she smiled, knowing exactly how he must feel—revealing something so personal to someone he didn't know that well. It was something she hadn't had the courage to do yet herself.

When you left, my heart nearly stopped,
the clouds rolled in and the temperature dropped.
The joy in my heart must have followed your path,
and left in its wake a dark aftermath.

I hadn't expected to miss you so much,
I hadn't realised I'd long for your touch.
When the night closes in and the darkness surrounds,
I think of you, darling, while my heart pounds and
pounds.

My days are so empty, and my nights are so cold,
the sun's lost its brilliance and it makes me feel old.
The one thing I'd hoped for, the one thing that mattered,
disappeared when you left me, and now I feel shattered.

I hadn't expected to miss you so much,
I hadn't realised I'd long for your touch.
When the night closes in and the darkness surrounds,
I think of you, darling, while my heart pounds and
pounds.

It's a hard road to travel, this thing we call life,
made harder by loneliness, brought upon us by strife.
I thought that you loved me, that I was your first,
You took me for a fool, and I couldn't have felt worse.

But the battle goes on, and one day you may find,
that the best love you had is the one you left behind.
As your days grow darker, you may long for my touch,
then perhaps you'll understand why it mattered so much.

'Wow, Nick, it's lovely,' Casey said, looking at him with a new level of respect. 'And I'm not just saying that to be nice. It was really good.'

'Do you think so?'

Casey gave a knowing nod. Her heart had been broken plenty of times over the years, and the heartbreak had often inspired her own lyrics. 'Travis was right. You should keep it up—it's a lovely song, and you've got a nice voice, too.'

Nick set the guitar against the end of the sofa and turned back to her. 'Thanks, Casey. It's good of you to say so, even if you are just trying to be polite.'

'But I'm not. I loved it. I suppose it could use some work, but couldn't we all?' When she grinned again, he shook his head slowly. 'Look, it's got so much potential. If you revisit it now, I'm sure you could improve it to where you're happy with it. I mean, the melody is beautiful, and there's so much emotion in it.'

He nodded slightly, and his lips turned up in a tentative smile. 'Maybe I should work on it ... although to what end I've no idea.'

Casey took a deep breath. Was he right to think it would go nowhere? Surely, it was as much worth pursuing as anything she'd written. She smiled. 'I think you should. Have you been playing long? Did it take you a long time to learn?'

She wasn't ready to give up on music, and this could be a massive step forward for her. She'd been thinking of learning the piano, but a guitar would be much easier to cart around with her. Maybe that's where she should concentrate. And maybe Nick could help her.

'I got my first guitar for my twelfth birthday and I taught myself to play by ear, by mimicking what I heard on the radio. I upgraded to this guitar a couple of years later, and I've got an electric one as well, but yeah, I've been playing ever since.'

'And you can read music and everything, right? I mean to write a song you must know how to write the music?'

'Sure. When I joined the band in college I had to learn to read music.'

Casey pondered the heartbreaks she'd had as a young girl. Finally, on a sigh, she asked, 'She must have meant a lot to you?'

'Yeah, look, it was a dark time for me ... or at least, I thought it was. You'd know what it's like—high school relationships were the most important things in the world back then. I haven't written anything since, nor have I been hurt by anyone like that. It was the heartache that inspired me.'

'Can you show me? How to play, I mean?'

When he cocked his head, his brow wrinkling, she was certain he would say no.

'Okay,' he finally answered. 'It's not that hard. Trust me, if I can do it, anyone can.'

He retrieved the guitar and showed her how to hold it. Then he helped her form a chord with her left hand, and had her strum the strings with the back of her nails. It didn't sound anywhere near as good as when he'd done it.

'Here, press harder with your fingertips.' He reached over and placed his hand over hers, helping her position her fingers. As it had with the letters, his touch sent shivers through her, and she pulled back slightly.

'Did that hurt?'

She shook her head. 'No, sorry, it's just an awkward position. Show me again.'

'You should find it easier than some do, if you're serious, because you've already got callouses on your fingers. Why is that?'

She lifted her hand and inspected her fingertips. 'Oh, that's from twisting the wires to make floral arrangements. I twist wire into them a lot of the time.'

'I thought it might have something to do with the flowers. Anyway, like I said, that should make it easier.'

She placed her hand as he'd shown her and pressed as hard as she could with her fingertips. This time, when she strummed, it didn't sound too bad. When she looked up at him, he smiled, and his approval sent warmth right through her.

'There, you've got it,' Nick said. 'I've probably got some of my old beginner books, but if not, they're pretty easy to come by. You'll pick it up quickly if you're determined to learn.'

Casey's heart filled with pride. She was finally playing an instrument. And that was the next step in her becoming a real songwriter—being able to write down the melodies in her head.

The sound of the front door opening announced Taylor's return before she even called out.

'Oh, hey Nick. Wow, are you teaching Casey to play the guitar?'

'Hi Taylor, and yes, I'm showing Casey a few chords to get her started.'

Casey made eye contact with Taylor, once again giving that look that said *don't say anything*. 'I've been meaning to learn an instrument for quite some time,' she said.

Taylor's slight smile indicated she'd gotten the message. 'Well then, I'll leave you to it. I'm just here to change my clothes and make sure you don't need the car for anything?'

'The car? No, not that I know of, why?' Casey asked. 'Where are you going now?'

'One of the ladies asked if I wanted to come over to her place tonight—there's a group of them getting together for a planning meeting ... for a bake-sale next weekend to raise money for the school. I said I'd love to help.'

'Are you having dinner here before you go?'

Taylor ducked her head apologetically. 'No, it's a dinner meeting. Sorry, I didn't even think of you as I knew you wouldn't be interested. There's stuff here, right? Or you can always go see what Alex is cooking.'

Casey grinned at her sister. 'Alex is busy tonight—something to do with some buyer for a couple of Travis' horses, but don't worry about me. I'll find something here. You go, enjoy your dinner party. I'll be fine.' She sniffed back a mock tear, and then winked.

'I knew you'd be okay. I'll leave you to your guitar lessons then,' Taylor said as she made her way toward her bedroom.

While Taylor changed, Nick showed Casey a few chords she could practise and then they made their way back to the study to read a couple more letters. There was nothing of particular interest in them, just more of the same: updates on the children, Daisy's job, and things she'd done and seen in the city.

When Taylor left, Casey added the letters they'd read to the stack of completed ones and turned to Nick. 'I think I'll make an omelette for dinner. We've got fresh tomatoes and plenty of eggs and cheese, and bread. Can I interest you in staying, or have you got other plans?'

~~*~~

Though the invitation caught him off-guard, Nick had to admit he wasn't unhappy about it. Casey, despite her rather unconventional appearance, was turning out to be good company. He'd never met anyone quite like her before, or at least had never taken the time to get to know anyone like her.

'No, I haven't got any plans, but you don't have to cook for me. We could pop into town and go to the hotel, or the steak house is pretty popular.'

Casey's face crinkled in obvious disgust.

'Didn't you like what you had at the hotel the other night?'

'It's not that, it's just ... I don't eat much meat. I'll have a bit of fish or poultry once in a while, if there isn't another choice, but I'm much happier having vegetarian meals. I definitely don't think a steak house is my kind of place.'

He nodded at the knowledge of yet another aspect of his future cousin-in-law that was a bit quirky. 'I did not know that. What did you have at the hotel the other night?'

'The mushroom risotto. It was ... okay,' she answered, shrugging.

He was glad he hadn't noticed or he might have made a wise-crack about that too. He made a mental note: don't invite her to a barbeque. 'Well then, I'd love a cheese and tomato omelette.'

A few minutes later as Casey set the kitchen table, the phone rang. She answered it, and told Alex that she and Nick were going to have an omelette, then explained where Taylor had gone.

There was a pause, and Casey sort of rolled her eyes as her sister obviously had something to say about all the news. After a few moments, she looked at him and made a fake yawning gesture before reminding her sister that she lived alone at home, was perfectly capable of cooking something for them, and that no, Alex didn't need to look after her tonight.

The omelette was delicious, and as they were finishing up, Casey surprised him yet again. 'You know, I've written a couple of songs myself.'

He swallowed his last mouthful with a bit of difficulty and then rested his elbows on the table for a moment. 'Really? You've written songs? But didn't you just say you can't play an instrument?'

'I can't ... but I make up tunes in my head, and I sing the songs onto my phone. I'm not saying they're great, but I've had a lot of fun doing them. That's why I got excited when you said you played the guitar. I've been meaning to take piano lessons, but a guitar might be way easier than the piano—it's certainly a whole lot more transportable.'

Nick most certainly hadn't expected this from Casey. He looked up at her and could see apprehension in her eyes. 'Can we listen to one? After I help you clean up the kitchen?'

She let out a relieved breath. 'Sure ... and maybe, well, I mean, maybe you can suggest some improvements? And could I ask you to write down the chords for me?'

He cocked his head, allowing another wave of surprise to wash over him. This girl was definitely not turning out to be anything like what he'd originally thought.

CHAPTER 10

As they washed up the dishes, Casey used the quiet time to think through which of her songs was the best to start with. She still couldn't believe she was going to share her songs with Nick, or that he'd agreed to try to write down some chords so she could learn to play it.

Suddenly, she had it—she'd play him the one related to the rose tattoo on her left forearm. Nick had reacted poorly when she'd explained about the oleander, but maybe the story behind the rose would make him appreciate her tattoos, or at least understand that they meant something to her.

Returning to the sofa, she opened her phone. 'Okay, this is a song I wrote based on the family of a friend of mine, Hayley, and her grandmother, Rose. Rose was given her name because the green rose was her mother's favourite flower, and one her father had bought her mother on their wedding day. Hayley's mother had it tattooed on her forearm and I liked the story so much that I took a photo and then had this tattoo done based on the photo.' She held out her left arm and showed him the delicate flower. 'See how it doesn't have actual petals like most roses? Its *petals* are formed from sepals, which is the outer part of the rose. It looks like a regular rose before it opens, like this one, but see how once open it has a totally different appearance?'

Nick leaned over and studied the tattoo. When he looked up, his smile held admiration. 'Well, that's something I certainly never knew.'

'Me neither, until my friend told me the story. I'd never even heard of a green rose, so I researched it and there you go. A few years later, I wrote this song.'

'She must be a very good friend—to get both a tattoo and a song.'

Casey swallowed. 'She was—she was my closest friend, actually. When she was killed in a car accident, I wrote the song so I'd never forget her.'

He reached across and gently ran a finger down her forearm, outlining the rose. His gentle touch caused her breath to catch. This time when he looked up, his face had saddened. 'It must have been hard to lose such a good friend.'

'It was. It was a few years ago now, but I still get upset when I think of her.'

She swallowed back her emotions as she searched through her recordings until she found the one she wanted. The sound quality wasn't brilliant, but it would give him an idea of the melody and speed. She pressed play, and then stared at her phone, not daring to watch his face as he listened to one of her most personal creations.

Red and yellow, lavender and orange, all of those roses combined
Tell of the givers desire and love, their messages can't be denied.
Yet green was her favourite, its story unique, telling of the renewal of life
So he raced round the country to find them, a gift for when she became his wife.

What do you see when you look at her arm,
Can you see beneath the dyes?
Can you find the truth buried oh so deep,
Or do you only see the lies?

When duty called him they were both still so young, he only twenty-three.
It was her birthday that day, she'd turned twenty-one and as they sat beneath a tree,
She gave him the news with tears of joy in her eyes; she was expecting their first,
On the day he left, her tears returned, fearing their love had been cursed.

What do you see when you look at her arm,
Can you see beneath the dyes?
Can you find the truth buried oh so deep,
Or do you only see the lies?

Struck down in the desert, so far from her side, the bomb took its terrible toll,

When the telegram arrived, her heart leapt from her chest,
and in its place left a gaping hole.
The baby came early, from the shock of the news, yet she
relished the physical pain,
Much easier to bear than the heartache, knowing she'd
never see her true love again.

When the child was brought to her all freshly bathed, she
looked at her babe's gentle face,
Gave thanks for a girl, said her name will be Rose, and
prayed for her new daughter's grace.
For the rose she most loved was the green one, symbolising
the renewal of life,
She'd always remember he'd bought them, on the day he'd
made her his wife.

As the recording finished, Casey looked up. Had he liked it, or did he think it was awful? Her throat began to ache as she waited, watching, fearful of his reaction.

Finally, after what seemed a millennium, he looked up and met her gaze.

'It's beautiful, Casey. The words and melody ... and your voice. You didn't mention you could sing,' he said, placing his hand over hers and giving it a gentle squeeze.

She could feel the blood rushing to her face. She'd never had any compliments about her music before because she'd never let anyone hear it. Alex and Taylor were the only ones who knew she'd written some lyrics, and even they'd only read the words. They'd said they liked her songs, but that's what sisters are for.

'You really think so?' she asked, tentatively.

'Absolutely. You put me to shame without question.'

Embarrassed, she looked down at the floor. 'No way. Your song's awesome—it had so much feeling.' She looked up, daring to meet his eyes again. 'I wouldn't have had the courage to let you hear my song, except I figured you of all people might understand.' She smiled as something between them seemed to click into place.

He squeezed her hand again. 'Let me see what I can do.' He released her hand and grabbed his guitar, strumming it a few times until he found the right key. 'Now, can you play the song again, and I'll see if I can join in as it plays. Mind you, I may have to change a few words here and there to get it to flow smoothly; if you don't mind, that is.'

Casey shook her head. 'Of course I don't mind.'

After the first chorus Nick began to play along with her singing. She could hardly believe how good it sounded. He had her play it one last time, and he played it right through. It sounded fantastic.

When the song ended, he looked up at her tentatively. 'How did that sound?'

'Awesome. I am so impressed. It would mean so much to me to be able to play it like that.'

When he frowned, she lost heart. Was it going to be too hard for a beginner? But then he shrugged, nodding his head up and down, and eventually the frown turned to a smile. 'It might take me a little while, but I should be able to write down some chords and teach you to play them. Later, you can embellish it when you've learned a bit more. I don't suppose you've got any lined paper? Like a notebook or something?'

Casey thought hard, trying to remember if she'd seen anything. 'Not that I know of—I've only seen plain printer paper, but maybe we can get a notebook in town. Would the hardware store carry any school supplies?'

'Wouldn't count on it, but they won't be open now anyway. I was thinking of going up to Sacramento tomorrow afternoon to see my old boss, and see if he can help search for Sarah's marriage record. He's a guru on this stuff—he's done all his own family's genealogy charts as well as for some of my colleagues. If you want to come with me, there's a music store nearby.' He smiled and cocked his head. 'We can get you some beginner books and get some blank sheet music at the same time.'

Casey clasped her hands excitedly. 'Seriously? Aren't you meant to be helping Travis all day every day?'

'Things have settled down a bit now that he's sold a few of the young horses. Besides, I already mentioned I'm planning to head up there tomorrow, and given he's the one who enlisted me into this project of yours for precisely this reason, he can hardly complain can he?' He winked and cracked a crooked smile.

Casey couldn't believe how things had changed. The song, the guitar lessons, beginner books—it was all happening. Impulsively, she leaned closer to Nick, put her hands on his shoulders and planted a closed-mouth kiss on his lips. 'Thank you,' she whispered as she leaned back.

It was only a peck, and clearly meant as a way of expressing her gratitude, but the look on his face made it clear she'd startled him. Was kissing him a mistake?

His face changed from startled to puzzled, and then from puzzled to intrigued. When intrigue turned to desire, his eyes grew darker and he bit his lower lip seductively. 'That was ... unexpected. Nice, definitely, but you caught me off guard. Perhaps we ought to try that again?'

He leaned toward her, put his hands around her waist and drew her into his chest. She closed her eyes and when their lips met a surge of energy raced through her whole body. When he released her, her heart was pounding as fast as if she'd just done a five-kilometre run.

'Casey?' Nick asked tentatively. 'Are you all right?'

She drew in a noisy breath, and let it out with a whoosh as she opened her eyes. 'Yeah, never better. I'm just ... I mean, I didn't exactly expect *that*.'

'Unexpected, but not unenjoyable, I hope?'

She lifted her head and stared into his eyes. What had come over them? Why was he staring at her like that? Finally, she remembered he'd asked a question. 'Yeah, no, I mean, yeah of course I enjoyed it. I mean, didn't you?'

He smiled. 'Very much so. But just to be sure, I wouldn't mind trying it one more time.'

Her eyes flew open and she tilted her head slightly. That seemed all the encouragement he needed. He leaned in, drawing her close, kissing her in a way she hadn't been kissed in a long time. Deep and probing, his tongue teased her into a state of euphoria and her whole body throbbed with desire. She could barely breathe. When he finally released her, she would have fallen down if they weren't already sitting.

'Wow. So ... that was ... we ...' she said, shaking her head, trying to gather her thoughts.

'It sure was. Who'd have guessed? Opposites attract, right?'

And that's all it took to shake some sense into her. He was right—they were complete opposites. No, she definitely had no business getting involved physically with him, even if he was a good kisser. All the reasons to back away from him swirled around in her head, battling with the physical urge to continue. He was a white-collar-day-job kind of guy, and practically family. Besides, she'd be going home soon, and he hated her tatts. No, this time she'd listen to her head and not give in to physical desire.

'Say something, Casey. Things aren't going to be weird between us now or anything, right? Just because we kissed?'

'No way, of course not.' She shook her head, feeling a frown tightening every muscle in her face—muscles that a moment ago had experienced bliss.

She stood and headed back to the study. When she heard him follow her, she sat at the desk. 'So, had enough of the letters for tonight?' she asked, desperately wanting to put the kiss behind them.

He didn't sit, but rather stood and stared at her, his face unreadable. 'I think I've had enough. I should ... get back. I'll need to be up at the crack of dawn tomorrow so I can finish what I need to do so we can be on the road just after lunch. Big day tomorrow, right?'

'Sounds good. I'll pop these away, and walk you out.' She quickly returned the letters to the drawer, and replaced it into the desk.

As she led the way down toward the front door she spotted his guitar. 'Do you want to grab your guitar?'

He hesitated for a moment, then turned to her, shaking his head. 'We'll need it for when I give you your next lesson. How about I leave it here?' He walked over, put the guitar in its case and leaned it in the corner of the room.

'That's fine. I promise I won't sell it or anything.' She grinned, trying to keep things light even though deep down she was thrilled that they'd be spending more time together—both with the letters, and now, with their music.

When she opened the door, he went to walk around her but bumped into her when she stepped back to pull the door wide.

'Sorry,' they both said at the same time.

She bit her bottom lip in confusion over the change in the dynamics of their relationship. Was she meant to kiss him goodbye from now on?

He saved her from dwelling on it too long by leaning over and kissing her cheek. 'I'll be here around one; if that's okay with you?'

'Absolutely ... whatever time suits you.'

He squinted for a second, nodded, then headed to his car. 'Yeah, I should be here by one. I'll give you a buzz if it's looking like I'll be much later. Good night then,' he said just before shutting the door and starting his car.

As his taillights disappeared, Casey ran her fingers across her bottom lip, remembering the sensation of his kiss. Then she pulled her hand away quickly and looked around for witnesses. There were none, of course.

Yet the sensation of being watched lingered unnervingly.

Or at least, that's what she thought had unnerved her.

This was definitely not how she'd expected to feel when Nick left tonight. She'd expected to feel as she had every other time she'd parted company with him—somewhat relieved, or at best, nonplussed. She drew in a deep breath and let it out slowly. She didn't really care that he'd gone. She couldn't. It was just Nick after all.

The epiphany that struck her frightened her with its power, yet the enlightenment it delivered seemed to set her free. She'd shown him her most vulnerable side, and she'd lived through it. He hadn't laughed or put her down, or told her she was wasting her time. He'd been supportive and encouraging.

And then they'd kissed.

And as far as kisses went, it was right up there. She'd always been a sucker for a good kiss—a kiss that would send her wild with anticipation. It had been a deal breaker if a man she dated couldn't kiss well. Yet, even if they were all good kissers, every one of her past relationships had ended badly because, as the spark of attraction had faded, there had been nothing left to hold them together. She'd been so focussed on the physical aspects of her past lovers, she'd overlooked their lack of substance.

And therein lay the secret to all her failed relationships. It seemed so obvious now.

Longing wrapped itself around her, and confusion followed quickly on its heels. She wasn't sure what she missed more however—Nick's kiss or this new-found connection.

She shivered as a cool breeze snaked along her bare arms, and she shook her head to get a grip on herself. She wasn't in a relationship with Nick. She had, until tonight, not even been sure whether she liked him.

Yet things had changed, and there could be no going back to where they were before.

She turned and went back into the house, leaning on the door as she closed it. The dynamics of their friendship would never be the same. And now the question was, what was she going to do about it?

CHAPTER 11

Pulling away from her house, Nick ran his tongue along his lower lip, hoping to find some of Casey's sweetness lingering there. It had been nice, but he knew it had been a mistake—especially when he recalled the way she'd looked at him afterward.

The not-so-subtle advice Travis had given him about Casey crossed his mind, reinforcing what he already knew to be true; it wasn't fair to start anything with Casey. He was going travelling for months, and she was going back to Melbourne. She was off-limits physically, no matter how nice it had been.

He definitely shouldn't have kissed her like that.

Yet, when he'd looked into her eyes after she'd kissed him, it was like he'd looked at her for the first time, as if some sort of protective shield she maintained had dropped. He'd seen her vulnerable side, and at that moment he'd wanted her more than he'd ever wanted any woman.

But what did it matter? She wasn't for him. He would head off travelling soon, and she would go home. He had to simply ignore any deeper feelings that threatened to surface, and keep things between them casual.

As he pulled up back at his house, he could see the glow of the lights. That would be Travis and Alex, in the kitchen or out on the back deck. Not ready to face interrogation, he decided to enter through the front door and go straight to his bedroom. He might have made up his mind that the kiss was not to be repeated, but he couldn't trust Travis not to pick up on some change in his demeanour and make a big deal of it.

He got ready for bed and switched off the light, but his mind wasn't ready to sleep. He played the chorus of Casey's song again in his head, remembering its rhythm as well as some of the words. He'd been surprised by both the tone of her voice and the emotion in the lyrics. She'd said she'd written it for a good friend she'd lost, but he couldn't remember if she'd said how her friend had died. It must have hit her hard, to have been able to write with so much emotion.

He replayed the song several times in his mind, which of course led to him remembering her face when she looked up at him after he'd listened to the song, which led to him remembering the kiss. And there he was, right back where he'd started. He should never have kissed her. She wasn't meant to get under his skin. And yet, it seemed, that was exactly what had happened.

~~*~~

Casey tried to drop off to sleep, but her mind wouldn't stop racing with the memory of Nick's kiss and the sound of his voice as he'd sung his song. Every time she thought she'd been successful at clearing her mind he returned, his blue eyes blazing and his voice crooning.

She was familiar with this routine—becoming obsessed with a man to the point of not being able to sleep. It was something she'd done far too many times.

But she certainly hadn't expected to be doing it with Nick Gold.

This routine had always been reserved for men with whom she'd had an instant connection—one based almost entirely on physical chemistry. Those men were sexy and intriguing, dark and mysterious. They had at least some ink and/or piercings, dressed in bohemian casual, and wore their hair a bit long or even in a man-bun. Most sported a beard of sorts. These were men who, once spotted, she hadn't been able to tear her eyes off.

And Nick Gold was nothing like any of them. In fact, he was the complete opposite of all of the men she'd ever dated. If she'd spotted him from a distance before she'd met him, she'd never have given him a second look. And yet, none of that seemed to matter anymore.

She threw the covers off and sat on the edge of the bed, trying to think this through. Nick had as much musical talent as any man she'd known. He'd picked up her song after only listening to it twice, and played it right along with her recording, embellishing it with riffs and interludes of music that she'd never have dreamt of, but that had sounded mind-bogglingly incredible. And he'd agreed to help her learn to read music and play her songs.

She had to concentrate on the letters, and the music, and drop all other thoughts immediately. She could not allow herself to become obsessed with this conservative Californian cowboy because, ultimately, she was going home to Melbourne. She was going back to real life, which meant beer-gardens with live bands, coffee with friends, and long walks along the beach with Taylor.

And that meant she could not kiss him again, no matter the circumstances.

She stood, pacing the room for a few moments, trying to convince herself she had this under control. It should be easy enough. After all, it was simply her excitement that made her give him that quick kiss in the first place. And his response, well, he was probably so caught off guard that he ... hmm.

She ran her fingers over her lips—slowly. Why had he kissed her like that? Surely, it couldn't mean anything. Especially given what he said as he left, right?

What exactly had he said?

A shiver ran down her spine, and she crossed her arms in front of her chest, rubbing them. He'd said he hoped things weren't going to be weird between them just because of the kiss. *Just.* He'd emphasised the word just, showing it meant nothing to him.

She made her way to the bathroom and turned on the shower. Climbing in, she let the soothingly warm water wash over her skin as she closed her eyes. Her attraction to him tonight meant nothing. It had to be just some weird form of admiration because he'd played her song.

She shut off the taps and stood there for a moment, letting the water drip onto her feet. She was here for a few more weeks, and after that she'd be back in Melbourne. And with a bit of luck, she'd know how to play the guitar well enough to put some of her other songs to music. She had to keep her head straight, continue to hang out with Nick the same way as before—casually—and learn as much as she could from him.

Surely, it couldn't be that hard.

After all, this cowboy was so clearly not her type.

~~*~~

Taylor was already dressed and finishing her breakfast when Casey made her way into the kitchen a bit later than normal. She'd slept in, which was out of character.

‘Where are you off to so early?’ Casey asked as she made herself a coffee.

‘Alex is picking me up. She’s going to drop me at Darleen’s house. A few of us are meeting there to get started with making things for the bake-sale. Then this afternoon when Darleen goes to work, I’ll go to the saloon with her and play some pool with Denver.’

‘Pool? With Denver?’

Taylor rolled her eyes dramatically, denying anything between them. ‘He’s been really bored not having much he can do around his property, and standing to play pool isn’t bothering him now. Better than him sitting in front of the television all day, don’t you agree?’

‘Oh, I have no doubt it’s good for him. I’m just surprised that you’re joining him. I gather you’ve taken to this game, have you? Or is there some other ... attraction?’ She raised an eyebrow, teasingly.

‘It’s a fun game, and I’m better at it than I’d ever have guessed I would be. And of course it’s nice because Darleen is always there, too.’

Casey shrugged and sat at the table across from her, disappointed that Taylor hadn’t bitten. She took a sip of her coffee before continuing. ‘I think it’s great that you’ve discovered something you enjoy, but you mightn’t think it’s as much fun when you get home as you do now. After all, you won’t have Denver playing with you.’ And as she said those words, she wondered how much of her wanting to learn to play the guitar was because of Nick.

Taylor tilted her head defiantly. ‘There will be other people to play with. In fact, it’ll be a great way to meet new people. Anyway, if you aren’t doing anything this afternoon, you should join us.’

‘I am doing something, as a matter of fact. I’m going into Sacramento with Nick. I don’t suppose you want to come with us?’

Taylor quirked a brow and replied slowly. ‘No, I’ll let you two go on your own. But you know it’s pretty rich of you to be teasing me about Denver, when here you are running off with Nick for the day.’

‘I’m not running off with him. He’s helping me discover Sarah’s maiden name so we can find out more about Daisy and her son. Then, while we’re there, we’ll go to a music store to get some beginner books for me.’ Casey stopped short of saying they were going to get music paper. She didn’t want to mention anything about her song yet. ‘And maybe they'll even have a guitar I can buy, so I don't have to borrow Nick's.'

Taylor didn't press her any further, but simply stood and carried her breakfast dishes over to the dishwasher. 'Well, you enjoy yourself. I do think it'd be fun to go to Sacramento one day—I've heard the tour of the Capitol Building is brilliant. Maybe we can get Alex to join us so the three of us can have a day together.'

'That's a great idea—we'll have to organise it. So, I thought I'd take the car and go to the gym this morning ... that is, if you don't need it?'

'Go for it. I won't need it at all today. I guess that means I won't see you for dinner either? You'll no doubt stop somewhere while you're out?'

Casey hadn't thought about that, but by the time they did everything they wanted to, it could be dinner time. 'Maybe, I'm not sure, but if you get an offer, don't turn it down for my sake. If we don't end up stopping anywhere for dinner, I'll find something here.'

~~*~~

Nick pulled into the driveway at the Mason's house and spotted the front door opening before he'd even shut off the engine. His heart thumped irregularly for a beat or two as Casey, dressed in jeans, boots and a heavy, cream-coloured sweater, caught his eye and smiled before turning to lock the door behind her.

'I don't have much American cash with me,' she said as she threw her tote bag onto the floor and jumped into the passenger seat.

His mind went blank, overwhelmed by her fresh, just-out-of-the-shower scent that reminded him of jasmine, and the gold flecks in her eyes that glistened as they caught the mid-day sun.

Struggling to regain his self-control, he threw the car in reverse and looked over his shoulder as an excuse to take his eyes off her. Once he pulled onto the road, he found his voice. 'They do take credit cards; it's not like we're a third world country or anything. I gather you do have at least one credit card?'

'Oh, sure, of course I do,' she answered, shrugging. 'I just didn't think for a moment.'

The meaningless chatter along with the need to focus on the road helped him find balance. He drove for several minutes without speaking.

Casey broke the silence. 'It's nice of you to take me with you. I've been thinking I should get my own guitar so I can practise every night, and not just when you have time to show me.'

'That's a great idea. Have you got other songs you're ready to put to music? Or just the one we listened to?'

She hesitated for a moment. 'I have a few, but I think the one you heard is the best. I've always dreamt of getting to where I could play the piano and compose music to go with the lyrics. I'm such a fan of both Missy Higgins and Delta Goodrem. They're both fabulous Australian singer/songwriters. And I also wanted to find out about something called digital audio workspaces. I heard someone talking about one once, and I think that's what I need. Maybe at this music store they'll know something about them.'

He turned to her for a moment, and immediately wished he hadn't. The feelings that had raced through him when she jumped into the car still lingered, and looking at her intensified them. 'I haven't heard of either of those singers, but I do know a little about digital audio workstations. I think I heard you say you have an iPad? GarageBand is a free app that you can get on the iPad.'

'Oh, that's right. I've heard of it, but haven't played around with it. You think it's good?'

'Yeah, it's pretty cool, and easy to use,' he said, keeping his eyes on the road this time.

'I'll have to check it out for sure, then. You know, you're the first person I've really confided in about any of this. I mean, Taylor and Alex know I've written a couple of songs, but not that I want to actually record them. They'd laugh if I told them I wanted to hear one of my songs on the radio one day.'

'Really? You think your sisters would laugh at you?'

'Well, possibly not. But I've dated a couple of musicians, and I was way too embarrassed to mention my songs for fear they'd want to hear them, and they would definitely have laughed and told me to stick to flowers.'

Nick swallowed back his thoughts about the jerks she'd obviously dated because there was nothing to be gained by starting on that conversation. Instead, he kept his eyes on the road as he made her an offer. 'I'll help you get started. It's not hard. Once I teach you the basics of the guitar, you can play around with it using the app.'

When she didn't reply he glanced over. His eyes were immediately drawn to her lips, which held a soft smile, making him want to kiss her again. He quickly turned back to the road.

The sound of her voice broke the spell. 'This is so weird. The last thing I expected to be doing on this trip was learning to play the guitar and how to record my songs. I figured we'd mostly hang out with Alex and do a bit of touristy stuff. I mean, we're all going to Disneyland with Annie soon ... and I figured we'd probably go to Lake Tahoe for skiing if there's enough snow. But learning to play the guitar and having someone help with song-writing and everything ... this is beyond my wildest imagination. I suppose I owe it to Travis for bringing up the fact that you'd written a song.'

He grinned, remembering his annoyance at the time and marvelling at how he could feel so differently about it now.

~~*~~

Casey couldn't believe that on top of teaching her to play the guitar, Nick was offering to help her get started on this recording adventure. She wondered if she'd been a fool to never show anyone before. If she'd had the courage to show Tom, her jazz-playing-ex-boyfriend, would he have thought the song had some potential? Or was Nick just being nice out of some sense of duty to his cousin?

On second thought, she couldn't see Tom helping her. He'd always been arrogant about his music, and would no doubt have thought her efforts amateurish and not worthy of his time and energy. But Nick, as an amateur songwriter himself, seemed to understand the effort that had gone into getting it to this point.

She shifted in the seat to angle herself slightly toward him so she could study him through her peripheral vision. He was a thoughtful man, and they did have some things in common. Should she allow herself to get to know him a bit better, even if she was going home soon?

They drove along in silence for a time, mostly through farm land and the occasional small town, and then it became obvious they were getting closer to Sacramento as the small towns began to meld into the outer suburbs of the city itself.

Eventually, Nick pulled into a multi-deck garage and parked.

'Shall we go see about the marriage records first, and then hit the music store?' he asked.

'Whatever you think.'

They made their way into a relatively modern-looking office building and to the elevator, where Nick used a small device on his keychain to press the button for the floor. Getting out, they went through a set of doors with a State of California logo, into a reception lobby where an older woman sat with her head down as she madly tapped away on a computer. After a few moments, she looked up.

'Nick, what are you doing here? I thought you were on extended leave? Couldn't stay away from us?' the woman asked as her broad smile lit up what was otherwise a rather plain face.

'Yep, that's it, Nancy. I've missed your smiling face every morning and had to drop in to see you.'

The woman raised a brow in mock coyness, and then made eye contact with Casey. Her scrutiny was quick, but thorough. 'So, trying to impress this lovely lady with your lavish workplace? Because I doubt she's all that impressed.'

Nick turned to Casey, shaking his head. 'Casey, meet Nancy. Nancy pretty much runs our department, and I honestly don't know what we would do without her. I'm serious; she's the glue that holds us together.' Then he turned to Nancy. 'Casey here is my soon to be cousin-in-law, and we're here because we want to look for an old marriage licence and thought Devin might be able to give us a hand.'

Nancy's smile widened. 'Ah, well then, you're in luck—even though you'd have been wise to make an appointment. He's in. Here, put these on, and you should probably sign in since you're technically a visitor,' Nancy said, handing him a couple of passes.

It wasn't long before Nancy's phone rang and she said they could go in.

They walked through a huge open-plan work area where dozens of people had their eyes glued to computer screens. Nick stopped in front of one of only a few offices on the floor.

'Knock knock,' he said as they entered the office.

A man with caramel-coloured skin and jet black hair, probably in his late twenties, stood and came over to shake Nick's hand. 'Hey, didn't think I'd be seeing you here quite so soon. Bored with civilian life already, are you?'

'Ha ha, not yet. Devin, this is a friend of mine, Casey. Devin's my boss—he may be a bit younger than me, but he's way smarter than all the rest of us combined.'

Devin turned to her and winked, pointed to visitor chairs in front of his desk, then went around and sat. When he faced them he asked, 'And to what do I owe the pleasure of your visit?'

'We're looking for the maiden name of a woman who was married in the early nineteen hundreds,' Nick said as he sat.

Devin cocked his head, blinking hard. 'You do know you can simply fill out a form over at the County Clerk Recorder over on 8th Street, right?' Devin asked, his tone dripping with sarcasm.

Nick drew in a deep breath. 'Well, we don't actually have all the information. We think we know the year—1918—but not the date. Makes it just a little bit trickier.'

When Devin shook his head, saying, 'and you want this because ...?' Casey feared he wasn't going to help them.

'The woman was my great-grandmother,' Casey said. 'We've found some old letters her sister wrote to her, but there isn't a return address on any of them, and the sister only signed them with her first name. If we find out my great-grandmother's maiden name, we'll know her sister's name too.'

Devin nodded, his brows knitting tighter. 'I see ...' he said slowly, which meant he clearly didn't. 'And you want to know her name because ...?'

Casey looked at Nick, who sort of rolled his eyes before squinting. She shrugged, having no answer for the direct question.

Nick turned to his old boss. 'Well, I suppose it's mostly curiosity, when you get right down to it. I mean, it's not like it's a life or death matter or anything.'

'Good,' Devin said. 'Because I'm really busy at the moment; I've got two reports that have to be done before I go home tonight and another by the end of the day tomorrow. If you'll leave it with me, I'll be more than happy to have a look for you over the next couple of days.'

They handed over the information they had about the marriage, and then after they'd expressed their gratitude, Devin stood, signalling the end of their brief meeting. As he ushered them out, he told Nick he'd be in touch when he found something.

'This is brilliant. So tell me again, how is it that he can do this when we can't?' Casey asked once they were back outside.

'Devin's done a lot of genealogy work so he knows what's easy to track down, and what isn't. And trust me, he'd have said if this wasn't something he could do quickly. He probably would have done it straight away if he wasn't so busy.'

'So ... once we have her maiden name, will it be easy to find birth records?'

'I believe so. And I think we should be able to use the on-line services for other searches. But if we do run into trouble, Devin won't mind helping us again—despite his very business-like demeanour, he's pretty cool. Now, music store?'

Over the next hour and a half, they looked at music books for beginners and strummed a number of used guitars for sale, until Nick finally found one they both thought would be perfect. Casey fell in love with the gorgeous instrument the moment she held it.

'Oh, I love this one. Should I get it?' she asked.

'I don't see why not. It's not going to break the bank, is it? You can even donate it to the school in town if you don't want to take it back to Australia with you.'

Casey smiled, knowing full well she wouldn't do that. She'd already grown attached to it after just the few moments of holding it; she was kicking herself for not having looked into getting one sooner.

After she paid for the guitar and case, they headed back to Nick's car. When he'd safely stowed the guitar in his car, he turned to Casey.

'I don't know about you, but I didn't have any lunch. I wouldn't mind getting something to eat while we're here.'

At the mention of food, Casey's stomach growled. 'Sounds great.'

'There are some nice restaurants down along the river. It's not far to walk.'

Thirty minutes later they were seated at an outdoor table. Casey munched on a salad while Nick looked quite content with fish and chips, and they both drank icy cold beer as they gazed across at the

Tower Bridge. Its bright gold structure reflected the setting sun, making it sparkle, like something from a fairy-tale.

'I thought the Golden Gate Bridge was in San Francisco,' Casey said with a wink, knowing full well this wasn't it.

Nick frowned. 'Yeah, I always did wonder why they called it the *Golden* Gate Bridge and then painted it red.'

She glanced back to the bridge, wondering if they'd have time to walk across it later. 'Has this one always been gold?'

'It's been gold as long as I've known it.'

'And how long is that? When did you move to Sacramento?' She'd heard someone mention he'd grown up in Masons Flat, next door to Travis and Denver.

'I moved here to go to college. When I got a job straight after I graduated, I stayed. And then I bought a house not long after that. Mom and Dad moved up here too, and even though Stacy and Tim are still there in our family home, I don't really feel any need to go back. It's great helping Travis out while Denver's recuperating, but I can't see me ever going back there to live.'

Casey finished the last of her beer, looking at Nick thoughtfully as she set the glass down. 'I get that. I mean, it's a quaint town and all, and Alex sure seems happy there, but I don't think it'd be for me either. Taylor ... well, I don't know about Taylor. If you'd asked me before we came over, I'd have said no way, but she and Darleen have become quite good friends. And she's been helping out with a bake-sale for one of the schools, and I'm amazed at how enthusiastic she is about it. She doesn't belong to the CWA at home, but maybe she'd want to be if we lived in a smaller town.'

'CWA?' Nick asked, a questioning frown appearing on his face.

'Country Women's Association. They do a lot of community work in small towns throughout Australia,' Casey said. When Nick's frown deepened, she continued. 'They're women who cook and do crafts and stuff, and raise money for charity to help rural communities in hard times. It's the kind of thing I could imagine Taylor being interested in, given how she's taken to this group organising the bake-sale.'

'Maybe she's just enjoying the company of like-minded women ... you know, women who like to bake and who talk about baking. Or maybe she misses her job.'

Casey hadn't thought of that. She certainly didn't feel an urge to hang out with florists while here, but maybe it was different with Taylor. 'Maybe. Anyway, she seems quite taken with the town, and playing pool at the saloon too.'

'And you haven't been tempted to join her at any of that?'

Casey tilted her head, thinking. 'No, not really, but it might be different if I hadn't found the letters.'

'Yes, the letters. I'm looking forward to getting back into them myself. Should I come around tomorrow afternoon when I finish up with the chores?'

Casey waited a moment before answering, not wanting to appear too anxious. 'Sure. I'll work on my guitar lessons when I get back from the gym, and wait for you before I start on the next lot of letters.'

'Cool,' he said, flashing a warm smile.

The sincere look on his face was so encouraging that she entirely forgot her resolve from the previous night, when she'd convinced herself to keep things casual, and asked the question she'd been pondering throughout the day. 'And do you think, maybe, we could write a song about them? About Daisy and Sarah and the letters, like Alex suggested? I mean, with your music skills and my lyrics ... I don't know, maybe it is worth a shot. Who knows, we might end up making really good partners.'

For a fraction of a moment, she imagined them becoming a real song-writing couple—like Sonny and Cher, or Beyoncé and Jay-Z—until the warmth on Nick's face faded with the speed of a light being flicked off at the switch.

He blinked, and turned toward the river. 'A good team ... yeah, okay. Kind of like Bernie and Elton, right? Turns out they were just really good friends when I'd always wondered if they were ... you know, a bit of a thing. I saw a movie about them not long ago—it was pretty good. They were certainly a great song-writing team.'

His words stung. Actually, it wasn't so much his words that stung as the change in his demeanour. He thought they could be friends, like Elton and Bernie ... not a song-writing couple.

He'd retreated from her.

Or had he ever been close enough to retreat? Perhaps watching the rays of the setting sun lighting up the river and turning that glorious bridge even more golden, all the while sipping drinks and watching boats pass by on the river, had caused her to read something into his manner that hadn't been there at all.

She forced a laugh, trying to think of a clever response, and softly sighed with relief when the waiter walked up.

'Can I get you anything else?' he asked as he began to clear their plates.

Nick turned to her. 'Did you want another beer?'

'No, thank you. Unless you want one?'

He shook his head as he looked up at the waiter. 'Nothing more for us. Just the bill if you wouldn't mind.'

Silence weighed heavily between them as they waited for the waiter to return. They had shared a moment, that's all. The sort of moment you have when you're sitting at a café in an exotic location and you feel as though you've been transported to another point in time. And then he'd ended it, in a flash, with a flippant response—not at all the response she'd hoped for. Casey couldn't believe she'd been so gullible.

When the bill arrived, Casey pulled out her purse and started to get her credit card.

Nick shook his head. 'My treat, you're the guest.'

'Oh, it's not necessary. After all, you helped me get the guitar and everything.'

'I insist. You can get the next one.'

She shrugged, and put her purse away. While he went up to pay at the register, she reminded herself of what he'd said quite clearly; their kiss hadn't meant anything. She shouldn't have asked that question about them being a team, and having asked it, she shouldn't have expected any better response than what she got.

When Nick returned, she stood and followed him out of the restaurant and to his car with barely a word uttered.

By the time they got on the road, the commute traffic had all but vanished and Nick manoeuvred them out of the city onto the road back to Masons Flat without a hitch. The atmosphere between them was no longer as convivial as it had been earlier in the day, but Casey did wonder if she might have misinterpreted Nick's comments regarding the song-writing. She wracked her brain for something trivial to talk about but before she could come up with anything, Nick turned to her with a question completely out of left field.

'So, have all women in Australia stopped having children or is it just the Mason women?'

CHAPTER 12

Casey turned to him, mouth open, at a complete loss for words. Had she actually heard what she thought she had?

Nick shook his head, glancing at her for a second before turning back to the road. 'Sorry, that didn't come out right. I just meant that you and your sisters are all ... thirtyish, right? And yet none of you have any children. If you're thinking of having them, aren't you leaving it a bit late?'

Casey's voice caught as she started to answer him. She'd been asked this question before, but never quite so bluntly. She cleared her throat, and tried again.

'Look, *mate*, we all have full lives. We have homes, and careers. Having children isn't the centre of our universes.' She thought about Alex, and how devastated she'd been when she learned she'd never have children, but that wasn't something she was going to discuss with Nick.

'So you've never even thought about having a family?' He kept his eyes on the road, his tone of voice bordering on judgemental.

'Never. And it's the same with most of my friends. I don't think *any* of them are desperate to have children, but it's not exactly something that comes up in conversation. It's not like we sit around and have whinge sessions about how our biological clocks are ticking or anything.' She tried to make it sound funny, but it just sounded defensive.

'Really? None of your friends?'

She bit on down on the inside of her mouth grappling with the fact that, only a short time ago, she'd been hurt by what she'd perceived as him pulling away from her. Given this line of conversation, maybe his change in demeanour wasn't such a bad thing. 'I have one friend with a gorgeous daughter, but she's a single mother, and I definitely don't envy her that.' Casey shifted in her seat, trying to read his face in the small amount of light reflecting from his dashboard.

'Right.' He paused for what felt like a long time. 'And you don't think you'll regret it if you don't end up having a family?'

She shook her head in disbelief. What was it with him and having to have children? 'I do have a family. I have two sisters who mean the world to me; I have my mother and her boyfriend, and his daughter, who's pretty much like another sister. Oh, and my mother's parents. Why do you ask? And why does it sound like you're judging me? Judging all of us?'

'Did it sound that way? Because that's not how I meant it. I was just ... curious.'

Casey turned to look out the passenger window while she drew in a couple more calming breaths. What a disappointment, ending such a lovely day together with this conversation. Bringing up the song-writing at dinner and using the word *partners* had been her mistake, but this—this was his fault. She turned back to him, again endeavouring to keep the edge out of her voice. 'So ... what, I suppose that all your friends have children?'

He turned toward her as the car came to a stop at an intersection. Street lights illuminated the interior of the car and she saw the seriousness on his face even before she heard it in his voice. 'Yes, as a matter of fact, most of my friends do. All the married ones either already have children or plan on having children. It's something I've always known will happen when the time is right. I want three, preferably.'

'Three? You're the same age as me, and you haven't started your family, but you want three?' Her tone dripped with sarcasm—exactly as she meant it to.

He huffed out an exasperated breath. 'It's different with men—you know that. I haven't met the right woman yet, but when I do, we'll start a family.'

'Seriously? Just like that? What if she doesn't want children?'

His look said it all, and when he chuckled, her blood began to boil and her jaws tightened. 'I suppose that answers my question—if she doesn't want children, she won't be the right woman.'

His slight chuckle before he spoke made her jaws clench. 'What? No, of course not, but every woman I've ever dated wanted to have a family someday, that's all.'

It was becoming increasingly obvious that her initial impressions of him were right: ultra-conservative, old fashioned, and totally not for her. 'Well, I don't ever plan on having children. There are too many people on this planet as it is, and I have no intention of contributing to that problem. You do know that over-population is the number one issue this planet faces, and is possibly the underlying cause of climate change ... and pollution ... and shortages of food and clean water, right?'

He didn't answer at first, focussing on the traffic as they went through a busy intersection. As the traffic began to flow easily again, he glanced at her. 'I'm sorry I asked—about children, I mean.'

She chewed the side of her mouth again for a moment, regaining her composure. Having begun this conversation, she wasn't about to let him off the hook so easily. She turned to him again. 'Don't tell me you don't believe in climate change either?'

'Climate change? Yeah, of course I do. I just don't necessarily believe it's been entirely caused by humans.'

'Right. So, what has caused it then?' she snapped, all her efforts to maintain composure having failed.

He sighed dramatically. 'Look, I agree that pollution is a real issue. The advent of plastic, for example, has turned out to be a double-edged sword. Cars pumping out carbon monoxide and factories spewing out God-knows what sorts of chemicals in the air and rivers, those are definitely things that our generation needs to address. But I also believe some of what's driving climate change—like sun spot activity and volcanic activity—are completely outside our control.'

'Yes, of course, but the rapid changes taking place now cannot entirely be explained by natural causes. I firmly believe over-population is at the heart of the problem. Surely you must agree?'

He turned to her briefly. 'Over-population? In some parts of the world, sure, particularly where there is a lack of natural resources to sustain the population.' He looked at her quickly again, then back to the road.

She fiddled with a rough spot on a fingernail, trying to decide how to continue. 'Well, I know for a fact that at home we're encroaching on natural habitat for housing, and farming ... and mining. And while efforts are being made to create new habitat areas, the issue is exacerbated by increasing bushfires. Which takes me right back to climate change and over-population. I believe we all need to reduce consumption, reduce waste, and importantly, reduce population growth.'

'I hear you, but I don't believe population growth in America is a huge issue. I mean, I don't feel like I shouldn't have kids on the pretence that I'll be saving the planet by not having them. Besides, looking at my family, there are four of us cousins, and so far only Stacy and Travis have just one daughter each so that doesn't even replace us. That's not growth.'

She had no comeback. His desire to have children was clearly as strong as her desire not to add to the problem. At least he'd acknowledged that there were problems, unlike some men who completely dissed any conversation about pollution and climate change. She continued to look out the window for a bit, but it was so dark now there wasn't anything to see. Finally, she turned back to him. Making an effort to keep the sarcasm out of her voice, she continued. 'I wish you well on your mission to find the perfect woman—one who shares your desire to give you three children.'

He made this funny little noise—she wasn't sure if it was a laugh or a sign of disgust—but other than that they drove along in silence for the rest of the trip, and all the while she stewed over their conversation. As he drove over the bridge into town, his voice startled her; she'd grown used to the silence.

'Home again, home again, jiggery jig.'

She turned to him, tilting her head, appreciating his small attempt to lighten the mood.

When he pulled into her driveway, he didn't turn the motor off. 'Shall I still come around tomorrow to go through the rest of the letters with you? Say around three?' The question sounded tentative.

She took a moment to answer, struggling with the disparity between still smarting from having had her momentary fantasy squashed at the restaurant, and trying to accept she wasn't going to change his views on climate change and pollution with one discussion. Regardless of both of those things, he was helping her and, for the most part, he wasn't bad company. She drew in a breath, and sighed softly, deciding to try to let it all go. 'Sure. I'll work through the guitar lessons until you arrive.'

He popped the boot from the inside, and didn't move while she went around and grabbed the guitar and music books out of the back. Then she came around to his side of the car and stopped beside the window.

He rolled it down and raised an eyebrow as he cocked his head. 'See you tomorrow then.'

'Yep, see you tomorrow.' She fished around in her bag for the house keys, but as she walked up to the door it opened and Taylor greeted her.

'Hey—have you bought a guitar? That's so cool. Hi, Nick. Not coming in? I made a cherry pie today. Would you like some?'

Casey turned back in time to see Nick shake his head.

'Thanks, Taylor, but I should keep moving. Another time, for sure.' He waved, rolled up the window, and backed out of the drive.

As his car disappeared, Taylor shrugged. 'His loss means all the more for us.' She looked at Casey, tilting her head, as a frown tightened her brows. 'Are you okay? You don't look so good.'

Casey scrunched up her face, giving in to all her uncertainties. 'I don't know. I mean ... I really don't know.'

Taylor threw her arm around Casey's shoulders and led her inside. 'Sounds like you need a piece of pie and a deep and meaningful. Come on, let's put your new guitar away and get started.'

CHAPTER 13

As he drove the short distance home, Nick cursed himself, wondering what force had made him ruin what had been a really nice day. He'd been enjoying Casey's company and, up until he asked that stupid question about children, it had seemed she'd been enjoying his company too.

He knew it wasn't just the nature of the question he'd asked, either. It was the way he'd done it. That stupid, blunt question had caused her mouth to fly open and her eyes to spit fire. He knew how to be subtle—he'd done numerous courses on negotiation and counselling skills as part of management training—and yet all that had flown out the window with one stupid, tactless question.

And the worst thing was that it wasn't even any of his business whether she or her sisters intended to have children. Not, that is, unless he was thinking Casey might become something more than his cousin-in-law. Was he subconsciously trying to ensure that could never happen by making her hate him?

When he was certain he was out of sight, he banged his hand on the steering wheel, shaking his head. He'd have to apologise tomorrow afternoon. But how? Bringing it up again might start another argument.

Could he simply pretend none of it had ever happened?

Chewing on his lip the rest of the way home, he weighed that up.

He might get away with pretending the conversation hadn't happened—maybe—but he couldn't pretend he hadn't enjoyed the earlier part of the day they'd spent together. And even more so, he couldn't pretend that he hadn't enjoyed the kiss they'd shared less than twenty-four hours earlier.

He stopped the car along the side of the house and sat there for a few minutes, taking deep breaths. He certainly didn't have to worry about getting too close to Casey now. He'd squashed any chance of that with just a few choice words—words he had a sinking feeling he might very well live to regret.

When he finally walked into the family room, three sets of eyes confronted him.

'How'd the trip to Sacramento go?' Alex asked.

'Great. My boss said he'll help us get some information on Sarah. Oh, and we found Casey a guitar she likes.'

Alex tilted her head inquisitively, but Travis asked the obvious question. 'Casey wants to play the guitar?'

He glanced at Alex before answering, noticing her eyes narrowing slightly. He took it as a cue not to say too much. 'Yeah, seems she's always wanted to learn to play the guitar, and when she heard I can play she asked if I'd mind helping her get started. It'll be easy enough to give her a few pointers next time I go over to help with the letters.'

Alex smiled, and Travis nodded, while Denver looked like he'd had some sort of epiphany. 'How's that going anyway?'

'The letters? Good. I mean, there hasn't been anything too interesting since we learned about the births of the boys though. Not sure what I expect to find, or what Casey hopes to find, but we'll keep going. We're over half way through them now.' He paused, but before Denver could get another question in, he turned the tables on him. 'But what about you? I'm sorta surprised to see you here tonight. From what I've heard, you're spending a lot of time at the saloon, playing pool with another of these Mason women.' He turned to Alex, and winked.

He'd never seen Denver blush, and wasn't sure that's what he was doing even now, but something was going on. He looked a bit like a kid getting sprung with his hand in the cookie jar. When Denver cleared his throat, both Travis and Alex turned to stare at him too.

'Pool? Yeah, it's become quite addictive. Something I can do that doesn't require a lot of mobility, you know?' His look pleaded for Nick to drop it there, so of course he couldn't.

'So ... it has nothing to do with Taylor?'

'Her company does add to the pleasure,' he said, looking at Alex, 'but it's more to do with the cabin-fever from hanging around the house all day. Once I got mobile enough to drive, and then Travis said I could use the Range Rover, well, that clinched it.'

Nick smiled, then glanced over to Alex and Travis and winked. 'Yeah, of course. I'm sure that's all it is. Well, if you don't mind, I think I'll have an early night—all the driving, you know?'

When they all said goodnight without any further questions Nick breathed a sigh of relief. He'd dodged an in-depth inquisition about

Casey, which was brilliant, because if they had asked anything personal he didn't know how he'd have answered it.

~~*~~

Casey stuck her fork into the pie, marvelling at the delicate crust as it flaked off into little bits onto the plate. The first bite confirmed that it tasted as good as it looked. There was good reason Taylor had such a following at her bakery.

Taylor's eyes were filled with pride when Casey looked up at her. 'Mmm,' she said with a full mouth. Then, 'this may be one of your best efforts yet.'

'I'm glad you like it. The ladies gave me a few tricks and I love how the crust has turned out. So ... I want to hear all about your day, and in particular, what went wrong?' Taylor stared at her, expectation written all over her face.

'He got me started on all the problems the world is facing. You know my biggest issue is over-population, so of course he had to ask why none of us have any kids yet.'

Taylor drew back, her face puckering with thought. Her mouth opened, but then she seemed to change her mind. She pursed her lips tightly as she continued to think for another moment. Drawing in a deep breath, she tried again. 'I take it from that he wants a big family.'

'Says he wants three children.'

'And you saw that as a reason to go down the whole climate-change-overpopulation-disaster path?'

'Well ... yes, sort of.'

'He's allowed his opinion.'

Casey knew how Taylor felt about having children; that while she wouldn't mind having one or two, it wasn't something she was prepared to do on her own. She would have to have a husband who also wanted to have children and would be prepared to share the parenting. 'Of course he is, and it wasn't so much that he asked, although I do get tired of defending myself sometimes, it was more the way he asked—with this *tone*. Anyway, you know what I'm like once I get started.'

Taylor laughed. 'Yes. I bet you would've given him an earful.'

Casey shook her head trying to see the humour in it. 'Says he agrees that over-population is a problem in countries that have issues with natural resources, but doesn't feel it applies to America.'

Taylor cocked her head, nodding. 'Well, I really don't know. He could be right. I do wonder what made him bring it up, though.'

'Yeah, me too. I mean, we'd had such a great day—his boss is going to search for information on Sarah, and then we went to the music store, and I bought the guitar ... and then we had dinner along the river, and it was so pretty there. And then not long after we got in the car for the drive home, things went haywire.'

Taylor frowned, thinking. 'Well, if it was me I'd just let it go—don't bring it up again. I mean, when you think about it, we're only here for a few more weeks; you're enjoying having his company to go through the letters with you, and he's going to teach you to play the guitar, and if you were getting along great up until then, why not just accept that he has a different agenda in life and forget it. You won't change his mind—all you'll do is make yourself angry.'

Casey suspected Taylor was right. 'I guess,' she said with a shrug. She stood and as she took the plates to the dishwasher, she turned back to Taylor. 'And how're you going ... with Denver? I mean, did you guys play pool again today?'

Taylor gave her a sideways look, but didn't bite at the first question. 'We sure did, and my playing has really improved. I hope I can find a pool parlour around home that isn't too seedy—or better yet, a nice pub with a pool table, one that isn't so popular you never get a game.'

'Right, I get that you're enjoying the pool. What about Denver's company? Are you enjoying his company as much as the pool?'

Taylor sighed. 'Of course. I mean, he's a great guy isn't he? I can see why Alex likes the family so much. And he's handsome, and has a wonderful sense of humour, and he's all-around good company. If we were sticking around, I could see myself getting quite attached to him, but ...'

Casey sighed. 'But we're not sticking around,' she said, finishing Taylor's sentence. When Taylor said no more, Casey sighed again. 'Anyway, I'm off to bed.'

Taylor was right. They weren't sticking around, so what was the point of her arguing with Nick about anything. He wanted to add to the problem of over-population, and she didn't—but so what? He wasn't going to change his views just because she said he should.

~~*~~

Casey was getting ready for the gym at seven-thirty the next morning when she heard voices.

'We're going to Yosemite,' Taylor said when Casey opened her bedroom door. Taylor and Alex were standing in the hallway, and Taylor was grinning from ear to ear.

'Now?' Casey asked, confused. She hadn't heard any talk of them going to Yosemite at all let alone on such short notice.

Alex raised her hands and then rubbed them together. 'Yes. I thought of it last night and made a few quick enquiries, and we're booked into a lodge right near the entrance to the park. I was hoping to get us into this beautiful old guest house in Wawona, but it turns out the Mariposa Grove isn't open in winter so we'll just be going to Yosemite.'

Casey's confusion grew. When she frowned, Alex continued.

'Mariposa Grove is where you see the Giant Sequoias, but we've got the Calaveras Big Trees Park not far from here so we can do that as a day trip instead. You look confused, Casey. Doesn't it sound good?'

'Sure, but I had no idea you were even thinking of this.'

'Well, we have to do something a bit touristy while you're here, and it doesn't look like there's going to be enough snow for a ski trip.'

Casey looked at Taylor's beaming face and tried to muster the same level of enthusiasm. 'Sounds great, Alex, but we *are* doing something touristy—or at least I thought we were. Aren't we going to Disneyland with Annie soon?'

'Yes, yes of course, but I thought this would be a perfect way for the three of us to spend some time together—just us.'

As it finally sunk in, excitement replaced her confusion. 'Well then, guess I'd better shower and get dressed. When are we leaving?'

'As soon as you're ready. I'm packed and ready to go, but no pressure. I'll go make some coffee and wait for you two sleepyheads.'

'Oh, Nick's meant to be coming over later ...' Casey said as she suddenly remembered their plans.

'No worries. Travis knows what we're up to—after all, I've got his Range Rover because it's 4-wheel drive, but I'll ask him to let Nick know not to come over.'

~~*~~

They were incredibly lucky with the weather as they drove to Yosemite; the sky was clear, and there were no storms on the forecast for the next couple of days. It was cold, but the air was fresh and Casey eventually found herself becoming more and more excited by the idea of communing with nature and bonding with her sisters for a few days.

'Have you stayed here before?' Casey asked when they pulled up in front of the lodge. She got out of the car and threw her overnight bag's strap over her shoulder and then tossed Taylor's bag to her.

'No, but it looked good on the internet. We've got a king bed and a queen sofa bed, so we'll draw straws on who sleeps where. I was disappointed to only get us in for two nights, but I was lucky to get what I did—they're fully booked out for the weekend as well as all of next week. Anyway, I figured we'd go have a quick look at the park this afternoon and then we'll have all day tomorrow to explore. How's that sound?'

'Sounds good to me,' Taylor answered.

Casey nodded and they followed Alex inside to check-in.

Once inside, Casey spotted some tourist flyers so she grabbed a couple on Yosemite itself, as well as a flyer on Mariposa Grove that Alex had hoped they could visit. She was gobsmacked when she read about the giant sequoias, some of which were taller than the Statue of Liberty and some over three thousand years old.

'I see what you mean about Mariposa Grove. It would have been great, but you say there's a park near Masons Flat that we can go see?'

'There sure is,' Alex replied, 'Calaveras Big Trees. I've been there once but I don't mind going again. It's beautiful—you'll both love it. Now, let's throw this stuff into the room and head into the park while we've still got the afternoon light.'

From the moment they arrived, Casey loved Yosemite. The views were awe-inspiring in every direction—from the sheer rock faces surrounding valleys filled with evergreen trees, to the cloudless cornflower blue sky.

After a quick visit to the information centre, where they bought detailed maps and a few souvenirs, they headed straight to Bridal Veil Falls. It only took two laps of the parking lot to find a spot, and they were off on their first real adventure.

After walking fifteen minutes along a reasonably easy path, they found themselves standing within view of the waterfall. They were pleased to see the small crowd begin to disperse so that they were able to get to the front and take a few selfies.

'Shall I take a photo of all three of you with the waterfall in the background?' a man asked. As Casey caught his eye, she noticed he had two small children with him. 'Sure,' she replied, 'then I'll take a couple of you with your children if you like.'

'That'd be great,' he replied, stepping forward to take Casey's phone while handing her his at the same time.

A minute later she positioned herself to take photos of the man and his two daughters. The two girls, who were either twins or very close in age, were both dressed in pink puffy jackets with red rubber boots sporting unicorns and rainbows. And they were, quite simply, adorable.

And as she watched them get into position for the photo, for the first time in her life Casey wondered if maybe she'd been a fool to think she'd never want to have a child of her own.

As she handed the man his phone, she caught his eye again and smiled. 'They're so cute. Twins?'

'Yes,' he answered, smiling.

'You and their mother must be very proud, indeed.' The moment she said that she realised it could sound like she was fishing to see if he was single and she regretted the question.

'We were, very much so. Sadly, the girls lost their mother last year, but we're doing great on our own, aren't we girls?'

The two little girls bobbed their heads in unison. Then, when he knelt down and reached his arms out, they ran to his sides giggling.

A rush of warmth washed over Casey as she watched the exchange, then she turned to find both her sister's staring at her. 'What?' she asked, defensively.

'Nothing,' Alex replied, then turned and winked at Taylor. Taylor just continued to smile.

'So, what's next on the itinerary?' Casey asked, turning to wave goodbye to the girls.

The man and his daughters waved back then continued to take in the view of the waterfall as Casey and her sisters headed back down the path to the parking lot. Once in the car, Taylor turned to Casey.

'They were awfully cute little girls, weren't they?' Taylor asked.

'Adorable. I wonder if we were ever that cute?' Casey asked.

'No way,' Alex replied, teasingly. 'You two were a pain in the arse, even at that age.'

'As if,' said Taylor. 'We were angels. Mum said so almost every day.'

'That was just some reverse psychology stuff. She was trying to get you two to behave like angels by telling you that's what you were.'

'No,' Casey said, smirking, 'we most definitely were angels.' But she couldn't help but laugh at the absurdity of her own statement. She knew for a fact that Alex was right—they were pains in the arse, forever playing with their older sister's toys and sometimes, unintentionally, breaking them.

'It'll be dark soon. I vote we head back to the lodge and have a quick dinner so we can make an early start tomorrow, since we've only got the one full day.'

'Sounds good to me,' Taylor replied. 'I'm starving after all.'

As they drove out of the park and made their way back to the lodge, Casey couldn't help thinking about the two gorgeous little girls, growing up without their mother. A tinge of sadness started to creep over her until she remembered that she and her sisters had grown up with just the one parent as well. It hadn't been that bad. Those girls would be fine. And their father seemed a genuinely nice person.

So why couldn't she stop thinking about them?

CHAPTER 14

'How was Yosemite?' Nick asked when he arrived Sunday afternoon.

As he stood there on the porch, waiting for her to invite him in, he looked a bit nervous. Seeing his unsettled appearance strengthened her, making the angst she'd felt toward him that afternoon when they'd driven back from Sacramento all but disappear.

'It was great,' Casey replied, opening the door wide for him to come in. 'The views were awesome.' As she said that, the image of the man with his two daughters at the base of the waterfall popped into her head, bringing a smile to her face.

Her smile seemed to help him relax. 'It's a spectacular place, isn't it? I went there several years ago, but I still remember the way El Capitan looked with the sun setting ... and those climbers who camp on the side of it. Crazy stuff.'

She shut the door behind him and led the way to the study. 'We didn't see that, but I heard some people talking about it. Maybe it's too cold this time of year for them to camp there.'

When they reached the study, Casey sat at the desk, and Nick took the chair beside it.

'I saw Taylor at the house just as I was leaving,' he said. Any anxious edge she'd thought she'd heard in his voice earlier was gone.

'Oh, yeah, she went over to show Alex how to make cherry pie.'

Nick nodded. 'I don't suppose you've had a chance to practise the guitar?'

Casey tilted her head, wondering if perhaps he regretted the way their conversation had gone on the trip back from Sacramento. For a moment she contemplated bringing it up, but decided it was best to just let it go. 'Not really, but I'll get back into it this evening. I'd like to practise as much as I can before I get home and back into my old routines, you know?'

'Yeah ... I haven't had a chance to do much with your song, either. I tried, but I couldn't remember it well enough. I should have had you email me the lyrics before you left. We'll do that today, okay? And then I'll see if I can work it out tonight.'

'Would you? That'd be awesome, if you've got the time.'

'I'll find the time,' he said, giving her a warm smile.

Calm descended upon her. It seemed they were starting over, and there was no point bringing up their awkward conversation again.

They settled into the letters and, after a few minutes, Casey asked, 'Have you heard anything from Devin?'

'Ah, yes, I meant to say. Sarah's maiden name was Carpenter. That gives us something to go on.'

Casey beamed. 'It sure does. It'll be interesting to see if any of the other letters will mention anything about either of them having children.'

As they continued through the letters, they found most were about the growth of the two boys and how Daisy was still enjoying her job. But then Casey picked up a letter dated 1926. After quickly skimming it she turned to Nick. 'Whoa—here we go.'

'What've you found?'

'Their father has died, and so Daisy's come clean with ... here, let me read it to you,' Casey said.

My darling Sarah,

Now that father is gone, I think I owe you the truth about the reason he and I had such a terrible falling out. But before I tell you, you must remember that this had nothing to do with you. I have never, not for one solitary moment, blamed you in any way. Take a deep breath and say to yourself that your sister loves you with all her heart and always will. Say it.

Now, secondly, you must promise to never divulge what I tell you to anyone. Especially David. Promise me, or stop reading and destroy this letter now.

Okay, if you're still reading then you've promised, and I trust you, Sarah, so here goes. You see, it all started when father caught me writing Mrs David Mason on a sheet of paper. He asked me what on earth I was doing so I admitted to him that I was in love with David, and that I hoped one day to become his wife. Father turned as red as a beet and demanded that I stay away from David because he was promised to you in an agreement he'd made with David's father many years earlier. He forbade me to speak of it ever again, and even when I begged him to release the two of you from the agreement, he told me to shut my mouth and behave like a decent sister. I knew you weren't in love with David. Not then, anyway. I'm sure you've grown to love him—I mean, who wouldn't have—but when you were first told of the match, I remember how terrified you were of the thought of marrying someone you hardly knew.

After telling me that David was promised to you, father began insisting that I marry the son of his friend George Stapleton. I'd always thought of George as a pleasant enough man but his son was so much older than me. I knew father was only doing it because he wanted me to forget about David. When I told father I would never marry George's son, he came very close to striking me, screaming at me and telling me that I was impertinent. I ran from the room, and from that day I barely spoke to father again. I started making plans to go to San Francisco straight away so that I could leave as soon as you and David were wed.

I'm over David now. Truly I am. Indeed, I rarely think of him and when I do it is simply with the fondness of a sister-in-law who is happy for her beloved sister. I feel terrible that you and I have been apart because of this, but you must believe me when I say that I never, not for one moment, blamed you.

You might think that with father gone I could return to Masons Flat but, other than you, there is nothing for me there. I love my job, and I love the man who has been like a husband to me and a father to my children even though, for reasons I cannot yet divulge, he will never be able to make me his wife.

I hope you accept this confession in the spirit it is given, as simply an explanation of past events that may have perplexed you for some time.

I will always love you, and hope that you will always feel the same.

Your loving sister,

Daisy

As she read out the final words, Casey sighed, overwhelmed with sadness. She searched Nick's eyes, anxious for his reaction. After a moment, when his face began to mirror her feelings, she spoke.

'What a horrible father,' she said. 'Making Sarah marry David against her wishes, while knowing that his other daughter was in love with him. I can't imagine a father behaving like that. Seriously, it's archaic. I wouldn't have thought that sort of thing happened here in America.'

Nick shook his head. 'No, I wouldn't have thought so either. I wonder if the two men had a purpose for having their eldest children marry, or if was it something stupid, like a pact made over too many drinks one night?'

Casey shook her head. 'Who knows, but any wonder Daisy left. She couldn't bear to watch her sister and David together. I wonder what David thought of all this?'

Nick rubbed his hand across his jaw. 'It's quite possible he never knew anything about Daisy's crush. Men aren't always good at reading subtle hints. There's been nothing to suggest any sort of tension in Sarah's life and if David had returned Daisy's feelings I think there might have been.'

'I think you're right. I think Daisy kept her feelings to herself. And now we know why she left, but it's still a mystery why she never married the father of her children.'

'True. The fact that she gave her children her own family name makes me wonder if he might have been married already. Maybe his wife had been committed to a mental asylum or something—then he wouldn't have been able to divorce her. I've heard of that sort of thing happening.'

Casey did a mental eye roll. Nick was giving the benefit of the doubt to the man in this case. 'Maybe, but it's just as likely he was happily married and liked having his cake and eating it too.'

Nick shrugged. 'Perhaps. Let's keep reading ... I wonder how Sarah reacted to Daisy's letter.'

The next letter made it clear that Sarah had apologised because Daisy reiterated that it wasn't Sarah's fault and that she had only told her what happened so Sarah could understand why she'd left. But there may have been some tension because for the next few years there were only Christmas cards.

Then, in 1931, Daisy wrote another long letter. This one told of the birth of a daughter, Mildred. After that, the letters became more frequent again, but revealed nothing that even came close to the letter about David. After they'd read a few more, Casey stood and stretched out her shoulders. They'd been hunched over the letters for the best part of two hours, and she needed a break.

'I'd kill for a cup of tea; would you like one?' Casey asked.

Nick followed her into the kitchen, watching her while she got the tea ready.

When she turned to him, he spoke. 'So, Daisy's got three children: Thomas, Ray and Mildred Carpenter. And they'd have been related to your family. Daisy was your grandmother's sister, right?'

'Our great-grandmother, yes. I'm anxious to keep reading to see if any of them married and then to find out if they had children. The solicitors who settled Uncle Steven's estate said there were no other Masons that had a claim to the estate, but these relatives wouldn't have been Masons—they were Carpenters.'

A frown crept onto Nick's face. 'Does that mean if you're successful at locating some distant relative, they might have a claim to some of your uncle's estate? Is that what you're saying?'

Casey shook her head. 'I don't think so. I mean, I suppose it's possible, but then again, why would they? Do cousins have any claim to an estate? And these wouldn't even be first cousins ... they're, like, distant cousins at best.'

'Yeah, I think you're right. I shouldn't have said anything. I wouldn't want you to worry about it.'

'I'm not—I'm just curious about potential relatives, but I'll talk to Alex and Taylor about it and see what they think. Alex has a pretty good legal brain so maybe before we do any additional records searches I'll run it past her.'

Armed with hot drinks, they continued with the letters which brought several sad revelations. Both of Daisy's sons, Thomas and Ray, were killed. Thomas died at Pearl Harbor, and then two years later, Ray was killed in a work accident. Daisy was devastated at the loss of her two boys. At least she had her daughter, Milly, who still lived with her in San Francisco.

They'd been at it for nearly two more hours when Nick, reading a letter dated in 1962, reached across and put his hand on Casey's forearm.

She looked at him, curiosity charging through her, and was about to ask what he'd found when she heard the voices of her sisters.

He released her arm as she called out. 'Alex, Taylor, we're in the study. Come say hello.'

A moment later, Taylor and Alex walked in and stood next to the desk. Nick jumped up and offered them his chair, but they both shook their heads.

'How's it all going?' Alex asked.

Casey quickly gave them the rundown on what they'd learned earlier in the day—the reason Daisy had gone to San Francisco and the loss of her two sons.

They chatted about it for a few moments, all saying how sad it was for Daisy, then Casey remembered that Nick had been about to say something to her just when her sisters had returned. And if his body language was anything to go by, it was something important.

'Nick, was there something new in this last letter you were reading?'

Nick's brows lifted as he nodded. 'Yes, there is something rather ... interesting.'

'Well, tell us. Or better yet, read the letter to us now that you've got us all curious,' Alex said with just a tinge of edginess in her voice.

Nick lifted the letter and began to read it out loud.

> *My darling Sarah,*
>
> *I was terribly sad to hear of the death of Albert Gold, the husband of your dear friend Emily. I am so sorry for his family's loss, but even more so for my own loss. I'm sure this will come as a shock to you, and please do not think poorly of me, but you see it was Albert Gold who I've been secretly seeing, and who fathered my three children.*

When Nick paused, Casey turned and met the gaze of her gobsmacked sisters, and then turned back to Nick.

'Did you say Albert Gold? I'm no historian, but I'd put pennies to pounds he's the same Gold family as you and your cousins, would I be right about that?' The wide-eyed look on Nick's face pretty much answered her question. 'Because if he is, that means the three children of Daisy Carpenter were not only related to our family, they were also related to the Gold family.'

Nick shrugged. 'Given the size of the town, I'd say that would have to be right. It's not like New York where there could be multiple Albert Golds. Not here.'

There was nothing surer. 'Go on, Nick. What else does the letter say?' Casey said, softly.

Nick continued reading.

I won't blame you if you feel you must abandon me because of my behaviour, for I have no real excuse for it other than that I was heartbroken when I left Masons Flat.

I was so lonely here without any friends or family, and then one day, about a year after I'd moved here, Albert appeared in the city. He bumped into me as I left work one evening. He claimed at the time that it was purely coincidental and that he was glad to have seen me and wanted to keep in touch in case I ever needed anything. It was wonderful to feel that I had someone I could turn to if I ever needed help.

After our first meeting, he began making regular trips to the city for business and always looked me up when he was here. It was quite some time later that he admitted our meeting hadn't been a coincidence. He'd heard from the postmistress that my letters were all postmarked in San Francisco and he'd begun to look for me. If he knew that, you have to wonder who else knew, but that's not the point I'm trying to make. You see, it turns out that he was always rather partial to me, but he fell for Emily's charms and when she became pregnant they married rather quickly. You may recall their first child was born prematurely, or so they said at the time. Anyway, Albert was so kind to me and convinced me that he was very much in love with me but that he could never leave Emily. Whether it was true or not, I believed him, and we continued to see each other in secret. I was never proud of my behaviour, but after a time it felt normal.

He was very attentive, and ensured that I had everything I needed to bring up the children—good food, money for doctors and dentists. We were happy, in our own way, and I will miss him terribly.

I hope that you can forgive me for my indiscretions, even though I know your dear friend would have been shattered had she ever found out. That's part of the reason I've had to be so careful. I heard that she passed two years ago else I would probably still not be telling you this even now.

If you are still reading this and haven't given up on me entirely, maybe you will find it in your heart to come to my daughter's wedding? Milly is going to be married in August to a lovely man by the name of Phillip Allen. She's so in love with him, and it warms my heart to know that at least one of my children has a chance at real happiness. Please give it some thought. We would both love to see you.

Your loving sister,

Daisy

CHAPTER 15

Casey wondered if the look of disbelief on the faces of her sisters and Nick mirrored the look on her own face. Daisy, their great-grandmother's sister, bore three children to the great-grandfather of not only Nick, but Travis and Denver as well.

'Well, that's crazy, isn't it?' Alex eventually said to the room.

Casey nodded, looking at Alex, then turned to Nick. 'Absolutely. So, Nick, I guess we were right about Daisy's benefactor being married. But I'd be leaning more to my idea of him having his cake and eating it too, than that his wife was locked up in an asylum.'

When Nick met her gaze, shaking his head slowly, she could tell he wasn't in the mood to be teased about it. She turned to Alex. 'Earlier today, before we'd seen this letter, Nick had raised an interesting issue about our inheritance. You see, Daisy's children would have been related to us. And although we learned that the two boys died while still fairly young, and presumably without having any children, there is the daughter, Milly, who we just learned got married in 1962. If Milly had children, they'd be related to us.' Casey turned to Nick as she continued. 'And now it turns out Milly was not only related to us, but also to you. So ... it begs the question ... do we continue to dig into this and potentially uncover someone who might have some sort of claim on our inheritances? Or do we simply put the letters back in the desk and never speak of them again?'

Alex shook her head immediately. 'No, you have to keep reading them. We can't just put this away. If there is a relative of ours out there, we have to find him or her, don't you think?'

Casey nodded. 'I agree—completely—but I wanted to be sure we have a consensus on this. I mean, if any of you have doubts perhaps we should consider this carefully, maybe even get advice on it.'

Taylor flashed a huge smile. 'I don't have any doubts. I think you need to keep reading the letters and find out everything. If we have a living relative out there somewhere, wouldn't that be nice to know? But if it turns out we don't, then I want to know that too.'

The three girls turned to Nick. He still looked a bit dumbfounded. 'I'm not concerned about inheritances, but ... this doesn't make us related to each other, does it? As in, most importantly, you and Travis?' He turned to face Alex, an eyebrow raised in question.

A collective "ewwww" came from the three sisters, followed by nervous laughter.

Alex spoke first. 'No ... no way. But it if turned out that either of us was directly related to Milly ... as in if she was Travis's or my grandmother or something ... that could be a whole different kettle of fish. Or at least I think that's right. Let me get some paper and a pen—I just want to check that I've got that right, okay?'

'I'll get some,' Casey said, dashing out to grab the pad of music paper they'd bought. She felt desperate to know if they were related to the Golds; she figured it was mostly on behalf of Alex and Travis, but could there be other reasons?

In a moment she returned, and watched as Alex sat and drew a rough family tree with the three family names: Mason, Gold and Carpenter.

After a few minutes Alex let out a noisy sigh of relief. 'No, look here. Sarah Carpenter had the Mason children, and Daisy Carpenter had some illegitimate Gold children who carried the name Carpenter, but the legitimate Gold children were completely unrelated to the Mason children. That means the Gold offspring would be related to Daisy's illegitimate offspring because they shared a father, obviously. And the Mason offspring would also be related to Daisy's offspring because Daisy and Sarah were sisters. But Sarah Masons children and the legitimate Gold children aren't related to each other. That means Travis and I aren't related in any way. Unless ... if Milly had a child who somehow came back into one of our families that could change, but seriously, that would have been recent enough we would have known about it, right?'

They all studied the tree structure Alex had drawn, nodding in agreement. It was Nick who answered. 'I think you're right, Alex. Let's continue to read the letters, and see if there is any mention of Milly having children, and take it from there. After all, if that family line died off then there's no issue in any case.'

When they all agreed, Casey picked up the rest of the envelopes while the others watched with considerably more interest than they'd shown previously.

There was a Christmas card in 1962 and in 1963 a Christmas card which also enclosed a brief letter. In that letter came the news that Daisy's first grandchild had been born. Caroline Darleen Allen. Daisy's pride came across clearly, but so did her pain, because the young family had moved to Los Angeles, meaning Daisy wouldn't see much of her grand-daughter.

'So, there is someone who would be related to both of us. Caroline Allen. Assuming she's still alive,' Casey said, looking first at Nick, then at her sisters.

Taylor frowned, then sort of shook her head. 'Don't you think it's a bit odd that there were no more letters after the one in 1963? It would have been nice to read a bit more about this Caroline Allen.'

Alex, frowning, replied. 'Perhaps by the mid-1960s telephone conversations were more affordable so they stopped writing long letters?'

'Possibly,' Taylor said. 'Kind of makes sense.'

The last of the Christmas cards was dated in 1975 and contained only Christmas wishes. Casey set the envelopes down and looked to each of the others in turn. As she looked at Nick, something changed. She suddenly appreciated Nick's desire to continue his family line, and she wondered if she'd been foolish to be so dead-set against having children of her own. She drew in a deep breath before continuing.

'So ... that's it. I guess that either Daisy or Sarah must have died in 1976. They'd both have been in their late seventies by then. Now we just have to decide if we're going to look further into Caroline Allen.'

They each glanced at the others with thoughtful expressions. Finally Nick spoke up. 'Let me run it past Travis and Denver tonight. I doubt they'll have any problem with it, but I'll ask anyway.'

Alex nodded. 'I guess these letters really were hidden all this time without Uncle Steven knowing about any of these people, because, surely, if he'd known, he'd have looked into them himself, don't you think?'

'I agree,' Casey said, 'but did I mention that Nick tried to work out the secret of how the drawer worked, but even knowing it was there he couldn't figure it out? That makes it a lot easier to believe that Uncle Steven knew nothing about the drawer or the letters. If we're taking a vote, my vote is to try to track down Caroline Allen, and find out if we have a relative living somewhere. What do you think, Taylor?'

Taylor threw her hands up. 'Definitely. Like I said before, if there is someone out there, I want to know about them.'

Alex chewed her lower lip for a moment. 'I also vote to continue.'

Nick cocked his head, then looking straight at Casey he answered. 'Yeah, my vote is we look into her, but let's see what Travis has to say. He could sway me ... it wouldn't be the first time his logic changed my mind about something.'

Alex huffed out a breath. 'Okay, you and I will talk to Travis and Denver tonight.' Then she turned to Casey. 'Oh, and before I forget, Annie is arriving tomorrow and we'll go to Disneyland later this week, which is great because that means we'll be back here for Christmas after all. Seems Annie's mother didn't feel the need to let Travis know she was heading off to a rodeo in Las Vegas and that she'd be pulling Annie out of school early. Anyway, I only found out today so I'll get onto the internet tonight and see if I can change our hotel bookings, or if not, I'll cancel them and find another hotel. It's going to be so much fun. It'll be like Travis and I have three children with us.' She grinned as she said the last bit.

Casey turned to Taylor, whose eyes grew wide as she rubbed her hands together. 'I can't wait! I've always wanted to go to Disneyland.'

'So have I,' Casey agreed. 'I've been to the theme parks in Queensland, and they're okay, but I bet they're nothing like Disneyland.' Then she turned to Nick, unable to hide her smile at the thought of spending time with him while having so much fun. 'You're coming with us, right?'

Nick shook his head. 'Someone has to mind all the animals. Denver and I will stay here. He can look after the house while I take over all the outdoor duties. You girls will have a great time, though; Disneyland's awesome, for sure. When I'm over in Europe, I might even go to the one in Paris—but I'm not sure it'll be any better than the original.'

Casey's heart sank. She'd all but forgotten about his overseas trip. 'Oh, that's right—you're heading off soon. Well, it sounds like a great trip,' she said, trying to sound happy for him.

When Nick turned and stared at her, she was certain he saw through her attempt.

Alex pulled her keys from her purse and rattled them. 'I'm gonna head back—are you coming now, Nick?'

Nick hesitated for a moment, making Casey wonder what he was thinking, but nothing he could say now was going to change the future. She put on a smile, and hoped it looked genuine. She had to change the subject. 'Do you still want me to email you the lyrics?'

'Sure—I'll text you my email address. I can work on it while you girls have fun playing at Disneyland.'

Casey could feel eyes on her back. She turned to find Alex with an eyebrow raised in question.

'Nick's going to try to write the music for one of my songs. That's why I bought the guitar—so I can learn to play it.'

Alex turned, directing the same look towards Nick. 'That's fabulous. So you *do* write music, Nick.'

'Sort of ... I was in a band a few years ago so I should be able to do it.'

Alex's eyebrow flew up again, and she gave Casey a subtle nod before replying to Nick. 'Quite nice of you. I'm sure Casey will really appreciate any help you can give her.' She turned back to Casey. 'I'll give you girls a call tomorrow and let you know how I go with everything.'

They all walked to the front door where Alex and Nick said their goodbyes, then Casey went back to the study and bundled up the envelopes to put them back in the drawer. She was grateful Taylor had gone to the kitchen so she could be alone with her thoughts.

General unease had plagued her since she'd returned the letters to their hiding place, but now the unease crystallised into something specific. She laughed at herself, shaking her head as she closed the desk drawer. Nick Gold wasn't for her—she'd known that right from the start when her intuition had gone on full red-alert toward the conservative cowboy who'd laughed at her tatts. So what difference could it possibly make that he would be travelling overseas where he might find a place that he liked so much that he never came back to California? How could that even matter to her life?

She'd be back in Melbourne soon, and her life would return to normal. And she'd have taken a huge step forward with her song-writing aspirations.

She threw her shoulders back and let out a deep sigh, then headed into the kitchen.

'So, what's for dinner?'

CHAPTER 16

The time at Disneyland turned out to be even more fun than Casey had imagined. Being with nine-year-old Annie made her feel like a kid again. It was a rare moment when Annie wasn't either laughing or telling silly jokes or stories, especially when they had to stand in long lines for some of the more popular rides. What really stood out for Casey, however, was the way Alex's eyes lit up in Annie's presence, and she wondered if Alex wished Annie could live with them all the time rather than only on school holidays.

They'd spent two full days at Disneyland, a full day at Universal Studios, and taken a drive down Hollywood Boulevard with a quick visit to the shops in Rodeo Drive. For their last day in Southern California, they would head to Santa Monica Pier. They'd have a nice lunch, Annie could go on more rides, and if the weather held, they'd spend the afternoon at the beach.

Everything about the little getaway had been perfect so far, yet as she was getting ready for bed the night before what would be their last full day, Casey was struck by a strange sense of melancholy. She sat, staring at the television in her room, but not hearing a word being said.

Rubbing her eyes, she tried to shake the feeling, but it refused to lift.

When an ad came on that had a cowboy in it, the realisation hit her: she was missing Nick. It was the only logical explanation, not that it was all that logical.

She flicked off the television, switched off the light, and tried to drop off to sleep.

~~*~~

'Look what the cat dragged in,' Denver said as Nick returned after a long day of working the horses. Denver, propped up against the stove, stirred a large pot of steaming spaghetti while an aromatic pan of sauce bubbled away next to it.

Nick was too exhausted to take offense at Denver's quip. He'd ridden the young horses that hadn't yet sold, plus Travis' stallion and Denver's mare. Afterwards, he'd checked the cattle and taken hay out to the young horses out in the back pasture. And that was on top of cleaning all the stables. It had been a long day of work, but he also knew the source of some of his exhaustion was waking most nights after only a few hours of sleep, unable to get Casey off his mind. He looked at his cousin and smiled. 'Mmm, smells fantastic.'

Clearly disappointed not to have gotten a rise out of him, Denver continued. 'Have you heard anything back about the searches on Caroline Allen yet?'

Nick watched as Denver heaped a huge serving of the spaghetti onto a plate and then smothered it with the sauce. As Denver set the plate down in front of him, Nick let out a tired sigh. 'Not yet. My boss is looking into it, but he's got some year-end reporting issues he's got to deal with today. I should hear something from him in a few days.'

'Cool. Not that it makes a great deal of difference to my life, I was just curious as I suspect Alex, Casey and Taylor may be anxious for the results.' Denver filled a second plate with the spaghetti and set it down on the table, then brought two glasses and a bottle of red wine over and sat.

Nick poured the wine, put the glass to his nose and inhaled the rich scent before taking a mouthful. It tasted as good as it smelled, and the warm sensation travelling down his throat was exactly what he needed. 'Yeah, they probably will be. I suppose they could have a bit at stake, given their recent inheritance, although none of them seem too worried about that.'

Nick remembered how thrilled they'd been when Travis had agreed with their plans to investigate the woman who was related to all of them, and Nick himself had been grateful when Devin had agreed to give them a hand again. He'd wondered what sort of favour Devin would ultimately ask in return, but he figured it would be worth it, whatever it was, because he'd be making Casey happy.

They continued to eat in silence, and were nearly finished when Denver started talking again. 'Been quiet around here without Alex and Travis. Must admit, I've enjoyed having Alex staying here.'

Nick gave him a sideways look, eyebrow raised.

'Oh, and you too. It's been great having both your company and your help, but I know you're leaving soon,' Denver added, quickly.

When Nick chuffed out a breath, Denver went on. 'I hope she decides to stay on once I'm back to full duties. She's turned out to be quite the cook—wouldn't have taken her for one when I first met her.'

'I wouldn't get used to it. The novelty will no doubt wear off soon enough.' He liked dishing it back to Denver, but he too had enjoyed the busy household. It would be lonely, especially at first, being on his own for the months he planned to travel.

They finished their meals in silence, then Denver cleared his throat. 'You know, I'm getting pretty fond of Taylor. I wish she wasn't going back to Australia. I don't know how she'd react, though, if I asked her to think about sticking around.'

Nick looked up in surprise. He'd been aware that Denver had been playing a bit of pool with Taylor at the saloon, and he'd enjoyed teasing him about it, but he had no idea Denver had developed that sort of interest in her. 'Really?'

'It took me a bit by surprise, too. She's ... not like most of the girls I've dated. She's a bit of a homebody ... and she's ... how can I say it tactfully ... a bit on the plump side. It suits her though, don't you think? Maybe that's part of the attraction—the fact that she is so different from all my old girlfriends. She loves to cook—I'd kill for some of her pastries and pies right now, ya know? And it's not like she won't ever be interested in dancing. When I told her how much a part of my life it normally is, she said she'd love to learn to dance one day.'

Nick shuddered dramatically. 'Wow, sounds serious ... like, you're really soft on her.'

Denver drew in a long breath. 'Yeah, she's so down-to-earth. There isn't anything remotely snobbish about her.'

Nick shook his head slowly, thinking how much that description reminded him of Casey. 'Well, sounds to me like she's really gotten under your skin. I think you've gotta just mention it when they get back from Disneyland. Tell her you've missed her company, and wish she wasn't planning to go back to Australia. Start the conversation fairly casual, and see what comes of it.' As he finished giving Denver the advice, he wondered if he should be doing the same with Casey, but he didn't say that out loud, and didn't even want to think on it too hard.

'Really? You think I should? Because it's pretty much what I was thinking too—just sort of sound her out, see if maybe she'd been thinking she'd like to stay.'

'I think it's a great idea. Let me know how it all goes.'

Nick was pleased for his cousin, but even more so, he had to wonder what that would mean with respect to Casey. If Taylor were to stay, would Casey too? He couldn't remember what sort of commitments she had at home—whether she had pets, owned her own place, or even if she had a boyfriend. As much as they'd talked, none of that had ever come up. It must mean she didn't have pets or a boyfriend because she'd have mentioned them, wouldn't she?

He stood and carried their empty plates and glasses to the sink, rinsed them and put them in the dishwasher. Then he rolled his eyes. Why even think about what it meant with respect to Casey? She'd made it pretty clear she wasn't ever interested in having a family, and wasn't that the most important factor to consider in every relationship he'd ever been in? Three kids. And a dog. He couldn't see Casey being that woman, not for a moment. Yet, if she was so wrong for him, why couldn't he get her off his mind?

When he returned to the table, Denver mentioned a movie coming on that he wanted to watch so Nick excused himself and headed to his room.

An hour later he'd finished writing out the chords for Casey's song when he realised there was a lot more to Casey Mason than not wanting to have a family. She was the sort of woman who brought out the best in him, and wasn't that more important than having children? Being with a woman who challenges you?

He picked up his guitar again and played the whole thing through from start to finish. It sounded pretty darn good. Then he played it again, this time singing the words. He'd changed a couple of the words to make it flow more smoothly, but he was pretty sure she'd be pleased with it. He sang it one more time, recording it onto his computer, and then headed to bed.

As he drifted off to sleep, images of Casey, with a small child sitting in front of her as she rode bareback across a grassy pasture, crossed his mind, and he felt a smile creep onto his face.

CHAPTER 17

Casey couldn't keep her mind from drifting to Nick. She was on her way to the gym for a workout the morning after they returned from Southern California. Having no more letters to read through, she'd struggled to think of an excuse to contact him. She'd hoped Alex might have suggested they all have dinner together tonight, but nothing had been said.

As she drove through Sonora she spotted a florist a few doors down from the gym. She was surprised she hadn't noticed it earlier.

All throughout her workout she tried to focus on the display panel of the cross-trainer, checking her heart-rate, calories burned, miles travelled and minutes worked, but it was no use. All she could see in her mind's eye was Nick, frowning as he concentrated on the chords she tried to play, or listening intently as she read out the contents of one of the letters. She had missed him more than she cared to admit over the days they'd been apart.

After a quick shower and a change, she decided to check out the florist shop. She went in and had a look at the arrangements, marvelling at the colours as she walked all around the small shop. Then she closed her eyes and took in a few deep breaths. She missed being surrounded by fresh flowers.

When a customer came in, it dawned on her that maybe the small area at the back of Alex's fruit and veggie shop would be enough room for her to do a small display, while concentrating on phone and internet orders. Would there be enough business to make it viable? It was certainly something she should give some thought to. If she could get it set up, Alex could run it in addition to the produce.

Having seen enough, she headed home, arriving shortly after ten. Taylor was finishing a coffee in the kitchen. 'Oh, you're back finally. I wouldn't mind going Christmas shopping ... don't suppose you'd be up for a drive to Sacramento?'

'Today?' Casey asked, frowning, not looking forward to a nearly two-hour drive in each direction, especially when getting a late start might mean driving home in the dark on the unfamiliar roads. 'What about tomorrow instead? I'll skip the gym, and we can get an earlier start.'

'Okay, that'll be fine. So, what are you thinking of doing today then?'

'I wonder how far it is to the Calaveras Big Trees that Alex mentioned. We could go there, since it's not raining.'

'I'll get my iPad and have a look.' Taylor headed to her bedroom and returned a moment later. 'Less than an hour. Shall we see if Alex and Annie want to come?'

Twenty minutes later, Alex arrived in the Range Rover. Annie jumped out, dressed in a denim jacket, black jeans and cowboy boots. A huge smile lit up her cute face as she called out to them. 'Hey, Casey, Taylor. Are you ready to go? I'm so excited. I haven't been to see the big trees before.'

Casey smiled. When Annie spoke it was easy to remember she was only nine, but to look at her, if not for her petite frame, you'd swear she was a teenager. Kids seemed to be growing up way faster than they did when she and Taylor were kids. 'Yeah, we're ready to go. Have you got your camera?'

It was cool when they arrived, but fortunately it was still dry. They parked and then wandered toward the Warming Hut where they had a hot drink and grabbed a map of the park. One of the first things they saw was a massive tree stump. Casey stopped to read the sign about the Discovery Tree, which had been chopped down in the mid-1800s. At twenty-five feet in diameter, it had been used as a dance floor by the people of the time. It sickened her, looking at the photos of people dancing on the stump, and she had to control her anger when she read that the tree was later determined to have been 1,244 years old when felled. She couldn't understand why anyone would want to destroy something so magnificent. Thankfully, it also said that in 1931 the whole area had come under the protection of the California State Parks, so never again would anyone destroy one of the majestic trees.

As they walked around the rest of the park, the one disappointment was missing the gorgeous flowering dogwoods that featured in many of the photos. They wouldn't flower until spring so they didn't see any, but Casey made a mental note to come back in spring sometime.

When they'd had their fill of the park, they headed toward home.

'Who wants to stop for a late lunch?' Alex asked, directing the question toward Annie mostly.

Surprisingly, Annie scrunched up her face, shaking her head. 'Could we go home for lunch? I'd like a P. B. J. and not many places have those.'

When Casey and Taylor looked at each other, Alex explained. 'Peanut butter and jelly. It's her favourite.'

'Ah, right, of course,' replied Taylor, winking at Casey.

It wasn't long back to Masons Flat and, as they approached the Mason house, Alex turned to Casey and Taylor in the back. 'Did you want to come in and hang around for dinner? I was thinking of grabbing some pizzas later.'

Taylor's eyes grew wide with pleasure. 'Pizza always sounds good, but I could go for one of Annie's peanut butter and jelly sandwiches right now.'

Casey shook her head at Taylor's appetite. 'I suppose I wouldn't mind trying a bite of one, but I'm mostly dying for some caffeine.'

As they approached the gates to the Gold's ranch, Casey's stomach began to do backflips. She'd see Nick for the first time since they'd returned from Disneyland. When they stopped at the front of the house, Casey got out and stretched, using the opportunity to glance over her shoulder toward the arena where she'd spotted movement. Sure enough, Nick and Travis were there, riding the horses.

She'd wondered what he looked like when riding a horse—whether he looked like a real cowboy or just a city boy pretending to be one. She turned her head back toward her sisters, making up her mind.

'Save me a quarter of your sandwich, Taylor. I'm going to watch them over at the arena for a few minutes.'

Taylor flashed a grin, and Annie shook her head. 'Daddy is fun to watch, but I'd much rather have my lunch.'

Casey smiled as the others headed into the house.

She approached the arena silently, stopping just shy of the rails. Travis sat on a large, dark horse, stationary at the other end of the arena. He spotted her and ducked his head in greeting, touching the brim of his hat gently. Nick rode a gold coloured and slightly smaller horse, making his way across the arena on a diagonal with his back to her.

She didn't know a lot about cowboys, or riding, or horses, or what they were even doing when they talked about *working horses*, but she knew one thing: Nick looked to her to be the real deal. As the horse did a slow trot across the centre of the arena, Nick seemed as one with it. His upper body appeared to be absorbing all the impact, and his backside never left the saddle. His hands were still, and the horse moved without encouragement. As he reached the edge of the arena, the horse turned to the right, heading toward Travis. Had Nick pulled on the reins? Or had he touched the horse with his heels? If he'd done either it wasn't obvious—she'd seen nothing to indicate he'd even moved.

As Nick rode past Travis, and then made the turn that would bring him toward her, she could see the concentration on his face. He seemed focused on a spot out in front of the horse, his eyes never wavering.

A moment later he was right in front of her. She drew in a breath, stepping back reflexively as the horse, still trotting, came within centimetres of the rails. When she looked up again, Nick had gone past, making a gentle turn to the right, following the curve of the arena.

When he reached Travis again, he seemed to sit back in the saddle, and perhaps he pulled on the reins slightly. Whatever it was, the horse stopped in its tracks in front of Travis. Travis reached across and patted the horse on the neck.

Now Nick turned, and a broad smile brightened his face. He reached forward, stroked the horse's neck, and then swung down out of the saddle. Leading the horse, he made his way across the arena and stopped in front of her.

'Hey, how was Disneyland?'

She had to think for a few seconds, Disneyland seeming a distant memory after today's trip to the big trees. 'It was awesome. I'm not sure who had the most fun—Annie, or me and Taylor.'

His smile turned into a laugh when the horse nudged him, pushing him toward her. He turned, patted the horse on the neck, and then looked back at her. 'Are you hanging around for a while? I'll have to cool this guy down and do a few other things, but it should only take twenty minutes or so. Will you still be here?'

'Yes, for sure. Alex said something about pizza for dinner.'

'Sounds great. I'll see you shortly then.'

As he turned to walk the horse out of the arena, she called out. 'You looked good out there. I mean, not that I know much about horses, but I was impressed.'

He looked at her over his shoulder and grinned. 'Thanks.'

Heat raced to her face when she realised Travis had been approaching, and had no doubt heard her compliment. 'He rides well. If he didn't, I wouldn't be letting him near my horses,' he said with a wink.

She wiped at some imaginary object on her face. 'Yes, well, I thought he looked like he knew what he was doing,' she said softly.

'He does. Now, more importantly, did I hear you mention pizza?'

~~*~~

They were settling back with drinks when Casey heard stomping on the back porch and the screen door creaked open.

'Hey, beautiful, did you have a nice day?' Travis asked, coming up and kissing Annie on the cheek. Then he walked over and gave Alex a hug from behind as he kissed her too.

Warmth washed over Casey as she watched the exchange. Travis, Annie and Alex made a good family. Seeing the three of them together begged the question, would she ever find herself in such a loving relationship?

'We had a lovely day, didn't we, Annie?' Alex asked, turning to give Annie a wink.

'We sure did. You should have come, Dad. The trees there are even bigger than you,' Annie said, giving her father a cheeky grin.

Travis shook his head, but then winked as he turned to walk over and pull out two more mugs. 'The coffee smells great. Is there enough for two more cups?'

'Probably not, but I'll make another pot,' Alex said, starting to stand.

'Stay there, I can do it. So, did I hear something about pizza for dinner?' Travis asked, as he made his way toward the sink to make another pot of coffee.

'I was thinking I could run over to Sonora and get a couple of pizzas later. Annie's just had a sandwich since we didn't get anything at the park,' Alex answered.

Annie's eyes opened wide. 'I still want pizza, and I want mine with cheese and ham.'

Annie took a sip of her milk just as the screen door creaked again. Casey's heart thumped at the same time, making her wonder if they'd all be able to see her chest moving with each beat. She leaned over, took a sip of her coffee, and then looked up to see Nick standing right in front of her, a warm smile on his face.

Annie broke the silence. 'We're having pizza for dinner. I'm having cheese and ham.'

Nick grinned at Annie and gently rubbed the top of her head. 'Sounds good to me. I could eat a whole pizza myself; your father has worked me that hard today.'

Annie's eyes grew huge. 'A whole pizza? Really?'

'Yes,' he answered, saying the word slowly as one eyebrow waggled.

Travis shook his head. 'What on earth are you talking about? You haven't worked hard today.'

Nick turned back to Casey and winked. 'It's all relative, isn't it? It felt hard to me, with you watching my every move. So, did you enjoy the giant sequoias?'

'They were awesome—quite amazing, actually,' Casey replied. 'I knew nothing about sequoias before this trip, and had never seen such massive trees. I mean, we have some huge gums in Australia, but these trees were ginormous.'

'Yeah, it's impressive. If you ever get back to Yosemite again, you'll want to take a look at Mariposa Grove too.'

She smiled, thinking there was a pretty good chance she'd be back here in the not too distant future, given that Alex was probably never moving back to Australia. She'd like another trip to Yosemite—perhaps in spring or early summer, when the waterfalls were at their peak. As she looked at Nick, she couldn't help but wonder if they might go there together.

The conversation stayed casual, and a short time later when they'd all finished their coffees, Nick stood. 'I should go out and check the cattle and those horses in the top pasture before it gets dark. Don't suppose you're up for giving me a hand, Den?'

Denver stood, gathered three mugs in each hand, and took them to the dishwasher while Nick put the milk back in the fridge. 'Sure, I'll give you a hand. Doctor says I'm fine to start light duties now, so I figure checking the cattle and feeding the horses in the top pasture will come back to me now.'

'When'd you see the doctor?' Nick asked, frowning.

'Yesterday.'

'On a Saturday?'

'Yeah, he's there Saturday mornings. Says I should stick to an automatic for at least a few more weeks, so it's a good thing The Beast is an automatic,' he said with a twinkle in his eye.

Nick glared at him, shaking his head. 'So you could have helped me yesterday then, right?'

'Well ... I suppose I could have,' Denver replied, dragging out his response.

Nick, still shaking his head, turned to Casey. 'See you a bit later?' he asked as his gaze bore into Casey's eyes for a moment.

'Yeah, sure. I'm looking forward to having pizza tonight.'

Alex turned to her. 'This place in Sonora makes them just the way we like them—with a super-thin crust so they're not as filling. I can get us a spicy vegetarian to share.'

'Sounds great,' Casey replied to Alex, watching Nick the whole time.

'Well then, see you in a while,' Nick said with a wave, then headed back out the screen door followed by Denver this time.

The casual banter had completely relaxed Casey, and she sighed as she drank the last of her coffee. 'So, Alex do you want to drop us back home so we can have a shower? That way I can drive back in the Buick and save you having to go out again?'

Alex made a face. 'It's pizza ... here ... in the kitchen. I hardly think you need to shower and change. You're fine as you are.'

Annie's eyes flew open wide. 'You can't go home. I've got a new game we can play,' she said, grabbing Casey's hand. Then she reached over to Taylor. 'You too, we need at least three for this game. Wanna play too, Alex?'

Alex sort of wavered back and forth a bit, then shrugged. 'Sure, why not.'

Annie ran to her room, came back with a huge box, and started setting up the game right there on the kitchen table. Travis excused himself to go out and finish some chores of his own.

An hour later, Casey was nearly bankrupt. She'd never been good at Monopoly, and while this one had slightly different street and place names than she was used to, it was just as difficult.

'I give up,' she said, throwing her hands in the air. Then she leaned over and checked out Annie's stash of money. 'Looks like we have a winner, ladies. Annie's clearly destined to become a property tycoon.'

'Oh, please, don't let that be true,' said Alex, her face screwing up as if she were in pain. 'Annie's going to be the next Serena Williams, right Annie?'

Annie grinned. 'I hope so, but I haven't been playing much since we moved to Seattle. It rains a lot up there. I miss California's sunshine. Maybe you can play with me while I'm here?'

'Of course,' Alex replied as she turned to look at Casey and Taylor.

'Don't look at me,' Taylor said quickly.

'Me neither, I'm hopeless at tennis,' Casey said.

Alex just smirked. 'Let me get something to write on and I'll start taking pizza orders. Nick and Denver should be back shortly.'

A few minutes later, the screen door creaked open and Nick and Denver appeared. Casey couldn't help notice how Taylor's face lit up as Denver walked over and stood beside her. As for her own state of mind when it came to Nick, Casey could only hope her face wasn't giving away her feelings the way Taylor's had.

'So, pizzas all around, right?' Alex asked, pen at the ready to take down their preferences.

Alex smiled as she jotted down the orders. 'So, that's five pizzas all up. Sure it'll be enough?'

Casey could hear the sarcasm in her sister's voice, but the men just nodded.

After Alex left with Annie as her co-pilot, Travis and Nick disappeared to have showers and Denver headed back to catch the weather report on the news, leaving Casey and Taylor alone in the kitchen.

Casey smiled at her sister and raised a brow. Speaking in a low voice so that Denver wouldn't hear them, she looked at her sister, raising an eyebrow inquisitively. 'Things seem to be getting serious with you and Denver. Am I right?'

Taylor winced, biting her lower lip. 'Oh, Casey, why did I have to meet such a nice man *here*? I mean, he's such a great guy—exactly the sort of guy I've always wanted to meet but never have. And I think he likes me too, but he lives here, and we don't. It's quite the dilemma. I mean, what have we got, a couple more weeks? And then what?'

Casey swallowed hard. Once again, Taylor was right. 'And then we go home, that's what,' she said; and even she could hear the melancholy in her voice.

In a few short weeks they'd be sitting on a plane headed across the Pacific Ocean. What use was it for either of them to form attachments here? They both had lives back in Melbourne, and as much as they loved Alex, neither of them had ever made any suggestions about staying on here. Casey wondered if she should suggest it—if she should confide her own misgivings about leaving. Her feelings about Nick were so complicated because, unlike what Taylor had said about Denver, Nick wasn't *exactly the sort of guy she'd always wanted to meet.* In fact, he was far from it. And yet she did wish they had more time to get to know each other.

'Yes,' Taylor said, her voice barely a whisper. 'Then we go home. And no doubt I'll forget all about him, right? And someone will walk into the bakery one day, and our eyes will meet, and I'll know that I did the right thing returning to Melbourne. That's how it'll go, won't it?'

Casey sighed, hoping Taylor was right for both of their sakes. 'Of course that's what'll happen. Doesn't it always happen that way in the movies? Now, how about we set the table? Wonder what they've got to drink?'

By the time Alex and Annie came back with the pizzas, they were all sitting at the kitchen table, nibbling on some peanuts and drinking beer. As Alex entered the room, the scent of toasted dough, melted cheese and tomato sauce made Casey realise how hungry she was. It only took a short time for them to devour every last slice.

'What say I run you two home?' Alex asked, grabbing her handbag.

'I'll take them a bit later, if that's okay with you?' Nick said quickly, turning to Casey.

Casey shrugged. 'Sure, I'm in no rush to get home. You, Taylor?'

'No, I'm fine staying here until you're ready. Unless Alex wants us out of here.'

'Not at all. I'm just weary and know if I plonk in front of the telly I'll be worse later,' Alex said.

Nick pointed toward his room. 'Good, I've got something I want to show Casey.'

Taylor gave her a questioning look, Alex smiled, and Travis looked away, perhaps trying to hide his expression?

Denver turned to Taylor and smiled as he gently placed his hand on her back and guided her toward the family room. 'Good, you can come watch TV with us. If I know Travis, he'll be asleep in a few minutes, as will your sister. Don't get me wrong, Annie, you're good company, but it'll be nice to have someone else with us, don't you think? How about we find a movie?'

Casey raised an eyebrow inquisitively when Nick gestured down the hall. She walked ahead of him, went into his room and sat on the corner of his bed. 'And what dark secrets are you planning to divulge?' she asked, not sure what demon inside her had made her ask that question.

CHAPTER 18

Casey waited anxiously as Nick closed the door. She half expected him to sit beside her on the bed but instead he sat at his computer desk.

He swivelled in the chair and faced her. 'I've finished your song, but I didn't know if you wanted me to say anything in front of the others. It occurred to me you might like to hear it alone.'

Casey's hands flew to her mouth, her eyes growing wide. She pulled her hands away and flashed him a big smile. 'Wow that was fast. Of course I want to hear it—and yes, probably best not to share it just yet.'

He winked, and swivelled back to face the computer. 'I recorded myself singing it to be sure the timing worked, and I've written it down as chords that you should be able to play fairly easily. Here, have a listen.'

He brought up the song file, and played it.

Casey couldn't believe she was listening to Rose's song. She knew the words were powerful, but his deep voice made it all the more chilling, giving her goose bumps. When he turned to face her, tears welled in her eyes.

'Oh, Nick, it's absolutely beautiful.'

A look that spoke of pride softened his features. She was certain he was going to come over and kiss her, but he didn't. Instead, he simply smiled and cocked his head. 'I'm so glad you like it. I spent a bit of time on it—wanted it to be perfect for you. So, you think it worked with a male singer rather than female?'

'Yes, definitely. It sounded so ... professional. I'd love to put it up on YouTube. Would you be okay with that?'

'Sure. I'm flattered you think it's good enough. Do you have a channel?' He turned to his computer again.

'A channel?'

'Guess that's a no,' he said. 'Never mind, I'll figure out what needs to be done to set one up and we can work on it together, and upload the song. There will no doubt be some sort of "about" page, so you'll need to work out what to say on it. Any ideas?'

'I'll have a look at a few others, and see what they put. This is so exciting. I can't begin to thank you enough. I can't even remember how long this has been a dream of mine. I mean, I'd love to hear one of my songs on the radio, but this is a step in the right direction, don't you think?'

'Of course it is. Lots of people get discovered by doing exactly this. I have to admit, I don't know a lot about the music industry anymore, not since our band split up, but maybe a few of the guys have some contacts. Mind you, none of them have gone on with music.'

Casey shook her head, still in a state of disbelief. 'Any help you can offer will be appreciated. I know so little, as I've said, but ... wow ... I can't believe it's going onto YouTube.'

Nick turned to his computer again and shut it down. 'It's late, so I won't do anything more tonight, but I'm sure it'll be easy to set up. Once it's up, you can add additional songs as they're ready. Or at least, I got the feeling you've got others. Am I right about that? That once you learn how to play you'll record a few of the others yourself?'

Casey couldn't stop grinning. She was going to have a song on YouTube. Soon. Like within a few days. Finally, Nick's question sunk in. 'Yes, I've got several others that I'll have a play with. This is just so amazing.'

Nick got up, walked over, and sat beside her on the end of the bed. 'It's been my pleasure. Working on your song has brought back a lot of good memories, and made me wonder why I ever gave it up. I mean, yeah, I know why I gave it up. All of us guys in the band got good jobs—time consuming ones—so we went our separate ways. Who knows where we might be now if we'd stuck at it. Nashville? Of course, we could have spent a lot of money getting there just to be sent packing along with the thousands of other failed artists.' He laughed, suggesting he knew it was a *fait accompli*.

Casey's heart sank a bit. He was right. There were thousands upon thousands of failed artists out there. She was silly to think this meant all that much. And yet, it was still a wonderful achievement. She shifted to face him and smacked her hand on his thigh. 'Don't burst my bubble. Not yet, anyway. Let me pretend that someday, someone will stumble onto my channel and say something like, "Wow, this girl can write! I must contact her." I mean, I can dream, can't I?'

Nick flashed another soft smile. 'Of course you can. And you should. I was talking about me and my friends. We had a blast, but I don't think we were all that good. We mostly did covers, and they were a lot of fun, but none of us was passionate enough about writing our own music.'

Casey didn't remove her hand from Nick's thigh. Instead, she turned her body slightly toward him and sighed, hoping he felt the same connection she did. Hoping he might even kiss her again.

He did turn, ever so slightly, but he didn't kiss her. Instead, he lifted his hands and placed one on each side of her face, giving her a wry smile as he gently rubbed her cheek with his right thumb. 'You're sweet, Casey. I'm sorry we got started off on the wrong foot when we first met. I can see now what a good person you are. I'm also sorry you live so far away and that you'll be going home soon, because I think you were right when you said we'd make a good team. Song-writing, definitely, and who knows what else might have come from that.'

Casey swallowed hard, determined not to show her emotions. Fearing her eyes might be tearing up, she turned away, wriggling out of his hands. 'Distance. It's a big issue, isn't it?'

'Maybe we can still collaborate on some music. Between emails and video conferencing, we'll be able to send stuff back and forth and chat about the songs. Of course, I'll be travelling for quite some time, so it'll have to wait until I get back.'

Casey turned back to him trying to look and sound unperturbed. 'Of course—when you get back. Where did you say you'll be going?' She knew exactly where he was going, she just needed time to regain her composure. She knew there was a big chance he'd lose interest in both her and their song-writing over time, but she didn't want to admit to him, let alone herself, that it mattered.

Nick stood, and began to pace the room. 'I fly into London, and then I'm heading over to Ireland to meet up with my friend, Patrick. He's there now, visiting family.'

Nick paused, so she looked up and met his gaze, forcing a weak smile onto her lips.

When he continued, Casey wondered if she could hear a touch of hesitancy in his voice.

'He's pretty stoked about me coming over. He's even booked a ski trip for us to Switzerland. After that, when he goes back to Ireland, I'll play it by ear. I mean, I really want to see Paris, and Rome, and parts of Spain, maybe Germany, but I thought it would be best to see what feels right, and maybe who I meet to travel with.'

Casey raised her arms and crossed them in front of her, rocking almost imperceptibly as she swallowed the lump in her throat. With all the places he was going, he'd forget her, for sure. There was nothing surer. 'Yeah, of course,' she finally managed to say, trying to sound positive. 'You might meet some nice people who want to go to the same places you do. Best to keep things fluid. Taylor wants to travel too. She mentioned something about us going on a cruise.'

'Yes, I remember her saying that. It sounds interesting.' He paused again, looking at her thoughtfully. 'So ... I'll sort our what's involved in setting up your channel if you'll work out what you want it to say, and we'll catch up to work on it in a few days.'

Still rocking, she stood, and put what she hoped looked like a genuine smile on her face as she headed toward the door. 'Thanks again, Nick. I'll definitely have a good look at it tomorrow. It'd be awesome if we can get that channel thing up before I go back to Australia.'

'I don't think it'll take long,' he said, walking toward her.

Every cell in her body wanted to step up to him, to wrap her arms around him and kiss him the way they'd kissed on the sofa that night. But as much as her heart wanted to, her head warned her away. She cleared her throat, listening to her head. 'Maybe Alex will still be awake enough to run us home,' she said, opening the door and stepping into the hall.

'Don't be silly, I'll take you—don't bother Alex.'

When they reached the family room, Alex sat snuggled up next to Travis. They were both breathing heavily, sound asleep. Taylor sat beside Denver, not quite touching him but it was questionable whether even a slip of paper could have fit between their legs.

'Ready to go?' Nick asked, speaking softly as he dangled his keys in his hand.

Taylor turned toward Denver, and took his hand. 'Best go while the rides on offer. I've seen this movie before, so I know how it ends anyway.'

Annie turned around from her spot on the floor in front of the television. 'I haven't seen it, so don't tell me,' she said with a giggle, then waved goodbye and turned back to the movie.

Denver looked at Nick, a wry smile on his face. 'You'll take good care of these girls, won't you? They're pretty special cargo.'

Nick chuffed out a breath by way of an answer.

CHAPTER 19

'Did I hear your phone ringing before?' Taylor asked as Casey walked into the kitchen after a night of restless sleep.

'Yes, it was Nick. He heard from his boss, Devin, this morning. It seems Milly's daughter, Caroline Allen, married Timothy Clarke in Los Angeles in 1989. But Devin didn't find any birth records associated with her, so he's not sure if she ever had any children. At least we know one thing; we have a distant relation out there somewhere, by the name of Caroline Clarke.'

'Did he find out where she lives now?' Taylor asked, a touch of a frown creasing her brow.

Casey shook her head. 'Nick didn't want to ask any more of the guy, he's already done so much. But he says it's not hard to track people down here in the US. There are all kinds of websites where we can look for her now that we know her full name, if that's what we decide we want to do.'

Taylor's frown deepened momentarily, then she shook her head and ran a hand through her long tresses. 'Well, I say we do our Christmas shopping today, and then we can have a nice lunch and talk it over. I'll ring Alex, see if she's interested.'

Alex appeared a half-hour later. 'I dropped Annie next door to spend the day with her cousin, Tammy, so it's just the three of us,' she said with a huge smile as Taylor and Casey bundled themselves into the Mustang.

'You didn't have any trouble getting away from the shop, Alex?' Casey asked once they were on the road.

'No, my part-timer is quite pleased to be getting extra hours while Annie is here. She's more than capable of doing just about everything. So ... Christmas shopping and lunch. Isn't this going to be fun?'

Four hours later, after they'd each bought several bags of presents, they were ready for lunch.

'Nick took me to a gorgeous place along the river. Want to see if we can get in?'

Taylor and Alex both agreed, so they popped all their bags in the car and made their way toward the river. It was late enough that they'd missed the lunch crowd so they got a similar table to where Casey and Nick had sat, overlooking the river and Tower Bridge.

As they were finishing lunch, Taylor's frown returned when she looked at Casey. 'Do you remember Caroline's full name? From Daisy's letters, I mean.' Taylor asked, tilting her head, a slight frown creasing her forehead.

'Caroline Allen, wasn't it? Before she got married and became Caroline Clarke,' Casey replied, not sure what Taylor was after.

'In the letter ... where Daisy mentioned the birth of her granddaughter, wasn't it Caroline *Darleen* Allen? I'm pretty sure I remember being surprised at the time because Darleen isn't a particularly common name.'

Alex's eye flew open wide. 'Darleen Clarke. How did I not put two and two together?'

Casey's brows knitted together as she stared first at Alex, and then Taylor. 'Clarke is Darleen's surname, isn't it? Darleen, who runs the saloon.'

Taylor and Alex both answered in unison. 'Yes.'

Taylor turned to Alex and answered her earlier question. 'There was no reason for you to put it together. Not before, anyway. But now that we know Caroline *Allen* married and became Caroline *Clarke*, it's not hard to imagine she might have chosen at some stage to go by her middle name, Darleen. A lot of people do that. Do you think it's her?' Taylor started fiddling with her napkin, tearing at the corners.

'She's the right age, but it seems so strange. I mean, if it's a coincidence, it's just too weird. And if it's not a coincidence, and she knows she's related to us, why wouldn't she have said something? If not to us, then at least to Uncle Steven? I mean, if she had said something to Uncle Steven, surely we'd have known about her, wouldn't we?'

Casey couldn't believe this. None of it had ever crossed her mind, and yet now that they were discussing it, it seemed quite plausible. 'We'll have to say something, don't you think? I mean, if it is her ...'

Taylor shook her head. 'I'll ask her, directly. I mean, she's either changed her name from Caroline to Darleen, or she hasn't. If she was christened Darleen, then it's not her.'

Casey turned to Alex. 'You've seen her payslips. What does it say on them? Is the name Caroline on there?'

Alex shook her head. 'No. But that doesn't mean anything. I don't think it's that hard to change your name. My intuition tells me Darleen Clarke is actually Caroline Darleen Allen. And that makes her a direct, albeit ill-legitimate, descendant of the original Masons Flat Gold family.'

'Wow,' Taylor said, her eyes growing wider by the second.

'Uh, yeah, wow is right,' Casey said, trying to quickly work out what that meant in terms of Darleen's relationship to Travis, Denver and Nick.

'I have the perfect idea. Have you two done enough shopping?' Alex asked, her face lighting up.

'I have, more than enough, actually,' Taylor said, frowning.

'Same. Why, what are you thinking?' Casey asked.

Alex stood, pulling her phone from her purse. 'Bear with me a moment, I need to make one call. I'll be right back.'

Taylor continued to fiddle with her napkin while Casey sipped her soda water, gazing out over the river. The serenity was palpable, and with only a few other patrons in the restaurant, it was easy to imagine being here all alone. The same feelings that had come over her while sitting here with Nick played at the back of her mind—the feeling of being at home here. It was eerie how grounded she felt.

Casey turned back to Taylor, who was still fiddling with the napkin, and wondered whether Taylor was thinking about Darleen Clarke, or if she was thinking about Denver. Could it be that Taylor wished she wasn't going back home to Melbourne? It was possible. But it was just as possible that Casey was projecting her own reservations about leaving California onto her sister.

A moment later, Alex reappeared, beaming. 'We have an appointment with Damien West in twenty minutes. Let's pay the bill and mosey over there.'

Taylor and Casey looked at each other, both shrugging.

'And he is ...' Taylor finally asked.

'He's the lawyer, the solicitor, who handled our inheritance. I have an idea—I'll tell you about it on the way there. We all need to be on board with it, but something tells me you're both going to be just fine with it.'

~~*~~

When Nick came in at lunchtime he found Denver in the kitchen, making ham and cheese sandwiches. 'Yo, cuz, these look great, but where are the ones for you and Travis?'

'Ha ha. If you can hold off a few minutes, they'll be even better. I'm going to grill them.'

Nick, who'd been about to grab one of the sandwiches, took a step back. 'Okay, should I make coffee?'

A few minutes later, having given up waiting for Travis, they sat at the table and began to polish off all the sandwiches.

Washing down the last bite of his sandwich, Nick noticed Denver staring at him, looking concerned. 'What's up, Den? Your leg bothering you?'

Denver shook his head. 'No, it's fine. It's just ... it's almost Christmas, and I'm at a loss for what to get in the way of presents, especially for Taylor.'

'Oh ... are we doing presents? I hadn't given it any thought other than for Annie and my niece. Do you think we need to get presents for everyone?'

Denver frowned, cocking his head to the side. 'Well, maybe not. Maybe I'm making too big a deal out of having a crowd at Christmas this year. Travis and I haven't bothered the last couple of years, but I just thought, you know...'

Nick nodded. 'Yeah, a tree with a stack of presents under it does look great. But with Taylor and Casey going back to Australia, any sort of souvenir we get them has to be small. And what on earth would we get Alex? No ... this is too hard. Why don't we suggest doing one of those Secret Santa things where we draw names out and then we just need to get a gift for the person whose name we've drawn? We did that at the office a few times and it was fun.'

Denver's expression lightened up immediately. 'That's a great idea. If we're unlucky enough to draw Alex, Taylor, or Casey, then at least it's only the one we have to worry about, not all three.'

'Done,' Nick said, 'let's suggest it to Travis and Alex tonight. But I think we should still spoil Tammy and Annie a bit—I mean, they're kids, and you remember what Christmas was like at their age.' Nick grinned, feeling relieved that they'd come up with an easy way out of worrying about women's gifts. However, as he looked at Denver, he could see he was still troubled about something. 'Have you had your chat with Taylor yet—about whether she might be thinking of staying here?'

Denver shook his head gently. 'There hasn't been a good time to bring it up. We haven't had a chance to talk since before they all went to Disneyland.'

'I guess you haven't been playing much pool. That's probably the perfect time, while having a quiet drink at the bar between games.'

'Yeah, maybe that's what I should do. Why don't you and Casey come too? You can be my wingman, so to speak. That way, while you and Casey are playing, Taylor and I can grab the drinks and it won't seem so much like I planned it.'

'Sounds good. Might as well put it out there ... see what she thinks. I mean, you're not getting any younger, and if she's special, who knows when, or even if, you'll meet someone else like her.' Nick stood up, getting out of arms reach. 'Especially living way out here in the middle of nowhere like you do,' he said with a chuckle.

Denver gave him a *watch-it* look, but he had to know he was right. When the right woman came along, it was foolish not to act on it ... not to give it a chance to turn into something more than a casual friendship. His stomach tightened as his thoughts sunk in, but he brushed the feeling aside, grabbed the plates from the table, and loaded the dishwasher.

Just as he stood up, Travis came in, his voice full of sarcasm as he asked, 'Hey, don't suppose you made any for me?'

CHAPTER 20

Casey was impressed by the law offices of Damien West, not that she'd been to many law offices. They were ushered into a meeting room, given glasses of iced water and told Mr West wouldn't be long. It was only a few minutes before a tall man with a full head of grey hair entered the room. The broad smile on his face complemented his fashionable glasses and well-tailored suit. Casey returned his smile briefly, just before he reached out his hand to Alex.

'Alex Mason, how lovely to see you again,' he said.

Alex stood, taking his hand, and introduced her sisters.

'And it's lovely to finally meet you both in person. Now, to what do I owe the pleasure of this unexpected visit?' Mr West asked.

Alex began by quickly telling Mr West about the letters Casey found in the desk, then turned to Casey gesturing for her to continue.

'Do you want me to explain ... everything?' she asked her sister.

Alex nodded. 'Yeah, briefly.'

Casey explained who Daisy was, and how she'd come to end up in San Francisco. She then went on to explain about Daisy's three children who, as it turned out, were fathered by none other than a member of the Gold family. She described the death of the two boys, the marriage of the daughter, Milly, and the subsequent birth of Milly's daughter, Caroline.

Mr West took brief notes, nodding throughout, but not asking any questions until Casey stopped. Then he looked up at Alex. 'And you think this Caroline Allen is a distant relative, and you want to know if she has a claim on your estate ... is that it?'

'Not exactly. You see, we think it's very likely that Caroline Allen, who later married and became Caroline Clarke, is actually the Darleen Clarke who has been running the saloon in town for the last twenty odd years.'

Mr West tilted his head and gave a tiny shrug. Then he raised his hands off the table making a steeple as he tapped his fingertips together. 'I see,' he finally said, but it was clear he didn't.

Alex scrunched up her face slightly. 'She isn't from the Mason side of the family, and her mother was certainly illegitimate, so I couldn't imagine she has a legal claim to our inheritance.' She turned to Casey and Taylor and sighed. 'But what we're thinking is that the saloon became part of the Mason estate through rather unconventional means. You've heard the story about how our ancestor won it in a drunken poker game from an ancestor of the Gold family, haven't you?'

'I vaguely recall something about it, but not the details,' Mr West said, still looking slightly baffled as to where Alex was going.

Alex drew in a deep breath. 'It seems our ancestor and the Mr Gold who was his contemporary were in a heated poker game one night—both drinking far too much. Gold threw what was then Gold's Saloon into the pot, and our ancestor threw in the Mason Hotel. Mason won, and Gold lost. Our ancestor then changed the name to Gold Nugget Saloon and refused to give it back, saying he'd won it fair and square. Years later, one of Gold's descendants, Mr Duncan Gold, who happens to have been my fiancé's father, tried unsuccessfully to get the original transfer reversed. After Duncan Gold died, Travis and his brother, Denver, tried, again unsuccessfully, to buy it back from our Uncle Steven.'

Mr West shrugged. 'I see what you mean about it being a somewhat unconventional acquisition.'

Alex nodded. 'Its loss remained quite the thorn in the side of the Gold family, and in particular my fiancé, Travis, who felt somewhat obliged to get it back for the sake of his father. The issue was nearly the end of our relationship, I might add.'

Mr West tapped his fingers together again. 'I see.'

'So, what we're proposing is that we gift the saloon to Darleen Clarke, thereby returning it, in some respects, to the Gold family. And given it's nearly Christmas, we thought it would be wonderful to do it as a surprise, on Christmas day.'

Mr West sat up taller. 'I see. That certainly is some surprise you have in mind. You do realise it would be worth a few hundred thousand dollars?'

Casey looked at her sisters, who both nodded. Alex answered. 'Yes, we do, but we reckon if Uncle Steven had known she was related, he most likely would have willed it to her. I mean, he trusted her to pretty much run it for the past twenty years, and she's done a brilliant job.'

Casey's heart swelled at the thought of doing what she knew was the right thing, and when she looked at Taylor she saw tears in her sister's eyes. Then she turned to Mr West again. 'If he'd known, if he'd found the letters and realised who Darleen was, I'm certain he would have left it to her.'

Alex, who had been looking at Casey, now smiled as she turned back to Mr West. 'I should have guessed she was related to us, right from the start. I mean, she even sort of looks like us.'

Taylor threw her head back, laughing, wiping at her eyes. 'You mean her hair? It's dyed. She's a brunette. She told me she started putting henna in her hair to hide the grey and felt it suited her, so she ended up going full red. Besides, I think the red hair comes from the Mason side of the family.'

Alex shook her head before continuing to speak to Mr West. 'I realise it's a huge ask ... getting paperwork done given it's so close to Christmas. If you can't do it, we can always mock something up on a computer to look like a gift certificate and get the real contract later.'

Mr West turned and gazed out the window for a moment before answering. When he turned back, he smiled. 'I think the best thing is to do a letter of intent first, rather than a full contract of sale. For one thing, you may want to make sure she actually wants the saloon. As you know, it's a lot of responsibility. She might prefer a cash payment of some sort rather than taking on that sort of commitment.'

Casey turned to her sisters who both had a blank look on their faces. Again it was Alex who answered him. 'Oh ... we never thought of that. I suppose it's possible.'

Mr West smiled. 'How about I prepare a non-binding letter of intent, giving her the option to purchase the saloon, and all its fixtures and fittings in their current condition, for one dollar, conditional upon determining that she is, in fact, the Caroline Darleen Clarke you believe her to be. When she receives the letter, if she isn't comfortable taking it on, you can discuss alternatives. I can get you that sort of letter relatively quickly. How does that sound?'

Alex turned to her sisters, raising her eyebrows as she suppressed a smile.

Casey reached across the table and placed her hand over Alex's. 'This is such a great idea, Alex—I'm so glad you thought of it.'

'Yes, Mr West, that sounds perfect. Thank you,' Alex answered.

When they climbed into the Mustang a short time later, Casey claimed the front seat, then turned to Alex and sighed. 'This is so wonderful, Alex. I mean, it's not an insignificant amount of money, but as you said, if Uncle Steven had known she was related, even as tenuous as the relationship is to our side of the family, I feel certain he would have left it to her. It's nice to think he would have, anyway.'

Alex glanced at her with a smile. 'From what I've heard of him, he was a very kind man. He cared for his employees and all the people in town, so I too am certain he'd have given her the saloon, maybe even more than just the saloon. But it's something, and having thought of it, I truly hope she's happy to accept it.'

Taylor leaned forward, speaking between Alex and Casey. 'Oh, I'm pretty sure she'll accept it. She's very proud of the saloon, and to be honest, I'm certain she practically thinks of it as hers anyway. I couldn't be happier about the decision; I'm just disappointed I wasn't the one to come up with the idea.'

'But you were the one who worked out the connection between Darleen Clarke and Caroline Darleen Allen. I mean, it has to be her, right? So you played a huge part in this. I just hope Travis sees it the same way we do—that it means the saloon will be going back to the Gold family.'

'Are you going to mention it to him beforehand, or let him be surprised on the day?' Casey asked, wondering if it might be best for Alex to give Travis a heads up, given what a huge issue it had been with him.

Alex reached up and placed her hands on the steering wheel, gripping it firmly. 'I think I'll tell him about it tonight, when we're snuggled up in bed. I think, or at least I hope, it will make him really happy, but you're right that it mightn't be fair to spring it on him as a surprise on Christmas day.'

'And what about Denver and Nick, will we tell all of them?' Casey couldn't imagine Nick would care one way or the other, but she didn't know how Denver would react.

'I don't think so, but I'll leave that to Travis. Oh, now before I forget, Nick's sister, Stacy, and her family are coming around for dinner tomorrow night. I'll make a couple of lasagnes, and maybe some salad.'

'I'll make a dessert,' Taylor chirped up from the back.

'I can make the salads if you like? Waldorf is always nice,' Casey said.

They arrived home just as the sun disappeared behind the trees. Alex shut the car off but didn't get out. 'Have either of you spoken to Mum this week?'

'We spoke to her last night, actually. She's getting pretty good at FaceTime. Why?' Casey looked back at Taylor who just shrugged.

'Oh, I thought we could do a group call if you hadn't spoken to her lately, but I'd just as soon get home, so I'll give her a call later.'

'No worries,' Taylor said, opening the door and climbing out.

'Yeah, that's fine. Drive safely,' Casey said, getting out of the car.

Alex had barely pulled out of the driveway, when Taylor's phone rang.

'Hi, how are you? ... we did a lot of shopping, and we bought lots of presents ... oh, really? Could have told us before we did all the shopping ...' Taylor said, her voice laced with sarcasm as she rolled her eyes. 'Tonight?' Taylor asked, looking questionably at Casey, who shook her head in an *I-have-no-idea-what-you're-talking-about* fashion, 'sure, we'll be ready when you get here. Bye.'

'What was all that about?' Casey asked the moment Taylor ended the call.

'The men have chickened-out with Christmas. They want to do a Secret Santa—you know, a Kris Kringle—so they don't have to think so hard about presents. We'll talk to Alex about it and see what she thinks, but for right now, Denver and Nick want to go to the saloon for a couple of games of pool. They'll be here in forty minutes, and we can grab something to eat at the bar. I don't know about you, but I'm starving, and Darleen's wedges—roasted potatoes, served with sour cream and chives—sounds absolutely divine. Now get your skates on, you have less than forty minutes to freshen up.'

CHAPTER 21

'I have played pool before, you know,' Casey said, as Nick came up behind her and reached around to show her how to hold the cue.

'But have you played it well?' he said into her ear, his tone unmistakable. He knew he was going to beat her.

'I haven't ever won, if that's what you mean,' she said, keeping her voice cool.

'Well then ... perhaps you'd be wise to accept my free advice.' He leaned in closer, the warmth of his body penetrating her jeans and light cotton shirt as he placed her hands on the cue, and then encouraged her to bend over to line up the ball.

It was too intimate, stirring feelings in her that she wanted to ignore. Feelings that should be reserved for someone she was dating, or at least someone she wanted to date. Not someone who she was determined to keep in the friend zone.

She turned and found herself face to face with him. The desire to kiss him overwhelmed her, but the desire to get away from him was even stronger. She drew in a breath, and twisted from his grasp. 'Uh, I think I'll give it a go on my own to start with, thanks.'

Nick stepped back with his palms up in surrender. 'Suit yourself—can't say I didn't offer to help.'

Settling herself, she turned to the table and struck the cue ball cleanly. As it broke the rack, the balls went flying and the red three went into the far left pocket.

'Bingo,' Casey yelled, spinning to look at the others as she did a fist pump. 'Guess that means I'm solids, right?'

Taylor walked over and gave her a high five while Denver grinned and said, 'Well done.'

Nick rolled his eyes and shook his head back and forth. 'Pool shark, right? And here I thought you needed some help.'

Casey, not certain if he was kidding or not, just smiled.

'Go get um, girl,' Taylor said, giving Nick a playful jab in the side with her elbow as she returned to where she'd been standing previously. 'Looks like she didn't need instructions after all.'

When she missed the next one Nick winked, barely supressing a smile, then took his turn. One by one he cleared all but one of his stripes before yielding back to her. She made one more but missed the next, and Nick ultimately won.

'Not a bad effort, for a beginner,' he said, flashing a cheeky smile.

'Considering I've only played a couple of times in my life, I reckon I did all right.' She grinned, walking up to stand next to him. 'But maybe you could give me a few tips now that I've got the feel of the table.'

Taylor and Denver were up next, so Nick said he'd get the next round of drinks. Casey followed him to the bar to help him carry the drinks, and stood admiring Darleen from a distance as she served a customer at the other end of the bar. Still in awe at finding out that they might be related, even if distantly, she couldn't wait to see the look on Darleen's face when Alex handed her the letter.

'What are you grinning about?' Nick asked, leaning close to her side.

'Me? Oh, nothing,' she said, not wanting to give anything away. 'Guess I was thinking about the game. I didn't expect to make that first ball. Beginners luck, no doubt.'

'You're probably a natural at it, as I suspect you'd be at a lot of things if you gave them a go.'

Casey turned to face him, wondering whether he meant that to be a double entendre, or whether she had read too much into his words. The look on his face seemed sincere, and once again regret returned. Regret that she was leaving, regret that it didn't matter because he was going overseas anyway, and regret that she had to choose between two sisters and two countries.

'What can I get you two,' Darleen said, breaking the silence that had grown between them.

'Three lagers and a light beer will do us,' Nick said, pulling out his wallet. Casey tried to offer some cash, but he pushed her hand away. 'You can get the next round if you like, this one's on me.'

They carried the four glasses back and then watched as Taylor and Denver finished their game. When Denver pocketed the last ball, Taylor took a few sips of her beer and then turned to Casey. 'I'm a bit peckish and wouldn't mind a burger. Did you want anything?'

Casey smacked her lips dramatically. 'Those wedges you were describing sounded pretty good.'

Nick and Denver, standing on the other side of the table, turned to them. 'A burger sounds good to me too. And some wedges. If you're going to be ordering food, that is,' said Nick. Denver quickly followed with the same order.

'Nick, you and Casey are back up. I'll help Taylor order the food, and by the time you finish the game, it should be ready. We'll also grab a table,' Denver said.

This time when Casey broke the balls, none went in, suggesting it had been beginner's luck after all. She mostly watched as Nick pocketed his balls, but occasionally she glanced over to see Taylor and Denver, who were now at a table, deep in conversation. She'd have loved to have been a fly on the wall, or on the table, to hear what they were saying because the look on Taylor's face made it obvious they weren't just discussing the weather.

'You're up, sweetheart, I missed that last one,' Nick said.

She knew he was teasing, but warmth still washed over her at the sound of his endearment. She didn't think anyone had ever called her sweetheart before. Well, maybe her mother when they were young, but not that she specifically recalled.

She got one ball in, then missed the next even though Nick had helped her work out the difficult angle, and handed the table back to Nick. He missed as well, so Casey had one more go, but could only get one more ball in before Nick took control back and finished the game.

Two hours and more games than Casey could recall later, Nick pulled up in front of their house and said goodnight. She'd hoped he'd give her a goodnight kiss, even though she knew she shouldn't want it to happen, but perhaps having Taylor and Denver with them made it too awkward. Then again, maybe he simply didn't want to kiss her. Either way, he didn't even get out of the car when he pulled up. He simply smiled and said goodnight as she and Taylor got out of the back seat.

Once inside the house, Casey turned to Taylor. 'That was fun. Such a great idea—I must thank Denver for thinking of it.'

'Actually, I'm pretty sure Denver said it was Nick's idea, but it was fun, wasn't it?'

The tone of Taylor's voice hadn't matched her words, making Casey wonder even more about that private conversation she'd had with Denver. Casey stayed quiet for a moment, leaving the door open for Taylor to keep talking, but Taylor just sighed, so Casey didn't press her. Instead, she changed the topic.

'Hey, why don't you come to the gym with me tomorrow? I always do a class, but there are loads of bikes and treadmills. You can work at your own pace. Or there's a water aerobics class if that suits you. There's a cute little café I spotted where we could have brunch afterwards.'

Taylor frowned. 'Oh, I don't know. I'd get all sweaty, and my hair would get wet if I do water aerobics.'

Casey rolled her eyes dramatically. 'They do have showers, you know. And it's not like we'll need to rush or anything ... unless you've already got plans?'

'I did say I'd make a dessert for tomorrow night.'

'Yes, you did. And I said I'd make a salad. So after we've had brunch we can find a grocery store and get everything we need and come home. Come on Taylor, it'll do you good.'

Finally, Taylor smiled. 'You're right. I haven't been doing much in the way of exercise. Sure, what time do you want to go?'

~~*~~

Nick could see Denver staring at him as they made the short trip home after dropping Casey and Taylor at their place. It made him incredibly uncomfortable. When they parked and went inside, Denver finally spoke. 'You and Casey seemed to be getting along pretty darn well.'

'Casey? Yeah, sure, she's nice. If she lived here, who knows, maybe we'd be dating.'

Denver threw his head back, laughing. 'And what would you call what you've been doing? Spending hours together reading through those letters, taking a trip to Sacramento to get her a guitar, working on songs together, playing pool—yeah, she might not live here, but you're already dating her, cuz.'

Nick knew Denver was right. He also knew he'd been sending Casey mixed messages all night. He'd told himself over and over not to get too attached, yet he'd done it anyway. There was no way he could defend himself against Denver's accusations when he wasn't even clear in his own mind how he really felt about her. He couldn't deny the physical attraction any longer—not after his performance at the pool table. He had to go on the offense, and get Denver off his case. 'Yeah, well you and Taylor sure seem to have a stronger connection every time I see you together. Did you ask her about sticking around for a while?'

Denver plonked down on the sofa, leaned forward and rubbed his hands through his hair. When he looked up, Nick saw the face of the kid he'd grown up with—tired after a long day of riding horses and herding cattle.

Running his fingers through his hair again, Denver sighed. 'I mentioned it. She said she likes it here, but she's got a bakery business in Melbourne that she can't walk away from. And besides, she said she couldn't imagine living anywhere without Casey, and she figures Casey would never want to live in Masons Flat.'

'She said that, did she?'

Denver frowned. 'Maybe not exactly like that, but she said everything she'd found quaint about the town, Casey had rolled her eyes at. Taylor looked sad when she was telling me all this, so there's that, but she is definitely going back to Melbourne.'

Nick cocked his head, grimacing. 'Sorry, man—wish I could think of something positive to say, but I've got nothing. Taylor definitely fits in here—hanging out at the saloon with you, playing pool, doing all this baking for the school and whatever—but I think she's right about Casey. I could no more see Casey living here than I could see myself coming back here. I mean, it's different for you and Travis ... you've got a successful business and everything, but it's definitely not for everyone.'

Denver raised his eyebrows, his face full of defeat. 'Guess there isn't anything I can do about it. I'd hoped maybe, you and Casey ...'

Nick shook his head. 'No, don't go pinning any hopes there.'

Denver sighed. 'Anyway, I'm gonna watch a replay of tonight's basketball game. You wanna watch it with me?'

Nick shook his head, 'Nah, I'm done. Catch you in the morning.'

As Nick headed to his room, Denver's insight plagued him. Denver was right about him and Casey getting along really well but, even if it was true, he was glad Casey would be heading back to Australia soon. She wasn't for him—even if they did get along well most of the time, had a lot in common with respect to music, and did have this undeniable chemistry. Maybe he needed to stay clear of her for a few days—maybe if he didn't see her, he'd stop thinking about her.

Wide awake now, he got onto his computer and pulled up YouTube. It was ridiculous to pretend he could stop thinking about her. It simply wasn't going to happen. She'd be here tomorrow night, along with his snoopy sister who didn't miss a trick.

CHAPTER 22

Stacy Reynolds looked a lot like Nick—blonde, attractive and conservatively dressed. The moment Casey spotted her she knew she'd made the right decision to wear the long-sleeved-high-necked-top that covered most of her tatts.

Stacy carried a platter laden with meats and cheeses and gourmet crackers, but that didn't stop her from leaning forward to do air kisses with both Casey and Taylor as she came through the door. 'It's so nice to meet both of you. I'm sorry it's taken so long ... what with us going back east for Thanksgiving with Tim's family, and then Tammy getting that rotten flu on the plane on the way home ... but we're here now, and we'll have Christmas in what ... could it really be only a bit over a week away?'

Stacy's husband and daughter walked in behind her, carrying bags of chips and containers of dip.

Nick gave his sister a quick hug, then stepped back to stand next to Casey. Casey wasn't sure if he'd done that on purpose, or if it was a coincidence, but Stacy seemed to take notice of it, staring at the pair of them for at least a full five seconds, during which the look on her face, which had clearly been pleasure, seemed to change to suspicion.

Casey shook off the discomfort of the stare as best she could. 'And it's lovely to meet all of you too,' she said, reaching toward the platter. 'Here, let me take that while you make yourselves comfortable. Taylor, you wanna take the chips and dips, thanks?'

Annie grabbed her younger cousin's hand, and the two disappeared down the hall while Stacy and Tim removed coats and made their way into the family room.

Casey and Taylor headed to the kitchen to remove plastic wrap and find bowls. When Alex turned down their offer for help, they returned to the family room. Stacy was now seated on the sofa between her husband and Nick.

Casey and Taylor set the platter, chips and dips on the coffee table and sat across from the others in a couple of comfy chairs.

'Travis is putting the beer on ice, and Alex will be out shortly. She's taking the lasagne out now, and wants it to cool for a bit. She said to put these out. Hope you don't mind?' Casey said, unable to shake a growing sense of unease.

'Not at all. So, tell me, what do you think of California so far? Have you seen much?' Stacy asked, her tone of voice not matching the innocence of her question.

'Oh, we've been having a great time,' Taylor answered excitedly, telling Stacy about the touristy places they'd been. Stacy smiled, but didn't look satisfied with the answer.

'Yes, yes, they're all wonderful places, I'm sure, but what I meant was how do you *feel* about being here in California compared to Australia?' She turned to Casey, her gaze piercing like needles. 'I mean, you all lived here before, am I right? I'm sure Alex mentioned you'd lived in Sacramento when you were young.'

Taylor glanced at Casey for a second, and when Casey narrowed her eyes as she tried to think of a polite response, Taylor jumped in and answered for them. 'Oh, I love it here. I've been hanging out at the saloon playing pool, which is something I'd never even thought of doing at home. And I've met some lovely people. There's Darleen of course, and Linda, who co-ordinated the school bake-sale, for instance, and Jenny, who taught me how to make the world's best cherry pie.'

Stacy smiled. 'Yes, Jenny's cherry pie is certainly to die for. You're lucky she shared the recipe with you,' she said, then turned and once again stared at Casey. 'And what about you, Casey? What do you think of our little community of Masons Flat?'

Casey looked at Nick, who simply raised his brows, and then she looked at Denver who was attacking the meat and cheese platter. Neither offered any assistance. 'Oh, it's a sweet little town, definitely. We have a step sister, who lives in a similar town in rural Victoria, but I have to be honest, I'm more of a city girl. I love going to beer gardens to listen to live music, and then there are the galleries, and clubs ... and theatres.' She could see a defensive look creep onto Stacy's face, but continued anyway. 'Of course, California is certainly a fantastic place—I loved the day we spent in San Francisco, and Nick took me to Sacramento where we had lunch on the bank of the river. Now Sacramento, that's a beautiful city.'

Stacy tilted her head, a wry smile touching her lips. 'It's nice there along the river, isn't it?' she asked, turning to Nick. 'You never mentioned you'd gone there, Nick.'

Nick leaned over and grabbed a chip, then shoved it into the dip and put the whole thing in his mouth before answering. 'Yeah, we went to catch up with my old boss, and to look at guitars. Neither of us had eaten, so we grabbed a late lunch.'

As Stacy turned back to Casey, she shrugged. 'Guess country living isn't for everyone. And thank God for that, come to think of it. I like this town just as it is ... wouldn't want to see hoards of people and a bunch of new developments popping up and changing it. You would have heard about that crooked real estate agent who had ideas of turning the town into a tourist attraction?'

Casey nodded, remembering Alex giving her and Taylor a full run-down on the events that took place earlier in the year—the events that had nearly ruined the budding romance between Travis and Alex.

When Alex called out that dinner was ready, Casey sighed with relief, and then the group moved to the kitchen to find lasagne and salads set out in a buffet style. The rest of the evening went well after the initial few moments of tension, and when Stacy, Tim, and Tammy got up to leave Nick walked them out to their car.

~~*~~

'I gather you and Casey have something going on, am I right?' Stacy had never been one to pull punches when it came to her brother, and she clearly wasn't going to start now.

Nick shook his head, searching for the words that would make her drop it. If he protested too much, she'd keep right on at him, so he tried a different approach. 'Oh, yeah,' he whispered into her ear, so that Tammy wouldn't hear, 'I've been banging her since they arrived. She's a pretty good catch, don't you think? What with this inheritance she and her sisters got, I mightn't have to work ever again if I can get her to marry me without a prenup.'

Stacy whacked his arm, hard. He jumped back, feigning injury, and the resultant laugh was a sorely needed relief.

'Well, she's got the hots for you. Women can see these things,' Stacy said, stepping toward him.

'Drop it, Stace. She's practically related to us.'

Stacy opened the passenger door and got in. 'Uh, no, she isn't. Masons and Golds, until now anyway, didn't mix like that. She's no relation, and she's either in love with you or infatuated. I can't discern it to that degree, but it's clear from her body language that she's interested.'

Nick stepped back as Tim came around the side of the car after settling Tammy into the back. 'Don't let her get to you, Nick. She can't help herself. She's only got you to pick on because I don't let her get away with it.'

Great, so Tim had heard everything.

'Good to see you again, Tim. Don't let so much time slip by between visits.'

'Well, with you heading over to London right after Christmas, I'm not sure how much catching up we'll be doing, but for sure, when you get back.'

When Tim shook his hand, Nick patted him on the shoulder with his left hand. 'You're a good man, Tim. You'd have to be, to put up with my sister.'

'I heard that,' Stacy called, rolling the passenger window down.

'Bye Stace,' he said, blowing her a dramatic kiss.

From the back seat, he heard Tammy calling out, 'Kiss, kiss,' as she blew him a kiss.

Returning to the house, Nick found Casey and Taylor getting ready to leave. He'd hoped to get a few minutes alone with Casey, to tell her what he'd found out about YouTube, but it could wait. They all said their goodbyes, and Nick watched as Casey and Taylor drove out of the yard.

~~*~~

'Wasn't she intense?' Taylor asked, as they drove away. 'For a moment there it felt a bit like the Spanish Inquisition.'

Casey let out a chuckle of relief. 'So, it wasn't just me. You felt it too?'

'Absolutely. She seems very defensive of this town. I mean, I get that it's her heritage, but it's ours too. Anyway, I wouldn't have picked her and Nick as siblings.'

'Physically, yes, but I agree that's where the similarity seems to end. So, I never got a chance to talk to Alex alone. Has she told Travis about the saloon?'

'Yep, and she said he thought it was a great idea, and that he believed it would have made his father happy, bringing the saloon back to the Gold family.'

'Great. So has Alex spoken to Darleen yet about having Christmas with us? And was Travis going to tell Denver and Nick?'

Taylor shook her head. 'Travis reckons the less people in on it, the better. Doesn't want the surprise to get spoiled. And yes, Alex spoke to Darleen today. She told her we're having a casual Christmas, with a Secret Santa, and that we'd all be delighted if she'd join us. Apparently, Darleen was really touched by the offer.'

'Awesome. So, we are doing this Kris Kringle, erm, Secret Santa, thing then I gather. We probably should have drawn the names tonight while we were all together.'

'Nah, Alex said she'll take care of it and let us know. She'll let the boys pick names from a bowl, then work out who is left and let us have the ones we've already got the best presents for. She's taking hers first, to make sure she gets Darleen. She'll put the letter of intent in a shoebox and wrap it up so Darleen will have no idea what it is until she opens it.'

'Cool. You know, we bought way too many presents.'

'Alex will return them after we leave. Or maybe we should all go into Sacramento together on Boxing Day and hit the sales.'

Casey couldn't believe how hearing those words out loud, *after we leave*, twisted through her gut. And yet, that's exactly what they'd be doing soon—going *home*. It was foolish for her to react that way.

She looked at her sister, and wondered if Taylor might be having similar misgivings, or whether she was happy about it. She had to ask, didn't she? 'So, are you glad to be heading back to Melbourne soon? Going home, I mean.'

Taylor stared at her for a moment. 'Glad? Well, yeah, obviously, because my life is there. All the work I've put into that bakery ... you know how important that is to me. Of course, there are a lot of things here that I'll miss, too. Like Alex, and of course I've made good friends here, like Jenny and Darleen ... and Denver. I mean, it's funny you should ask, because Denver asked me the same thing the other night when we were playing pool.'

Casey tilted her head. 'Did he? I wondered what you two were talking about that night, but you didn't seem to want to talk about it when we got home.'

'Yeah, I guess it made me a bit sad at the time. It's strange ... having a foot in two different countries. It wouldn't be so bad if it was here and Canada, or Australia and New Zealand. But this business of taking a full day to travel between the two ... it's just too hard to comprehend.'

'I was thinking the same thing. It's nice here ... and it's great being around Alex ... and everyone. But our lives really are back in Melbourne, aren't they?'

They were both quiet the rest of the trip home, and less than ten minutes later, they were standing in their own kitchen. It wasn't particularly late, but Casey headed off to bed anyway. As she closed the door behind her, melancholy took over. They would be going home soon, leaving Alex behind. But was it only Alex she was concerned about, or did it also have something to do with a certain cowboy—one who she'd wished had kissed her goodnight?

CHAPTER 23

Rain the following morning made their expedition with Alex and Annie to find a Christmas tree a bit less than ideal, but even so, Casey was enjoying the scents of fir, pine and spruce trees as they made their way around the large gravel enclosure filled with hundreds of trees. After looking for over an hour, they finally selected one, and the attendant helped them get it onto the top of the Range Rover, however the tree was far too wet to bring into the house so the decorating would have to wait.

Annie, not ready to relinquish the attention of both Casey and Taylor, pulled out her Monopoly game and insisted they play. Alex made some sandwiches and they settled in.

'So,' Alex said when Annie was declared the clear winner, 'I thought I'd make spaghetti for dinner. I could do some sauce without any meat for you, Casey, if you want to stay?'

Casey turned to Taylor. 'I'm easy, if you want to stay.'

Taylor's face scrunched up before answering. 'I thought I'd make us a quiche and some salad for dinner, if that's okay with you, Alex?'

'Absolutely—let me run you home then.'

Casey looked longingly at the back door, disappointed that Nick had never come in for lunch but he was nowhere to be seen. She wouldn't have minded staying for dinner, as at least she'd probably have seen him then.

After Alex dropped them home, Taylor began preparations for the quiche, and Casey made a pot of tea. 'I would have thought you'd have wanted to stay and have dinner with them?'

'Me?' Taylor asked, her cheeks flushing slightly. 'No, I wanted something a bit healthier, and figured you'd be up for quiche and salad. Besides, Denver is picking me up at seven and we're going into the saloon to play pool again, so I wanted to come home and change.'

Casey raised an eyebrow, trying not to smirk. 'I see. So, pool ... again.'

'Yes. Why don't you join us?'

Casey thought about it, but she knew that if Taylor had really wanted her to join them, she'd have mentioned it earlier. 'You go and have fun. I'm pretty tired tonight, so I doubt I'd be good company anyway. I'll use the time to practice my guitar.'

That night, after several attempts, she played Rose's song the whole way through without having to look at the sheet music. It didn't sound as good as when Nick had played it—the timing wasn't quite right as she laboured with finger placement—but to her ear it still sounded amazing.

The following morning, Casey and Taylor went over and helped decorate the now dry tree. When they were done, a sense of nostalgia washed over Casey as memories of the last Christmas they'd had with their father flooded her mind. She and Taylor had only been eleven, still young enough to have insisted on a real Christmas tree.

She hadn't had a real tree since.

Now, as they sat and gazed at the finished product and lunchtime was approaching, her nostalgia turned to disappointment; once again, neither Travis nor Nick appeared.

'Travis seems to be avoiding us. Have I said something that offended him?' Casey asked, making sure her tone was tongue-in-cheek and following up the question with a little laugh.

Alex shook her head, her brows creased. 'Hardly. He sold some horses to a lady in Bakersfield, and agreed to deliver them. Nick's gone with him. They stayed the night last night and were going to work with the lady this morning to make sure she was happy with the horses before they left.'

'Ah,' Casey said, dragging out the word while wondering whether Nick had mentioned it. Then again, why would he have? He owed her no explanations as to his whereabouts.

Later that afternoon, when Casey was back home pottering in the garden, her phone rang. She looked down at the caller ID, seeing Nick's name. She let it ring several times before answering, trying to keep her voice calm and even as she said hello.

'Hey Casey, I've worked out how to set up your YouTube channel. Travis has given me the rest of the day off, so I wondered if you might want to come over and work on it. After all, you'll be leaving soon, right?'

When she arrived, Nick greeted her at the door, looking and smelling like he'd just stepped out of the shower. Annie came running up behind him and was the first to say hello.

'Hey, Casey. Have you come to play Monopoly again?' she asked with a giggle.

Casey rolled her eyes dramatically. 'You know, I'd *love* to play, but Nick and I are going to do some work on the computer.'

Annie shook her head. 'Okay. I'll set up the board in case you change your mind. There are a bunch of Christmas movies on ... you do know tomorrow's Christmas, right?' She snickered and put her hand over her mouth, then dashed off toward the family room.

Casey looked up at Nick, and shrugged.

He just smiled. 'Shall we get started?'

A wave of excitement rushed through her. This was happening, really happening, and it was all thanks to Nick.

As they ducked into the kitchen to grab a chair, she said hello to Alex, making sure she didn't need any help with the food for the next day. Then Nick grabbed one of the kitchen chairs and she followed him to his room.

Sitting close to him in front of his computer, their shoulders almost touching as Nick typed away on the keyboard, Casey wasn't sure which was more exhilarating—taking a giant step forward with her dream of becoming a songwriter, or the fact that Nick was helping her do it.

Stealing the occasional glance sideways, she watched as Nick downloaded several photos from her phone—a few taken of the waterfalls at Yosemite as well as some she'd taken a few years earlier in the Dandenong Mountains near her home—and made a collage for the banner. Then, using her initials, CM, Nick created a simple logo. The "About" section was easy—she wrote songs from the heart. It all proved to be incredibly simple and then Nick showed her how to edit it if she wanted to expand the about section.

He uploaded the song, put his name next to hers under the copyright message, and then it was done.

She was officially Casey Mason, Songwriter.

'Are you happy with the way it looks?' Nick turned to face her, staring intently into her eyes for the first time since they'd started the process. The intensity of the gaze took her breath away.

'Happy?' she finally managed. 'That doesn't begin to describe how I feel. I love it. It's something I've wanted to do for so long, and now it's done.'

His answering smile was a reflection of her own feelings—excitement laced with pride and a sense of awe as to how this small thing might change her future.

'Do you want to show it to the others?' Nick asked.

One side of her wanted to shout it out to the whole world, to tell them she was now an official songwriter, but a niggling hesitation crept over her. 'Not yet. It's awesome, but I think I want to sort of ... take it slowly. Maybe after Christmas?'

'Sure, whatever you want to do is fine by me.'

She let out a noisy breath. 'Thanks. I'm probably being overly cautious but I think I'll shoot it across to the solicitor Alex has been using to do all our legal stuff—to see if he thinks I need to set up a proper business or tax entity or anything like that before we encourage too many people to look at it, you know? And I'm not sure how the whole copyright thing works either.' As soon as she said those words she felt better. This was all so new, and she needed time for it to sink in. Sending it to Mr West would give her that time.

Nick nodded. 'Yeah, that sounds like a good idea. Not something I know much about, I assure you.'

When he smiled, happiness practically exploded in her. They'd done this. Together. The desire to lean across and kiss him swept over her, but it felt too late. Like the perfect moment had passed. If she'd done it the moment the song finished loading that would have worked—now it would seem forced, or even worse, planned. Instead, she stood and put her hands in her jeans pockets. 'So ...'

'Yes ... it's done,' Nick replied as he too stood, staring deeply into her eyes.

Casey had to lighten the intensity between them, and what better way than to talk about Annie. 'You realise the moment we walk out of here, Annie will round us up for a Monopoly game, don't you?'

Nick turned back to the computer, leaned over and switched it off. 'Yes, there's nothing surer, but what better way to spend Christmas Eve than losing at a board game to a ten-year-old?'

Casey shook her head. 'Well, at least I know the rules to that game. I wouldn't even know where to start with any of her video games.'

As she started to move toward the door, Nick stepped to the side, partially blocking her way. When he made eye contact, she thought she felt the slightest touch on her forearm, making her wonder if he wanted her to wait for a moment ... like he was going to say something, or do something, significant. A moment, heavy with indecision, passed. Then he shrugged, almost indiscernibly, and stepped back.

'After you,' he said with a sweep of his hand toward the hall.

An hour later, Casey was once again bankrupt, and while Alex said she was welcome to stay for dinner with them, Casey decided to go home and finish wrapping the last of the Christmas presents.

~~*~~

Nick let out a sigh of relief as Casey drove off.

He'd enjoyed her company more than he should have. If truth be told, he'd enjoyed having her in his room more than he'd enjoyed anything for quite some time.

With her sitting only inches away from him, he'd felt her breath on his hands as he'd typed, and he'd breathed in her fresh jasmine scent. So close that if he'd leaned just an inch to the side he'd have rubbed up against her shoulder. He'd enjoyed it, but at the same time, it had been like a slow form of torture. It had taken every ounce of his self-control not to kiss her.

He'd been grateful when Travis had mentioned the trip to Bakersfield, knowing it would keep him away from Casey for the better part of two days—physically, anyway. Nothing could stop him from thinking about her, though. Of course, it hadn't helped that Travis didn't like to talk much when he drove with horses on board. Getting conversation out of him over the four hour drive had been nearly impossible, leaving far too much time for thoughts of Casey to surface no matter how much he tried to stop them.

He swallowed hard, then shook his head. This was dumb. She'd be leaving just after Christmas. There was seriously no point thinking about her. He'd be in Europe. She'd be in Australia. Their brief little ... whatever this had been ... would come to an abrupt end shortly. They'd keep in touch, perhaps, if she wanted his feedback on another song, but something told him once she got back to Australia, she'd forget all about him.

And that really would be for the best.

~~*~~

Christmas morning dawned with the promise of clearing skies.

Hearing no movement in the house, Casey got up, dressed and snuck out as quietly as possible to head across the road to the park for a brisk walk.

As she drew in a deep breath, the familiar scent of eucalyptus met her nostrils. At first, it was welcoming—like she'd come home—but a moment later it felt more like homesickness. Could she be missing Melbourne, or was it something else? Perhaps it was an awareness that her time in California would end soon, and she'd be leaving more than just her sister behind.

Walking as fast as she dared on the slippery ground, she focussed on breathing in through her nose and out her mouth, trying to simply enjoy the moment: the fresh air, the smell of the gum trees and wet earth.

By the time she returned to the house, the sun was making its way up over the trees. She closed her eyes and tilted her head toward the sun's rays. Its warmth seeped into her body and, coupled with the endorphins from her walk, her optimism returned.

It was Christmas Day, after all, and it was going to be a lovely day.

~~*~~

Shortly before eleven, Casey and Taylor arrived at the Gold residence, where they joined Alex in the kitchen to give her a hand setting up the buffet. Given the number coming, they'd decided a hot meal would be too hard, so instead they were having cold ham and turkey, both cooked the day before, enough bread rolls to make sandwiches for a whole football team, a huge bowl of potato salad, Casey's salad, a variety of relishes and cranberry sauces and, of course, Taylor's pumpkin and cherry pies for dessert. When everything was laid out to Alex's satisfaction, they covered it with a light cotton cloth and the three made their way to the family room.

While they'd been busy in the kitchen, Stacy and her family had arrived, and Annie and Tammy were already parked next to the Christmas tree, gently moving the presents around, clearly trying to count how many they each had.

Taylor quickly claimed a spot on the sofa next to Denver, while Alex went and stood behind Travis' chair. Casey, unsure where she should sit, stood in the doorway. Her eyes gravitated to Nick, who sat in one of the big comfy chairs near his sister and her husband. The blue shirt he wore made his cobalt-blue eyes even more engaging today, and Casey struggled not to stare. Nick nodded toward the arm of his chair, seeming to suggest she sit there, when the doorbell rang.

Casey immediately headed to the door, feeling Alex come up behind her.

She opened the door to find Darleen looking slightly sheepish, holding a large casserole dish.

'Here, let me take that into the kitchen. Casey, can you take Darleen into the family room?' Alex said, leaving Darleen with Casey.

'We're so glad you could join us,' Casey said with genuine warmth. She hadn't gotten to know Darleen as well as either Alex or Taylor had, but she certainly liked her.

'It was such a surprise when Alex invited me. I generally spend Christmas on my own because our family never did big Christmases. I make myself a huge bowl of popcorn and watch old movies with a glass of red wine. But this, well, this invitation was completely unexpected. And appreciated.'

Casey could hear the breathless tone in Darleen's voice and desperately wanted to make her more comfortable. 'Here, let me take your coat. We'll probably do the presents soon so we can put those girls out of their misery,' she said, nodding toward Annie and Tammy.

Darleen let out a soft chuckle, and turned toward the room where Taylor had jumped up to make room for her on the sofa.

When Casey returned from hanging up Darleen's coat, Nick shifted over, making it clear he wanted Casey to sit on the arm of his big, comfy chair.

Once everyone was settled, Annie and Tammy jumped up from the floor.

'Are we handing out the presents now?' Annie asked, with all the nervous energy of a horse at the starting gate of the Melbourne Cup.

'Yes,' Alex answered, walking into the room, 'but remember what we talked about ... you're to hand them out one by one so that everyone can see what everyone else gets. That's part of the Secret Santa rules, so no rushing.'

Annie selected the first present and handed it to Alex. Then she stood in front of her, watching as Alex carefully tore the paper.

'Oh, my favourite,' Alex said, turning to Nick.

Nick had no doubt sought help from Travis to get the right perfume.

The next present was for Tammy. Her young face sported a deep frown as she uncovered a hoof pick buried amongst wads of crinkled newspaper in a huge box. She looked at her mother in confusion, but then her face broke into a wide-eyed smile.

'If you're getting a horse of your own you'll need a few things to care for it,' Stacy said.

Tammy ran to her mother and threw her arms around her, saying thank you over and over. 'When can I see it?' she finally asked.

'You'll have to talk to your Uncle Travis about that. He's going to take you to see a friend of his—a man who rescues horses.'

Tammy ran to her uncle and threw her arms around him too, squealing with delight. When she finally settled down, Annie chose the next gift. This one went to Denver who got a red checked shirt from Stacy, and then Annie opened one of hers, finding a tin of tennis balls, a cute visor with rainbows on it and a bottle of sunscreen. Annie giggled, thanking her cousin. Next, Tim got a bottle of Jack Daniels from Denver, and Taylor got a Neiman Marcus Cookbook from Travis. Finally, Tammy handed a box to Darleen.

Casey quickly scanned the room. Alex and Taylor both had their eyes glued on Darleen, and when she caught Travis' eye he gave her a subtle nod.

When she turned back to Darleen, she'd opened the box and unfolded the single sheet of paper it held. Confusion was written across her brow as she read the letter. Then she read it a second time, shaking her head slowly the whole time. When she finally looked up, there were tears in her eyes.

'I don't understand,' she said, turning to Alex first, then Taylor. 'You're giving me the saloon? Am I reading this properly?'

Alex stood and walked to Darleen with her arms outstretched. Darleen stood too, and they embraced for what seemed a long time. When Alex stepped back, Darleen wiped her hand across her eyes.

'Yes, you're reading it properly,' Alex said, her voice soft. 'And it's simple, really. Do you know who your grandmother was? And your grandfather?'

'My grandparents?' Darleen glanced around the room, stopping as she stared straight at Travis. She swallowed hard, and then turned back to Alex. 'My mother told me a story once—said she'd pried the truth from her mother not long before she'd died—but I didn't know if it was true because she'd also said Grandma was losing it toward the end. Either way, Mom said there was no way I could ever prove it and not to even think about trying because Grandma had listed the father of her three children as unknown.'

Alex appeared to be processing all that. 'And yet you came here, to Masons Flat? Did you ever say anything to Uncle Steven?'

Darleen shook her head. 'How could I? It would have sounded like I was trying to make some sort of claim, which I wasn't. It was just that after my divorce, I felt lost—both my parents and Grandma were gone, and I had no family to turn to. I thought I'd come up and just see how it felt to live in a small town, one I might have some connection to. When I got here, it felt like I'd come home. Your uncle gave me a job at the saloon within a few days, and not long afterwards asked me to be the nightshift manager. Masons Flat became my home.'

Alex nodded slowly, then eventually drew in a deep breath. 'So you never said anything to him? Even after years had gone by? You never thought about getting a DNA test or anything?'

'No, none of that mattered. I'd found a home, and the last thing I wanted to do was anything that might jeopardise that. But ... how do you even know about any of this? How could you possibly know anything about what my mother told me? And why would you think any of it was true? And even if it is true, why are you giving me the saloon?' Darleen spoke to Alex, but then she turned and stared at Taylor and Casey in turn. 'I mean, I still can't believe it—there has to be some sort of catch, right?'

Alex shook her head. 'There's no catch. Casey found some letters that your grandmother, Daisy, had written to her sister—our great-grandmother. The truth was in those letters. Daisy explained about how she'd fallen out with her father and gone to live in San Francisco, how she'd eventually met someone and had three children with him. And then, many years later, she'd finally told her sister who the father of her three children was—Albert Gold.' She turned to Travis, speaking softly, 'Your great-grandfather.'

Darleen shook her head in disbelief, her brows tight as her eyes darted from one sister to the next. 'You have letters? Written by my grandmother all those years ago? May I see them?'

'Of course you can see them,' Casey exclaimed, before describing how she'd found the letters. She went on to explain how she and Nick had looked for clues and how they'd finally worked out Daisy's identity, which had led them to Milly and Milly's daughter, Caroline.

Darleen ducked her head and ran her hands through her long strands of hair. 'This is so unbelievable. Finding out that I have a family ... and that it's you ... I mean, it's just incredibly hard to take in. This is the best Christmas anyone could ever ask for.'

Casey glanced at Alex, whose face was displaying all the emotions Casey felt. It was, indeed, the best Christmas. And although she hadn't known them, something told her both the Mason and Gold ancestors would also be happy with this outcome.

Casey heard a quiet mumble and looked up to see Denver deep in a quiet conversation with Travis—they looked pleased with the outcome. Then she looked at Nick. When he caught her eye, he mouthed the word *wow*, and shook his head softly as a smile crept onto his lips. Casey just nodded, unable to supress a smile herself.

Alex threw her arm around Darleen's shoulders. 'Welcome to the family—and congratulations on becoming the new owner of the Gold Nugget Saloon.'

Sometime later, with the remains of the buffet put away and the kitchen tidied up, everyone headed into the family room again, this time to watch an old Christmas movie. Excusing herself, Casey made her way out onto the back porch with a glass of wine. It was cold and dark but the soft pale green woollen scarf, which was her Kris Kringle present from Nick, kept the chill away. She closed her eyes and drank in the scents of wet grass and fresh country air. After a time, she heard the soft sound of cows bellowing far off in the distance. She stepped out onto the grass and looked up at the clear sky—amazed by how many stars she could see—a site she'd rarely been privileged to experience at home.

She took a sip of the wine, let its warmth fill her, then closed her eyes again as she drew in a long, slow breath.

She'd known Alex was taken with the community here in Masons Flat—that she'd embraced the challenge of running her own business and being the landlady of a number of others. And of course, it helped that a handsome cowboy named Travis Gold, and his adorable daughter, Annie, had made her part of their family. But perhaps there was more to it even than that. Maybe it also had something to do with the clean country air and the luscious earth and the never-ending sky here in Masons Flat; to the way life moved at a slower pace.

Opening her eyes, she gazed at the stars again. The peace and tranquillity here astounded her, and for the moment, she luxuriated in its simplicity. Yet as lovely as it was here, and as certain as she was as to why Alex had made this her home, she knew it could never be hers.

~~*~~

Nick couldn't believe the generosity of these Mason women. As he sat, pretending to watch the old movie that he'd seen several times, he watched the way the group interacted. They looked like they'd always been one big happy family.

Nick knew the history of the saloon; about how his great-great-grandfather had put up the saloon in a drunken poker game and lost it to his Mason counterpart. He'd heard the story many times, and had never given a hoot about it other than to think it had been pretty stupid. But he also knew it had started some sort of feud at the time, one that Travis' father, unlike his own father, had perpetuated. Nick remembered the animosity that still existed when Travis had first met Alex, and wondered if giving the saloon to Darleen might have been Alex's idea as a way of ending, once and for all, all remnants of the rift between the Mason and Gold families that began all those years ago. If so, smart move Alex.

Still glancing around the room, he figured it had to have been at least ten minutes since they'd all gone into the family room, and yet Casey still hadn't joined them.

Gently pushing Tammy away from where she sat leaning up against his legs, he made his way to the kitchen. When he discovered the back door ajar, he suspected he'd found her.

He opened the screen door and headed to the centre of the deserted porch before spotting her in the middle of the lawn, gazing upwards.

He stepped down from the porch and walked toward her just as she turned to see who was approaching.

'Oh, Nick, it's you. I figured it would be Alex. She can be such a mother-hen sometimes.'

He chuckled softly. 'Nope, just me. Disappointed?'

She tilted her head, and a rush of warmth washed over him as he watched her pull the scarf, the one he'd personally selected for her, tighter around her neck. He could almost feel its softness as he watched her fingers adjusting it.

Finally, she answered. 'Not at all. It's beautiful out here, don't you think? I don't know when I've seen so many stars,' she said as she looked back up at the sky.

He followed her gaze, taking in the sparkling diamonds above them. After a time, he looked at her again, staring until she finally made eye contact. 'You're missing the movie. Have you seen it before?' He knew it was a lame question, but didn't know what else to say.

'Only about a dozen times,' she said. 'You know, I'm not sure I thanked you enough for the work you've done—both with Rose's song, and with setting up YouTube for me. I might have figured out YouTube, but I don't think I'd ever have been able to sing Rose's song as well as you did.'

He cleared his throat, not having expected the compliment. 'You'd have gotten there, in time.'

He'd never been so intimidated by silence. He wanted to wrap his arms around her and kiss her, yet he knew it wasn't the right thing to do, even if he was attracted to her on every level. He would leave for

Europe soon, and she would return to Australia. There was no point complicating their parting.

When she finally spoke, her voice was soft, hesitant. 'We'll still write songs together, right? I mean, if I send you some of my other lyrics, or write some new ones, you'll have a go at putting them to music, right?'

He chewed on his lip, wondering how quickly her interest in his help might wane as distance separated them, but decided to say what she'd want to hear. 'Of course I will. I'd love to stay involved ... in your song-writing. We shouldn't let the distance between us matter.' He forced a smile onto his face even though his heart ached; even though part of him felt broken, and he had no idea how to fix it.

She looked at him for a long moment, a wry smile touching her lips as her eyes, shot with flecks of gold, glistened in the light from the porch. Her eyes said what her voice hadn't—she didn't believe his words any more than he did.

CHAPTER 24

Unease had plagued Nick from the moment he'd said goodnight to Casey on Christmas night. Unease borne from the knowledge that even though it made no sense logically, his heart kept insisting there was a strong connection between them.

He'd thought about ringing her many times since. He'd thought about offering to take her horseback riding, since she'd asked about it early on. He'd thought about asking if she wanted to send him any other lyrics. He'd also thought about simply calling to say hello.

He'd thought all those things, but he'd done nothing, because logical demanded it was best if they drifted apart.

Now, in just a few minutes, they'd be seeing each other one last time before she flew home. They were all having dinner together, at the hotel, and probably at the same table where they'd eaten the night Casey and Taylor had arrived.

He, Alex, Travis, and Denver were the first to arrive, so Nick situated himself at the table's far end. He watched hopefully as Alex sat at the other end near Travis; it left a spot for Taylor across from Denver, and with a bit of luck, Casey would take the seat across from him.

And that's exactly what happened.

Talk at the table seemed formal, subdued even, as if everyone was on edge. Nick figured Denver was no happier about Taylor and Casey heading back to Australia than he was, and there was little doubt that Alex was sad to be saying goodbye to her sisters. Even Travis couldn't seem to find anything comical to say to break the mood.

Finally, while they were finishing dessert, Alex turned to Nick and asked about his trip.

'I leave for London on the fifth,' he said, glancing at Casey, who continued to look down at her plate.

Alex nodded, tilting her head as if in deep thought. 'Nice. I'm sure I would have told you that I was a good tennis player, before my accident, right? Did you know I played at Wimbledon once? I only made it to the first round, but I had a couple of days to look around afterwards. I loved

London. I think perhaps my favourite thing of all was seeing the Crown Jewels. Of course, I was there in the middle of summer and the weather was divine. I can't imagine what it'll be like in winter. And after London, where to after that?'

'Ireland. I'm meeting up with a friend of mine, Patrick, who has family in Dublin. We'll stay with them for a few nights, and then do some travelling.'

Alex frowned, doing a mock shiver. 'I loved Ireland too but, as I said, it was summer. I bet it'll be terribly cold. You'll want to rug up.'

Nick didn't comment on the weather—he knew it was going to be cold. He also didn't query her expression "rug up" as he'd heard her say it before and knew it meant keep warm. 'We're heading to Switzerland to go skiing after Ireland. Then, when Patrick goes back to Ireland, I'll think about Amsterdam, France, Spain, maybe even Italy. I'm not sure yet.'

He glanced at Casey again, but she was still looking down, playing with her fork as she attacked the last of what had been a slice of lemon meringue pie.

It seemed Alex wasn't done yet. 'And Europe in the dead of winter too—I hope you've got good boots and a heavy coat.'

It seemed odd that she was harping on about the weather. He knew it wasn't the best time to be going travelling but this was how it had worked out, and he planned to make the most of it. 'Yeah, I bought some stuff a few weeks ago, so I'm all set. I know it'll be cold, but it's not like it isn't cold up here all winter.'

When Alex took the last bite of her chocolate cake, Nick hoped she was done with the topic. When she spoke again, he finally saw where she'd been heading. 'You should think about going to Australia after your ski trip. It's summer there—warm weather, great beaches. And I know a couple of nice ladies who I'm certain would be happy to put you up and show you around.'

Travis leaned forward, nodding enthusiastically. 'That's a great idea. I wasn't there very long, but from what I saw of it, it's an awesome place. What was the country town we visited, Alex?'

'Willows,' Alex replied, turning back toward Nick. 'It's where our step-sister lives. Travis and I went there for her wedding. It's a nice town, but there are lots of quaint country towns not far from Melbourne—all of them perfect for day trips, or overnight getaways.'

Nick glanced across at Casey again, and this time she looked up and met his gaze. Was it hope he could see in her eyes as she waited for him to answer? He kept his gaze locked on Casey as he raised an eyebrow. 'That's a thought. I'm not due back at work until the end of April. Who knows, maybe I will drop in and say hello. Or should that be G'day?'

Casey gave him a weak smile, but Taylor didn't hold back.

'Seriously? You might come to Melbourne? Oh, that would be awesome. There's so much stuff we could take you to see, and even though Queensland skites about having the best weather, Victoria's got some of the best surf beaches in the world. Do you surf? We could take you to Bells Beach. Oh, I do hope you'll come see us. It'd be so much fun.'

'Thanks, Taylor. I'm sure it would be fun, although I have to admit I've never tried surfing,' he said, trying to match Taylor's enthusiasm.

Then he turned back to Casey.

Her eyes had changed, becoming distant. When she spoke, her voice was almost mechanical. 'Sure, like Taylor said, it would be great if you came down for a visit.' Casey looked straight at him, yet it felt like she was looking through him—as if he'd already gone and she was talking about him, not to him.

~~*~~

Casey struggled to look at Nick as he talked casually about his trip, and then about how he would give some thought to visiting them in Australia.

She'd never been good at maintaining friendships with ex-lovers. She simply relegated them to her past, where they became one of the many.

The problem was—Nick hadn't been a lover.

He wasn't one of the many.

She couldn't just relegate him to her past.

She wished she hadn't reacted so badly to him when they'd first met; wished she hadn't been so quick to judge him as someone utterly undesirable. Would something more have happened between them if they hadn't had to spend so much time repairing the damage done that first night?

The phrase "*what might have been*" never meant as much to her as it did right now.

Then, as quickly as those thoughts materialised, she realised it would be even worse. Far worse. If they *had* become an item it wouldn't just be "*what might have been*", it would be "*what now?*" and she would be facing hard decisions.

She glanced at Taylor in her peripheral vision, careful not to make the eye contact she was certain would give away her feelings.

What had Taylor said? That she'd wished she could have met Denver in Melbourne? Yes, that was it. But at no stage had Taylor said she wished she could stay here in California. That was a whole different thing. Taylor had as full life back in Melbourne as she did.

Casey knew her voice hadn't reflected the same level of eagerness Taylor's had when Nick mentioned a potential visit to Australia, but then she'd never been good at pretending to be enthusiastic when she didn't feel it. But did she feel it? Did she want him to come to Australia? Would she welcome him with open arms? Or would it simply be awkward?

She looked up, met his eyes, and tried again. 'Of course you should come. Alex is right; it'll be summer—hot days, and it stays light well into the evening. It makes me cold just thinking of heading further north.'

There, she'd done it, and as far as she could tell it had sounded genuine. She looked up at Alex, then at Travis. They both looked normal. There was a good chance she'd managed to pull it off without giving away her innermost doubts.

Nick rubbed his hands together as if they were in front of a warm fire. 'Now I'm torn ... cold winter days, or hot summer ones? Decisions, decisions. I'll see how things work out, but it sounds good. Thanks, ladies.' If his body language was any indication, he didn't particularly want to visit them, he was just being polite, not wanting to dismiss the invitation outright.

But when he continued to stare at Casey, she sensed something more, and suddenly wished they were having this conversation alone rather than in front of an audience. Even so, it probably wouldn't have changed the outcome. She was going home to Melbourne, and he was heading to Europe. They were heading in opposite directions, and nothing was going to change that.

And soon, he'd be nothing more than someone she'd met once, and had gotten to know, if only just a little.

She was grateful when the hotel manager came over to see if anyone wanted anything else as the kitchen was getting ready to close.

~~*~~

Nick stood near the back of the old Buick, watching as Casey chewed on her lower lip. Alex, Travis, and Denver were making their way down the street to where Travis had parked, and Taylor, having said she was cold, had already climbed into the passenger seat of the Buick and shut the door.

Exhausted from keeping up the pretence of a jovial mood throughout dinner, he had to summon his innermost strength as he faced Casey to say goodbye. Once again, he fought the urge to reach out and stroke her cheek, to pull her into his arms and allow his true feelings to show themselves in the tenderness of a last kiss. He wanted to, but it didn't feel like the right thing to do. Instead, he cocked his head and gave her a crooked smile as he tried to keep his voice light-hearted. 'You won't be a stranger, will you? I mean, we can Skype or FaceTime or whatever, right?'

When she sighed, he almost gave in to his desires. Almost.

'Sure,' she finally replied. 'We can do that. We can talk about songs, and ... whatever.'

She looked different tonight. The defiant Amazon Woman she normally channelled seemed to have deserted her, leaving her vulnerable. And it was her vulnerability that strengthened his resolve not to kiss her. It would be wrong.

Completely.

Surprising him, just as he had that thought, she reached forward out placed her hand on his forearm, giving him a slight smile. 'I wish we had longer,' she said, making his heart skip a beat.

'Do you?' he asked, revelling in the warmth of her touch.

'Yes. I mean, who knows what we might have created ... if we'd had more time.'

Was she talking about the music? Or was she implying something more? Her words made him want her more than ever, and not just in a physical sense. He knew she was right—if they'd had more time, things wouldn't be ending like this. He swallowed, then leaned over and gently kissed her cheek.

'Yes, who knows,' he managed to whisper into her ear. Swallowing back his emotions, he stepped away, grateful for the darkness surrounding them. 'It's cold—I better let you go.'

She nodded, unspeaking, and turned to open the car door. When she hesitated, his heart skipped a beat. When she turned and looked at him, once again chewing on her bottom lip, he felt certain she was about to say something. Instead, she shook her head, opened the door, and got in.

He continued to stand there until she'd started the car, and pulled away from the parking spot. He'd have liked to have stood there longer, but knew the others were waiting for him. So instead, he forced his feet to move and made his way down the street, fighting the urge to turn and run after her.

CHAPTER 25

Casey took a sip of her drink and then sighed as she looked at Alex. With a couple of hours to kill before their flight, the one that would take her and Taylor back to Melbourne, they'd headed to the small food court near the international departures gate. Now, looking at her sisters, it was clear they were all feeling the strain of the pending separation.

'It's going to be quiet around here without you guys,' Alex said. 'And then with Nick going next week and Annie's mother coming to get her soon, it'll be like a ghost town. It's been so much fun having everyone around—one big happy family. Are you sure you don't want to extend your stay?'

Taylor pulled a face and shrugged before answering. 'One side of me would love to stay longer, but I've worked so hard to get the bakery to where it is, you know?'

'Of course I know that,' Alex said with a shaky smile. 'Just as I know Casey's going to be run off her feet as soon as she hits the ground.'

Casey bit her lower lip. 'I'm going to miss you, too, and ... everyone. It's been great being here. But, even if it wasn't for my job, I could never see myself living in a town like Masons Flat. I get why you love it, but it's far too quiet for me. I need more entertainment options. Places like night clubs and beer gardens and movie theatres. I don't know how you survive without at least one movie theatre?'

Alex smiled as she reached across and put her hand on Casey's forearm. 'There is more to life than movie theatres, but I know you both have your own lives. I'm being selfish. I'm the one who left, so if I'm a bit lonely for a few days I'll just have to build a bridge and get over it. I think I'll move in with Travis and Denver, though. He suggested it ages ago, and now that I've gotten used to being there, well, it makes so much more sense than me rushing back and forth, trying to maintain our huge house. Do you guys think I should put a tenant in it?'

Casey nodded. 'Sounds good to me, Alex, about you moving in with Travis, that is. You two are definitely a match made in heaven, so I can't see any point in putting it off. As for the house, you should do whatever you think is best. I mean, don't hang onto it for our sake. Oh, maybe I shouldn't speak for both of us?' She looked at Taylor.

Taylor sort of frowned before answering. 'Yeah, I guess you should put a tenant in it. It's not likely I'd want to live there, but it's nice to think there are options so I'd rather we didn't sell it yet.'

'My thoughts exactly,' Alex said. 'Let's not rush into anything. I'll have a chat to the local estate agent and see if he can find a tenant. We can always sell it later if that's what we decide.'

Casey drank the last of her soda water and turned to Alex. 'You don't have to hang around here the whole time. You've got a long drive back.'

'I know, but it's just hard to say goodbye. I'm not going to hang around to watch your plane leave or anything.'

Casey smiled at her big sister. 'Thank you for everything. It's been a wonderful holiday and so much fun with the three of us getting to spend time together.' Casey glanced over at Taylor, and the sadness on Taylor's face mirrored her own.

They all hugged, and Alex walked to the security gates with them, but when she could go no farther she gave them a weak smile, her eyes filled with tears. 'I really am gonna miss you guys. We'll have to FaceTime more regularly, okay?'

'Of course we will,' Taylor said, brushing a tear away from her eye as she gave Alex one last hug.

Casey rolled her eyes as she fought back her own tears. It was hard, ignoring the growing lump in her throat. She knew she'd miss this place, but she wasn't entirely sure who she was going to miss the most.

~~*~~

Nick couldn't remember ever feeling so tired. He'd spent the afternoon cleaning the stables to the point where they practically sparkled, but even being exhausted wasn't enough to make him forget about Casey.

He ate his dinner without tasting it, and then plonked on the sofa to watch basketball. He woke to the sensation of being shaken by the shoulder.

'Why don't you go have a shower and call it a night?'

Blinking a few times to clear his vision, he looked up at Travis. 'Me? I'm fine. I'll head off when the game's over.'

'You were snoring so loud we couldn't hear the commentators,' Travis said with a laugh.

'Yeah, all right, all right,' he replied, getting up.

The shower seemed to invigorate him, so he switched on his computer to check his emails and read the news. And that's when he spotted her name. There was an email from Casey, sent that morning.

Nick,

I know I've thanked you already, but I wanted to do so again. I am just so grateful for what you did with Rose's song. Seriously, I don't think I explained just how much it means to me.

You've inspired me, with both your voice and your ability to play the guitar. I've been practising most nights and will continue when I get home, but I suspect I could practise for a million years and not get as good as you.

Anyway, I've been playing with the words for a song about Daisy over the last few days and I thought you might like to take a look. I mean, if you want to, and if you have time. I know you're going away shortly, and you'll no doubt be busy, but if you do find yourself alone in a hotel room somewhere and feel inclined to turn your mind to it, I'd be thrilled to hear what you think you can do with it.

I've called it TORN, but I'll take your advice on the name, like I did with Rose's song. Anyway, here goes:

Torn with indecision, more times than she could say,
should I? she had asked; but never more than on this day.
She wanted to confide her love, let her feelings be known to all,

but she knew that those dearest would be the ones to fall.
There are special bonds with sisters, ones miles can never break,
but even strongest bonds are tested, when there's much at stake.

She'd let the miles grow between them, and retreat to distant lands,
leaving truth behind her, to blow over the pasture's sands.

She wrote when she was settled, keeping all her secrets hidden,
for other hearts might break if they knew what had been forbidden.
She yearned to see her love reflected in another's eyes,
yet knew it best to leave love buried, beneath secrets and lies.

There are special bonds with sisters, ones miles can never break,
but even strongest bonds are tested, when there's much at stake.
She'd let the miles grow between them, retreating to distant lands,
but kept in touch with letters, written by her lonely hands.

One day another came along, charming in his own way.
He chipped at her resistance 'til she agreed to let him stay.
But the shadow of her first love had never left her side,
and even if he'd asked her, she'd have never been his bride.

When children came she wrote of them, to her sister, dearest of all,
yet kept her pain still hidden, through winter, spring, summer and fall.
When those involved had finally passed, she wrote her sister once again,
and with the truth revealed, was free to dream of what might have been.

There were special bonds with these sisters; ones the miles could never break,
and though those bonds were tested, they held strong, through life's heartbreaks.

I'd love to hear your thoughts on it, any changes you'd suggest to get it to flow better. Or maybe you think it's too depressing. I'm pretty close to the subject at the moment, as you can probably tell, so who knows ... I might read it myself in a few weeks and toss it out.

Anyway, I hope to hear from you at some stage. You said I shouldn't be a stranger, so that works both ways.

Thank you, for about the hundredth time,

Casey xxx

He sat staring at the screen long after he finished reading the email for the third time, dwelling upon the xxx at the end. Didn't that mean kisses? And what about the song? Was it entirely about Daisy and her dilemma, or had Casey been torn about leaving Alex behind too? And if that were the case, did he dare to wonder if he played a role in her dilemma?

This would drive him crazy if he let it, trying to decipher a hidden meaning in her email. He'd probably be awake all night, thinking about it.

But then again, he probably would have been awake all night anyway, wondering if whether he'd kissed her the way he'd wanted to as they'd stood beside her car, things would have turned out differently.

He pulled out his phone and pressed her number. He didn't know when the flight was leaving, but if she didn't answer he could at least leave a message. When it went to voicemail his heart dropped, but he was determined not to let it come across in his voice.

Hey, Casey - I just spotted your email and thought I'd ring to say goodbye, but maybe you're already on the plane. Look, I love the lyrics. I'll have a play around with them, and see what I can do about putting them to music.

Anyway, I'll be in touch. Safe flight. Let's ... talk soon.

CHAPTER 26

When her phone rang, Casey was pretty sure it would be her boss, Maree.

She'd given up hope that it would be Nick. In the six weeks since he'd left the message on her phone saying he'd received her email and would work on the song when he could, she'd only heard from him once. He'd sent a quick email to say he was enjoying Ireland but, while he definitely intended to work on the song, he wasn't sure how much time he'd have after all.

Since then, she'd tried to forget him and move on with her life.

Tried. And failed miserably.

She'd thought of him most days, if not every day. Every time she spotted her guitar leaning against the wall in her bedroom, every time a lyric flitted across her mind, and every time she saw a clean-shaven man with short blond hair, her heart sank a little more.

At least work had kept her busy. Maree, who had celebrated her sixtieth birthday a few weeks earlier and was clearly wishing to scale down her own work hours, had become more and more reliant on Casey. She was treating her more like a partner than an employee. She'd taught Casey how to prepare profit and loss statements, how to update and maintain their website, and had even bounced ideas off Casey for new ways to grow the business. Casey had learned more about running a florist business over the last month than she had in all the years she'd been working there. But while her ego liked that she was now considered second in charge, a part of her regretted that she'd had to put her lyric writing on the backburner due to the longer hours she'd been putting in.

Casey had no doubt that Maree wanted her to buy into the business and become a full-fledged partner. And it was tempting. Casey adored working with flowers—loved the colours and the scents, mixing and matching them to make arrangements that were suitable for everything from the simplest flower girl's bouquet to the most elaborate corporate centrepiece. But she missed the days when that was all she did—the floral arrangements—when Maree handled all the administration, and she had time to work on lyrics.

Turning her attention back to the ringing phone, she grabbed it from the kitchen table. It wasn't Maree after all. It was her long-time party-partner friend, Elly.

'Hi,' she said, trying to disguise the surprise in her voice. She'd successfully avoided going out to nightclubs since she'd returned from California and had forgotten she'd let Elly talk her into going to a new one across town.

Elly's voice was as bubbly as ever. 'What are you going to wear? I'm thinking nice jeans with this gorgeous red top I just bought, but if you're going to wear a dress or skirt I might reconsider.'

'Oh, well actually ... I mean, about tonight...'

Elly's dramatic sigh spoke volumes about the deflated look she would have on her face. 'Don't tell me you're going to pike out on me again? You know how much I've been looking forward to tonight,' Elly said. 'Besides, I've got no one else to go with.'

Frustration burnt behind Casey's eyes—she didn't want to go, but she and Elly had been party-partners for years, supporting each other whether they were both single or not.

'If you really want me to, I'll go, but I've got to be honest, I'm not in the right mood. I mean, I'd much rather go see a live band, somewhere we can actually hear each other speaking.'

'Oh Casey, you know how much I've wanted to check this place out. There are three levels with different themes, and there will be lots of new men there.'

In the past, she would never have let Elly down, but since returning from California she hadn't been able to conjure up even a smidge of enthusiasm about nightclubs. 'The thought of getting groped on the dance floor by sweaty men simply isn't doing it for me.'

'Whoa. Where's my friend Casey? And who is this stick-in-the-mud who's impersonating her?' Elly said with a laugh.

Casey rolled her eyes, trying to find humour in the situation. 'Okay, I'll go tonight, but from now on, it's Sunday beer gardens or small venues with live bands, got it?'

Elly giggled nervously. 'Got it—sure thing. So, what are you going to wear?'

Casey knew full well this wouldn't be the last time Elly coaxed her into going. Elly loved the clubs—the volume, the intensity, the flashing lights, the *men*. And Casey loved them too—or at least, she used to.

After ending the call with Elly, she rang Taylor.

'We're going to check out a new club tonight. Do you want to come?' Taylor had sometimes joined them when they went out, but normally only on a night when she didn't have to work the next day.

A few seconds passed before Taylor replied. 'No, I've gotta be up at four tomorrow, so I'll take a raincheck. If you think it's worth a second look, I'll go along another time.'

Although it wasn't out of character for Taylor to stay home on a Friday night, she hadn't gone out with them even once since they'd returned from their trip.

'You're sure you don't want to get out? Meet some new people? It doesn't have to be a late night. You could grab a taxi home when you've had enough?'

'Thanks for the invitation, but I'd rather stay in if it's all the same to you. Next time. Promise.'

Casey wondered if Taylor still missed a certain cowboy far too much to be interested in meeting someone new, but she wouldn't bring that up. They'd talked about it while waiting to board the plane—Taylor had again voiced her regrets at leaving California, and Casey had admitted she'd enjoyed the time she'd spent with Nick—but they'd made a pact not to dwell on it. Taylor hadn't broken that pact, and Casey wasn't about to either.

'No worries. I'll ring you tomorrow and tell you how much fun you missed out on,' Casey said, not sure whether she was trying to tease Taylor into changing her mind, or trying to convince herself it was going to be fun.

~~*~~

Nick sat at the small outdoor table, looking across The Seine as he drank espresso and watched people walk past. It wasn't as cold today as it had been the day before, so he'd decided to take advantage of the sunshine and head to the café recommended by the proprietor at his small hotel.

This pastime was something he'd never dreamed would be so enjoyable—drinking coffee and watching people. The commonalities between people in London, Dublin, Zermatt, Amsterdam, Stuttgart, and now Paris were stronger than the differences—no matter the colour of their skin, the shape of their eyes or the clothes they chose to wear. There were those walking quickly, clearly on their way somewhere; those walking slightly slower with their heads down, staring at a phone; and those who walked even slower yet, meandering along and taking in their surroundings, snapping a few photos along the way. It was with those in the last category that he'd discovered the joy of making eye contact with a stranger and watching as a smile erupted on their face. Some faces were so unusual they seemed to burn into his memory, and he wondered if one day he'd write songs about them.

Working on Rose's song had awoken a passion in him that he'd set aside while developing his IT career. Now, while working on Casey's latest song in his hotel room on the nights he had no other plans, that passion was growing even stronger.

As thoughts of her swirled around in his mind, he spotted a tall woman, with hair the colour of rusted steel, walking toward him with long, self-assured strides. His imagination replaced the woman's face with Casey's, but as she got closer her details became undeniable. Of course it wasn't Casey. Just like it hadn't been each of the other times he'd thought he'd seen her: in London at the Horse Guards, in Dublin at the Guinness Storehouse, and in Amsterdam sitting at a café not unlike the one where he sat right now.

A shiver ran down his spine as the wind picked up, sending a draft up the back of his loose jacket. He pulled it close around him as he thought how warm it must be in Melbourne. The sun would have just started to drop toward the horizon. He knew the time difference—he'd checked it out each of the times he'd come close to punching her number into FaceTime.

He pulled out his phone, twirling it around in his hand, wondering what she'd say if he called her. Would she be getting ready to go out tonight? It was a Friday evening, after all. Had she reconnected with an old boyfriend? Could they be going out for a romantic dinner? Or would she be going out, hoping to meet someone new?

Did any of that matter? She asked him to work on Daisy's song, so he could call. It wouldn't be weird. They'd both agreed they should keep in contact.

He set the phone onto the small table and took the last sip of his coffee as he thought about how she'd react. No, Friday night wasn't a good idea. Besides, he had to get back to the hotel, grab his bags, and make his way over to the train station. Maybe he'd call from Barcelona—one morning, early, when he first woke, catching her in the afternoon.

Three days later, as he returned to his hotel in Barcelona after dinner, his phone rang. He hadn't called Casey—was it possible she'd somehow felt his desire to speak to her? He shook his head—that had to be one of the dumbest thoughts he'd ever had.

He pulled out his phone and saw it was his boss. 'Devin. I didn't expect to hear from you. What's happened? Nothing's wrong I hope?'

'No, relax, nothing's wrong. How's the trip going? Where are you now?'

'Barcelona. I've just come in from dinner.'

'Good. I got that right then. Barcelona's a great city. Hope you're having a good trip. Now look, I don't mean to be bothering you, but a project has come up that you'd be perfect for, and I can just roll you right across into it—same salary, same everything. The thing is, though, it needs to start by the first of April. So if you're not interested, I'll have to begin advertising for a manager fairly quickly.'

'Where, and what, is it?'

Devin explained the project, which would be run from their office in Sacramento.

'Yeah, sure, of course I'm interested.' The words left his mouth before he'd thought it through, but why wouldn't he be interested? It still gave him over five weeks before he'd have to be home.

As they continued to chat, the sense that he'd answered too quickly refused to lift, however, and by the time they ended the call Nick wished he'd asked for a day to think it over.

The room was cold; maybe that wasn't helping. He rubbed his hands together, trying to get the blood circulating, wondering if his post-dinner stroll hadn't been such a great idea. Somehow, he'd expected Spain to be warm, even in winter. But he'd been wrong. While Paris had been slightly warmer than Amsterdam, and now Barcelona was a little bit warmer than Paris, it had still only reached a top of 59F as he wandered around the city checking out the architecture. The previous day, as he'd headed over to Camp Nou, the largest football stadium in Europe, it had only reached 58F.

As he continued trying to blame the weather for the cold seeping through to his core, the answer struck him—hard. He missed Casey.

He missed her smile.

He missed her laugh.

And, mostly, he missed the way she made him feel.

The amazing thing, the thing that he'd been refusing to see but was now blatantly obvious, was that somewhere along the line his image of his future home life—of a fair-haired petite woman surrounded by several small children who were exact likenesses of his own childhood self—had changed.

And now, he only had five weeks before he'd have to be back at the office.

If he was going to do anything, he had to do it now.

He grabbed his iPad and logged into the airline's website. There was one flight that worked. He rang the airline, and in less than a half-hour he'd changed his flights.

CHAPTER 27

Casey had just finished the morning's flower arrangements when her phone rang. As she picked up the phone and saw the caller's name, her heart skipped a beat.

'Nick,' she said, surprise pushing her voice up an octave.

'Hey, Casey. Hope I haven't caught you at a bad time?'

His voice sent shivers down her spine—it was a sensation she'd missed.

She took a couple of settling breaths, then answered as calmly as possible. 'No, not at all. I was about to make myself a coffee, as it turns out, so I've got time to chat. Where are you? Oh, let me guess ... somewhere exciting, perhaps a ski resort in the Swiss Alps?'

'Ha ha; been there, done that, but I was growing a bit tired of the cold weather, as Alex had predicted, so no, I'm actually a lot closer than that.'

She chuffed out a breath. Closer than Switzerland. And warmer. Well, that narrowed it down to something like half the planet. 'On safari in Kenya, perhaps?'

His laugh was little more than a soft chuckle.

She'd missed that sound, too.

'You know, that never even occurred to me. Africa would definitely have been warmer than Barcelona. But no, I'm much closer than Africa. Maybe an hour from your place?'

'An hour? What ... are you in Sydney?' she asked, shaking her head in disbelief.

'No, actually, I'm in Melbourne. I just collected my luggage, and I'm in line at the taxi stand trying to decide what to tell the driver when I get in. I assume I'm about an hour, by taxi, from your place?'

'Oh. My. God. Nick, are you serious? You're here?'

'Yeah, I probably should have called first. It's just, when I checked with the airline there was only the one seat available and I thought I'd better grab it and then the time was all wrong to call you so I just figured I'd take my chances when I got here.'

'No, it's okay. I mean, I'm surprised, but it's a nice surprise.'

'Great! Look, I don't expect you to put me up. I mean, it would be nice, of course, but I'd be happy to go to a motel if you could make a recommendation ...' he said, his voice trailing off hopefully.

Still in a state of disbelief, it took her a moment to react.

'Motel? No way, you'll come here. I've got a spare room. And so has Taylor for that matter. You'll come here, and we'll figure things out when you get here.'

She gave him the address, then ended the call and raced out to explain the situation to Maree. When she asked for a few hours off, Maree flashed a huge grin and told her to take the rest of the day.

Pulling up at her unit, she could barely remember how she'd gotten there. She hurried inside, checked to make sure she'd made her bed, tidied up the dishes in the sink and ran a duster over the furniture in the lounge room. Then she remembered the bras drying over the shower nozzle. After retrieving them, she sat, trying to relax. When it wasn't working, she jumped up, poured herself a large glass of water and gulped it down.

She checked the time. It had been roughly forty minutes since he'd rung. How long would it take a taxi to get to her place? Forty-five minutes? An hour if they hit traffic? She raced into her room and changed into a soft green top, its colour similar to the scarf Nick had given her for Christmas. Then she splashed cold water on her face, and applied a small amount of mascara and fresh lip gloss. As she finished, she heard the knock at her door.

Her heart pounded so hard she could see it thumping through her shirt. Her hands felt numb. Were these the signs of a panic attack? She forced herself to take three slow breaths as she walked to the door, and took an extra deep breath as she opened it.

'Hey, you're a sight for sore eyes,' Nick said, stepping forward and kissing her cheek as he held out a small bouquet of flowers. 'I wanted to get you green roses—or any roses for that matter—but this mixed bouquet was the best I could find.'

He looked different. Firstly, he hadn't shaved in a while, and his hair was longer than she'd ever seen it. But it wasn't just that. He looked refreshed. It made no sense, given he'd just flown half-way around the world. Maybe it was just that she was really glad to see him. Whatever it was, there was no question that he was happy to see her too—his warm smile made that clear.

She reached forward and took the small bouquet and held it up to her nose to draw in the luscious scents. 'I can't believe you brought me flowers. They're beautiful. And no, you'd struggle to find green roses at the best of times. But come in, come in,' she said, stepping back from the door.

He swept his now empty hand through his hair, pushing it back off his forehead. She hadn't seen him do that before—his hair had never been long enough to get in his eyes—but she hoped she'd get to see him do it again. She licked her lips nervously.

As he walked through the door, she took yet another deep breath, willing her nerves to settle.

'Here, I should put these in water,' she said as she headed to the kitchen and pulled out a vase from under the sink. The simple task of filling it with water gave her something grounding to think about.

But when she turned, he was right behind her, watching. A slow smile touched his lips, and then his eyes. When he swept his hand through his hair again, a shiver ran down her spine.

'So ... what exactly are you doing here? I mean, I had no idea you took our invitation seriously.'

He smiled. 'Nor did I. Not at first, anyway. You're not unhappy that I did, are you?'

She shook her head. 'No, of course not. Just ... surprised.'

'Yeah, sorry about the lack of notice. I guess I should have sent you a text and given you a heads up at least.'

'Not to worry. It's a nice surprise. But I'm sure you must be exhausted? You'll feel better after you've freshened up, so if you want to jump into the shower I can show you around afterwards?'

'I could use a shower and a shave—since you've offered—and I'd like to change out of these clothes.'

Casey tilted her head. 'A shave too? I mean, of course you're welcome to, but I'm kinda liking this slightly more rugged version of you.'

A slow grin touched his lips, and then his eyes began to smoulder. 'Yeah, okay, I'll skip the shave.'

She showed him through to the small second bedroom, pulled out some fresh towels and placed them in the bathroom. Her hands were shaking. 'Did you want a coffee or something to eat first? Sorry, I'm not a very good hostess. I don't have a lot of house guests.'

'Think I'll go for the shower first. Then I'll take you out somewhere for a late lunch, if you like.'

He shut the door and a moment later she heard the water running. She couldn't stop pacing. It was hard enough to deal with Nick being here in her unit, but on top of that, he was naked, in her bathroom. She was so glad she'd remembered the bras hanging there.

She raced to the kitchen, made herself a strong coffee, then topped it off with cold water so she could drink it immediately while watching a neighbour's cat study a bird out on their shared fence. The temporary distraction helped—she'd gone a whole thirty seconds without thinking of Nick.

No, probably more like ten seconds.

What was he doing here? He hadn't really answered her when she asked him. Was it simply the weather? She couldn't dare presume it was to do with her, could she? When she heard the bathroom door open, she jumped.

'Man, that felt great,' Nick said, as he walked into the kitchen wearing only a pair of jeans. As he rubbed his hair with the towel, his fresh bath-soap scent nearly floored her.

'You were quick,' she said, trying not to stare at his bare chest.

'Was I?'

When he grinned, she relaxed.

Slightly.

'How long was the flight? I mean, it was bad enough from here to San Francisco.' Her voice nearly sounded normal. Hopefully, he wouldn't have picked up on the difficulty she'd had in breathing and talking at the same time.

'I had to fly back to London from Barcelona—that was a couple of hours. Then London to Sydney via Singapore was a long stretch. Then, what, a bit over an hour from Sydney down to here?' He stopped rubbing his hair but continued staring at her.

'Oh, I'm so rude. Here, let me take your wet towel. And can I get you a coffee now? It's not as good as barista coffee, but it's all I have.'

'I'd love a cup,' he said, taking a step closer to hand her the towel.

She took the towel and tossed it into the laundry, then returned to make his coffee. As she reached up to grab a cup, Nick's hand engulfed hers.

'You're shaking. Have you developed some affliction over the past weeks?' he asked, his voice a deep whisper in her ear.

She turned around, and he was right there—his peppermint-scented breath teasing her nostrils and his chest so close she could feel the heat from his skin.

'I ... it's probably some form of shock—like, from the surprise,' she said, hoping to sound cool and clever, but suspecting she'd missed both. As she looked up, his gaze captured hers. She'd half expected a mischievous grin, but instead she found passion and longing on his face.

'I was hoping it had something to do with you missing me. I sure have missed you,' he said as he reached out and brushed his knuckles along the side of her face.

She leaned into his hand, closing her eyes, as a soft moan escaped her lips. She quickly turned the sound into a question. 'You've missed me?' She opened her eyes to search his, looking for a hint of laughter or something to suggest he was just toying with her—still not ready to believe this was real.

'Very much,' he replied, his voice low and filled with emotion.

'I wasn't sure I'd ever see you again,' she said, wanting to trust that he really meant it.

'And that bothered you, the thought that you mightn't see me again?' he asked.

'Yes. It bothered me a lot,' she said, her voice barely more than a whisper.

He leaned forward and placed a soft kiss on her lips. When he pulled back, his eyes were smouldering, and she suspected her own would look much the same. Then, he reached up and put his hand behind her head, pulling her forward as his other arm circled her waist. When he kissed her this time, there was nothing soft about it. Her hands sought the strong muscles of his shoulders, pulling him closer and holding him tighter until their bodies merged as one.

She wasn't sure how long they'd kissed, but when his lips finally released hers, dizziness engulfed her. She licked her lips, still tasting the minty freshness of his toothpaste on them, as she opened her eyes.

He was still right there—his pupils dilated, making his eyes darker than she'd ever seen them.

He drew in a ragged breath, and when he spoke, his voice was low and full of passion. 'You don't know how much I've regretted not doing that the last night we saw each other in Masons Flat. Would it have made a difference?'

She could barely muster a whisper as her mind raced to remember the details of that night—they'd stood awkwardly beside her uncle's old Buick for quite some time. 'A difference?'

He cocked his head, giving her a sheepish smile. 'Would you still have left? If I'd kissed you like that, and told you how much you'd grown to mean to me? It's something I've been pondering for weeks.'

She closed her eyes, trying to get her head around what he'd asked, trying to make sense of it. 'I ... well, I think ... I don't know ... maybe?'

He shrugged. 'Of course you would still have left. I'm being a hopeless romantic, thinking a simple kiss might have changed your plans. It's just ... I've missed you, Casey. I thought I'd forget you once I got overseas, but how could I? Everywhere I went, I saw you. It was never you, of course, but the disappointment that followed each time made it even harder to forget you.'

Casey looked down, confirming that her feet were still on the floor. Then she reached out and ran her hand across his chest so lightly that she could just feel his golden chest hairs on the tips of her fingers. Yes, he was definitely there—standing right in front of her.

As she looked into his eyes, an involuntary frown tightened her brow as she concentrated, trying to recall every word he'd said but all she could remember were the four most important ones; *I've missed you, Casey*. She forced a smile onto her face, realising it had been a long time since he'd stopped speaking, and thinking that he must be anxious for her to respond with something. Anything.

'I ... I tried to forget you, too ... to put you in that special place I have for exes who I know I'll never see again. But you didn't fit there. You didn't belong there because ... you know, it's been really hard not to think about what might have happened if we'd both stuck around in the same city for a bit longer.'

He let out a huge sigh, and when his eyes met hers there was so much warmth resonating in them her desire for him became almost unbearable.

He reached forward, trailing a finger across her cheek as he looked deeply into her eyes. 'I was hoping you felt that way—that's why I'm here.'

Casey had to break eye contact. She looked down, trying to catch her breath. So he *was* here for her, not just the summer sun. After several calming breaths, she looked up, finding her desire mirrored in his eyes.

He smiled, staring deeply into her eyes. When he finally spoke, his voice was lower and sexier than any she'd ever heard before. 'I've got four weeks.'

Her heart was pounding and she wasn't certain she'd find her voice. 'Four weeks—the time will fly.'

He stepped back slightly, flashing a mischievous grin. 'I don't have to stay here the whole time—I mean, just say the word and I'll take off. I can go to Sydney, or up to Queensland. I've heard snorkelling at the Great Barrier Reef is a must-do.'

She couldn't keep the smile from creeping back onto her lips. He wanted them to have a chance to get to know each other. They could take things one day at a time and see what came of it. And if it didn't work out, he would take off and see other parts of Australia. Of course, if the way she felt right now continued, that wouldn't be happening.

She looked into his questioning eyes and took his hand, pulling him close to her. Mustering up her sassiest voice, she leaned forward and whispered into his ear. 'I don't think I'll be pushing you out the door, mate. If anything, I'll be sticking to you like cling-wrap on a glass bowl.'

When she faced him, they picked up where their last kiss had ended.

CHAPTER 28

They never made it to lunch. They spent the rest of the day in Casey's bedroom, getting to know each other all over again, but on a much more personal level. Nick's only regret was the weeks he'd wasted.

By five-thirty, they were both in need of a shower and they were famished. He showered quickly, and unpacked while she had her shower.

When Casey came out of the bathroom, with only a towel wrapped around her body, the desire to throw her back onto the bed and make love to her again was nearly irresistible, but there'd be lots of time for that later.

'Do you mind if I ring Taylor to see if she wants to join us? She'll be offended if I don't at least let her know you're here,' Casey asked in a voice as smooth as warm honey.

'Sure,' he said, following her into her bedroom and making himself comfortable on the corner of her bed. 'But first, come over here and let me have a closer look at those tattoos of yours—'

She cut him off, her voice edging toward testiness. 'Not that again. Puh-lease, let it go.'

He stood and grabbed her around the waist, gently dragging her toward him. He sat back on the bed, and pulled her onto his lap. 'I wasn't going to criticize them. I was going to say I wanted to have a better look at them because, believe it or not, I love them. Never, in a million years, would I have thought I'd say something like that, but seriously, they're each so beautiful, and they say so much about you.' He let his finger trail softly down her forearm, then dropped his voice to a loud whisper. 'Like this oleander you showed me that first night when we met, and this green rose.'

She laughed, the edge completely gone from her voice. 'Okay, you're allowed to compliment them all you like.'

'This one is awesome,' he said, turning her so she faced away from him, and sliding the towel down enough to completely expose the large red, orange and green tattoo. Running his hand gently down her back, he asked, 'Are they poppies?'

When she pressed herself into his hand, he rubbed her back softly.

She made a sound he could only compare to a cat purring, then answered in a voice that made him remember what a strong woman she was. 'Yes. Poppies symbolise sorrow and death—that's why they're used with the Anzacs.'

'Anzacs?' He'd heard the expression but wasn't exactly sure what it meant.

She spun around, staring at him in disbelief, one delicate eyebrow raised. 'Don't tell me you haven't heard of our Anzacs?'

He cocked his head, trying to remember the context in which he'd heard the term. 'Maybe ... sort of? No, not really.'

She shook her head and smirked, like a school teacher chastising a lazy student—a look he knew all too well.

'It stands for Australia New Zealand Army Corps, and is the name given to the expedition that was sent to capture the Gallipoli peninsula in World War One. A great-great-uncle of mine died at Gallipoli. That's one of the reasons I get so emotional about Rose's song. It combines the story of Hayley's grandmother and my own relative.'

He ran his hand up and down her back, rubbing her shoulders in the most comforting way he knew. He dropped his voice to a whisper. 'And that's why you have the poppies?'

'Yes, partly. They also symbolise imagination, which is something I truly treasure.'

He bowed his head slightly before replying, finally realising how much he treasured everything about this woman. 'And so you should. It's stunning.'

She leaned into him and threw her arms around his shoulders, speaking into the fabric of his shirt. 'It's my favourite too. I was afraid you mightn't like it because it's so prominent.'

'I love it, Casey. In fact, I'm beginning to think I love everything about you. I'm thinking I've been a real fool up until now and that I've got some ground to make up.'

When she shuddered against him, he wrapped his arms around her and hugged her to his body. When her shivering stopped, he loosened his hold, encouraging her to lean back until she looked squarely into his eyes.

Her voice was husky and full of mischief when she spoke. 'And I'm beginning to love a lot of things about you, too, Mister Gold, much to my surprise. I mean, seriously, who'd have put the two of us together?'

Relief exploded from him in laughter. She got him, as much as he got her. They were utterly different in so many ways, but not in the ways that mattered. They could work through most things, but only if they gave themselves a chance.

He kissed her tenderly. And then, as much as he'd have loved to take the towel away and throw her naked body back down on the bed, he gently slid her off his lap and went back out to the living room so she could get dressed.

~~*~~

Casey ordered takeaway from her favourite Thai restaurant and they picked it up on their way to the beach. Taylor's car was already there when they arrived, and the three headed to a bench overlooking the water to eat while they watched the gentle bay waves rolling in.

'Tell us about your trip,' Taylor said, between bites of her spring rolls.

'It was cold, just like Alex had said it would be, but other than that, everywhere I went was incredible. Ireland was possibly my favourite, although that's probably because of being there with Patrick and his family.'

'Oh, I'd love to go to Ireland someday. And Scotland, of course, where our ancestors came from. But I think you're right—I doubt I'd want to go on my own. I think I would find it too lonely. Maybe if I ever find Mr Right we'll go there for our honeymoon.' Taylor grinned, and Casey just shook her head.

When they finished eating, they took their shoes off and walked down to the edge of the surf. Taylor bent and picked up a rock, throwing it into the water. 'I've always wanted to get a rock to skip across the water, but I've never been able to do it.'

Nick picked one up and failed just as miserably. 'I think the water needs to be still—like a lake.'

Casey smiled at them both, marvelling at how normal this felt—as if it were something they'd done hundreds of times before.

Taylor did a dramatic hip bump into Casey, then took her hand and squeezed it. Casey wondered if it was tears she saw in Taylor's eyes or simply a reaction to the salty breeze?

'I still can't believe you're here,' Taylor said, shaking her head gently as she leaned across Casey to look at Nick. 'You didn't seem all that keen on the idea when we talked about it in California.'

Nick shrugged, raising his hands in defeat. 'No? I guess the freezing northern winter changed my mind.' Then, after a few more steps he threw his arm around Casey's shoulders. 'That, and the fact that I missed your sister.'

'Awww ... you guys are so cute together,' Taylor said, grinning.

The way Taylor's voice trailed off spoke volumes. Casey knew Taylor had mixed feelings about leaving California, but did she still regret the way things had turned out? Would Taylor possibly even be open to the idea of giving things in California a go?

By the time they got back to where their cars were parked, Nick looked like he was asleep on his feet. Taylor cocked her head. 'I was going to suggest you follow me back to my place for a drink, but you look like you've had it, Nick.'

'Yeah, I think all the travelling has finally caught up with me. But I'd love a raincheck if that's okay?' he asked, smiling at Taylor.

'Of course it is. Casey and I will organise a dinner or something. I might even cook for you guys.'

'Sounds good to me,' Casey said, clicking the unlock button on her car's key fob. She could tell by the look on Taylor's face that there was something more Taylor wanted to ask—privately. 'Hop in, and I'll just be a minute.'

Once Nick was in the car and had shut the door, Taylor's eyes flew open wide. 'Did you have any idea he would turn up?' she asked, her voice low and filled with curiosity.

Casey shook her head. 'None. In fact, the last time I heard anything from him before today was a quick email when he arrived in Ireland, and that was weeks ago.'

'But you two are ... I mean it seems as if ... you're together, right?' Taylor's eyes sparkled with interest. This mattered to her.

'I guess—for the moment anyway. It's just so ... I never thought of him as the kind of guy I'd end up with, and yet his being here seems completely natural.'

Taylor shook her head slowly as a wide smile took over her face. 'From the moment I saw you two come back from that walk on Thanksgiving Day, I thought he was perfect for you.' She leaned forward and planted a kiss on Casey's cheek. As she pulled back, she winked. 'I'll talk to you tomorrow and we'll work out a night for dinner.'

CHAPTER 29

Casey couldn't believe how understanding Maree was about Nick's visit, proving, once again, that she was the greatest boss of all time. Casey was able to delegate most of her work to the two part-timers who, luckily, were more than happy to get the extra hours. What she couldn't delegate, Maree did herself.

So without feeling the slightest bit of guilt, Casey took Nick on three short trips, ticking off some of the most popular tourist hotspots along the east coast of Australia. They went to Hobart, where they visited the Port Arthur historic penal colony, Battery Point, and the Salamanca Market; they flew to Queensland where they went across to Hamilton Island to go snorkelling; and then they spent a long weekend in Sydney, where they climbed the Sydney Harbour Bridge, took a tour of the Opera House, and rode the ferry over to Manly Beach for an afternoon swim.

On the days in-between their trips, when Casey went to work for a few hours, Nick either took the train into the city to explore Melbourne or hung around Casey's place and worked on their songs. They'd also had dinner with Taylor several times, and had ventured to some of Casey's favourite beer gardens for pub meals with a few of her friends, including Elly.

Yet even though they'd spent every day together for three weeks, and Nick seemed to be enjoying their time together as much as she was, they never touched on the future—on what would happen at the end of Nick's stay.

By the end of the third week, Casey had grown somewhat anxious.

She knew what she wanted their future to be. She'd weighed up all the pros and cons several times and had come up with the same answer each time. Following Nick back to California was the right decision, even though it meant she'd miss Taylor, and she'd be giving up a really good job. Still, he was worth it.

She just hoped he wanted the same thing.

Now, as they prepared to visit Casey's step-sister in the small town of Willows on Nick's last full weekend in Australia, Casey felt certain that the peaceful country setting would encourage them to discuss their future. And if Nick didn't bring it up, she would have to overcome her fear of rejection and find the moment to do it herself.

~~*~~

Casey pulled off the freeway just before six, and within a few minutes, she and Nick were driving down the centre of the small town of Willows. Although bigger than Masons Flat, Willows was still a small town with mostly just one main street through the middle of it and the instructions on how to find the bed & breakfast couldn't have been simpler. After checking into their quaint little cottage, they made their way to the restaurant where they were joining Casey's step-sister, Summer, and her husband, Max, for dinner.

Summer, who had met Travis briefly nearly a year earlier, appeared thrilled to now be meeting his cousin.

'I wouldn't have picked you as being related to Travis. You're so fair, and he was tall, dark, and handsome if I remember correctly,' she said, emphasising each word. Then, turning to her husband she continued, 'Oh, not that you're not handsome—I didn't mean it like that—and you too Nick, of course. You're both very handsome.'

Nick shook his head back and forth slowly, quirking a brow. 'I take after my mother's side of the family.'

Casey wondered how many times he'd heard this before.

Summer nodded, then continued. 'Travis was like this Knight in Shining Armour, coming over here to track Alex down. It was right before our wedding so of course I was somewhat distracted,' she said, turning to give her husband a quick peck on the cheek. 'From memory, Alex and Travis and been squabbling about something, but he couldn't let things end that way. It was so romantic. And so ... what brings you all the way over here, Nick? Have you come out on business?'

Casey was surprised when Nick grabbed her hand under the table and gave it a slight squeeze. 'No, I'm actually taking a break from work. As I'm sure you know, Casey and Taylor spent Thanksgiving and

Christmas in my home town in California, and they suggested I come down to Australia for a visit.'

'I see. Yes, I'm sure it's lovely being here for our summer rather than being in the northern hemisphere's winter.'

Nick grinned. 'Besides, while she was in California, I promised Casey I'd take her horseback riding and since it never ended up happening, I thought I'd better come down here and fulfil that promise.'

Summer frowned. 'Really? Quite a long way to come to go horse riding, don't you think?'

Casey glanced at Nick in surprise. This was the first she'd heard of this.

Nick appeared to be struggling not to laugh.

Seeming oblivious to Casey's confusion, Max jumped into the conversation. 'Well, we've got a few horses on our property that don't get out nearly often enough. Why don't you come out tomorrow and we can head up to the lookout? It's a nice ride from our place, only about an hour in each direction. We can take lunch with us and have a picnic up there?'

Two hours and two bottles of Shiraz later, they said their goodnights and walked back to the cottage. Being alone in the small room should have been the perfect time for Casey to bring up California, but the urge to discuss their future evaporated as Nick pulled her into his arms and covered her mouth with a passionate kiss.

~~*~~

The following morning, they made the short drive out of town to the large ranch-style home of Summer and Max. Casey pulled up in front of the house shortly before eleven.

After a quick catch-up on their verandah, Max led them to the yards where four horses stood, saddled and ready to go. Casey had been a bit anxious ever since Max had suggested the ride, but she chastised herself as she looked at the calm horses. It couldn't be that hard.

'This here is Missy. She's Summer's little mare, and she's sweet as they come,' Max said, pointing to the smaller of the two grey horses. 'If you want to take her, Casey, Summer can ride one of the younger horses.'

When Casey stepped up to the mare and gently stroked her nose, the mare lifted her head and sniffed at Casey's mouth.

'See, she likes you already,' Max said with a laugh. 'And this little bay here is Tom, short for Phantom. He's mine, Nick, but I understand you're no beginner so you shouldn't have any problems with him.'

Nick patted the horse's neck and then began to check out the saddle. 'Can't say I've ever ridden in one of these stock saddles—I'm looking forward to the experience. Thanks for offering to take us.'

Casey tilted her head, looking at the saddle, trying to remember how it differed from the ones she'd seen from a distance in America. Then it dawned on her, these had no horn, but they did have what looked like pads where your thighs would be once you sat down. These actually looked like they could be easier to ride in—or at least she hoped that would be the case.

'No worries, I'm glad you wanted to come—it's a great opportunity for us to get these younger horses out on the track. They've been ridden, but not nearly as often as they should be. Now, I'm not entirely sure the weatherman knew what he was on about, but he did mention the possibility of some storm activity a bit later today, so I've taken the liberty of tying these oilskins onto the saddles. Casey, you'll need to really lift your leg when you get on to swing over the top of it. And Summer insists you wear a helmet, given you're a beginner. She always wears one herself, just in case she comes off.'

Casey put on the helmet, which was similar to a bike helmet, and then accepted a leg up onto the grey mare. Max put his hand on her ankle and asked her to stand in the stirrups. 'They look about right to me, but if they feel too short, we can adjust them for you later. Now, this is how you stop her. And you don't need to kick her. She'll go along just fine for you if you simply let her follow the other horses.'

When Max winked, a flash of doubt once again crossed Casey's mind, but she quickly dismissed it when Nick got on his horse and came over beside her.

'We'll go up through the state forest to the lookout,' Max said. 'It's a gentle climb, with a few good spots for a little trot or canter.'

'Sounds good to me,' Nick said, reaching down and patting Tom's neck again. The horse blew what Casey would call raspberries.

Summer climbed up onto a tall chestnut, and Max quickly swung himself up onto the other grey horse. 'Everyone okay to go?' Max asked.

They headed off, with Max leading the way, followed by Summer and Nick, and Casey's horse followed at the rear of the group, which suited her just fine. They made their way along dirt roads, but it wasn't long before they reached a track that led up through the forest, and by then, Casey was getting the hang of it.

They hadn't gone far along the gently sloping track when they came across a small mob of about a dozen Eastern Grey Kangaroos. They looked to be mostly females, with a few joeys still in the pouch. Casey drew in her breath, expecting Missy to panic, but Missy barely seemed to take any notice of them. The other horses didn't seem fussed about them either.

'Those are my first kangaroos,' Nick said, his voice full of excitement. 'Guess the horses are used to them. This guy didn't even flinch.'

'Yeah,' said Max over his shoulder, 'we've got skips bounding through our paddocks on a regular basis, so it's nothing new to these horses.'

'That's what we should have done,' Casey said, feeling stupid for not having thought of it earlier. 'I should have taken you up to Healesville to the native animal sanctuary. Maybe we can still go one day this week.'

Nick looked over his shoulder and smiled. 'If we don't get there, that's okay. It's always good to leave a few things on a to-do list for the next visit.'

Casey was stunned by his comment. If Nick was thinking of coming back here for another *visit,* he couldn't be thinking too hard about her going to California with him. She couldn't put off the conversation any longer. One way or another, she was going to have to find the courage to bring up the subject herself.

She was just contemplating how to do it casually, when he changed the subject.

'Are there many snakes around? I am watching for them, of course, but do I need to worry about them?'

'You don't need to worry,' Max answered, 'but I wouldn't stray off into the long grass.'

'Yeah, I was just thinking the same thing,' Summer called back over her shoulder. 'Just stay on the track.'

As they continued to walk along in silence, the horses all seeming quite relaxed, Casey began to enjoy the familiar scents of eucalypt and woody soil, and the sounds of the native birds. Then, when Max called back to see if Casey was okay to do a bit of a canter, she gritted her teeth and called out faintly, 'Okay'.

Max started off, followed by Summer, and then Nick's horse began to pull ahead as well, but much to Casey's relief, Missy seemed quite happy to keep walking. When the gap between her and the other horses continued to grow, Casey grabbed hold of the front of the saddle and leaned forward, allowing the reins to go slack. It seemed all the encouragement Missy needed and she surged ahead. Surprisingly, Casey barely left the saddle as the mare made her way closer to the group.

When Missy caught up to the other horses, she went back to a walk. 'Wow, that was awesome. Are all horses as smooth as this one?' she asked, looking at Summer.

'Not all. She's a purebred Quarter Horse, and she's got that classic Quarter Horse lope that lots of people call a rocking-chair lope. I wouldn't sell her for anything,' Summer answered, patting the neck of the horse she was riding. 'No offence, Charity. You're sweet too, just nowhere near as comfortable to ride.'

Content with walking now, they continued along the track until they reached a ridge and followed this for a while until they finally stopped at a small clearing where they could see back to the town.

The town looked bigger than Casey expected, sprawling in all directions. From here, she could see that it was more than just the main street. In the distance there were rolling hills scattered with homesteads and paddocks. Most of the paddocks were golden, but some were still dotted with patches of green even this late into summer. She patted Missy's neck, amazed at how much fun this was turning out to be, and chastising herself for her earlier trepidation.

'This is the spot,' Max said, jumping down off his horse and walking over to take Missy's reins while Casey dismounted. As she stretched her legs, Max walked over and tied their horses to a tree. Summer brought over the other two horses and grabbed some saddlebags off the back of her saddle.

They sat on huge boulders and ate cheese and salad rolls, and drank cans of lemon squash while Max told them about the town, pointing out new buildings and landmarks.

'It seems a nice town,' said Nick, nodding his approval. 'You should see the place I grew up—now that's a small town. Mind you, it's grown a little bit since I moved away, but most people do their shopping a bit further away. Looks like you're pretty self-contained here.'

'Yeah, we can get most things here in town, but you've gotta drive a fair way if you want to see a movie— either up to Bendigo or Ballarat, or down to Melbourne.'

'And I take it you both work here in town then?' Nick asked.

'Yeah, Summer's just started working part-time in the news agency, and I do a bit of fencing here and there, but we make most of our money running cattle—Black Angus,' Max said, still looking out over the town.

'That's right. You mentioned it last night.'

A few minutes later, they'd just begun preparing for the ride back when a sudden strong gust of wind came through, sending leaf and dust everywhere. Both of the younger horses jumped back for a moment, but Tom and Missy just turned their faces away from the wind. After a moment, when the wind stopped, they all settled down.

'That was kinda weird,' Casey said. 'Don't know what brought that on.'

'They did say the weather could turn. We should probably get a move on. Do you want to wear that oilskin, just in case?' Max asked.

Casey looked down at her lightweight cotton shirt, realising that it would afford little protection if it did start to rain. 'I guess. Let's see if it fits.'

The oilskin was a good fit, as was the one given to Nick. She liked the way he looked in it—it gave him a real *Man from Snowy River* look.

Now, with all four ready to go, Nick quickly checked the saddles and gave Casey a leg up onto Missy. She'd just gathered her reins and gotten the oilskin even under her seat when another strong gust of wind blew, followed by what sounded like a herd of elephants tramping toward them through the bush.

~~*~~

Nick knew the sound all too well—a tree had come down, and not far from them. His horse jumped, but Nick had no trouble keeping control of him. Missy, Casey's horse, was only a few feet away from him. He turned to grab her reins but, before he could reach them, Summer's horse bolted in-between him and Casey. Missy spun on a dime, nearly tossing Casey off in the process, and took off full speed hot on the heels of Summer's chestnut.

Nick dug his heals in, urging Tom to follow, and was impressed with the instant speed the horse attained. Luckily, the track here was fairly wide and he was able to put his horse between the trees on the edge of the track and the two mares, urging Tom to get in front of them. Once he was well past, he turned Tom and pulled him up across the track, forming a barrier. The two mares sat back on their haunches and skidded to a stop. Casey, who'd been barely hanging on, toppled off to the right.

She landed with a thud and went immediately silent.

Nick jumped to the ground, throwing his reins to Summer, who had finally gained control of her young horse, while Max raced up and grabbed Missy, moving her away from Casey.

Nick reached Casey in two long strides. Her eyes were open, but were wide with fear.

He pulled off her helmet and quickly checked it for cracks. Finding none, he ran his hand over Casey's head, looking for any signs of bleeding or injury. 'Does your head hurt, sweetheart? I don't see any obvious injuries, but that was a nasty fall.'

As her eyes filled with tears he realised she was still struggling to draw a breath, her mouth opening and closing like a dying fish. She didn't answer.

'Casey, I think you've had the wind knocked out of you. Can you sit up? That's it ... now try to breathe in through your mouth. Push your stomach out, if you can. That's it. Now, suck your stomach in, and try to exhale. It should start getting easier.'

The panic in her eyes began to lessen as she started to take small breaths. But she still didn't say anything.

Finally, after what seemed ages but was probably barely more than a minute, she drew in a loud breath and reached up and threw her arms around his neck.

'What happened?' she asked, her voice scratchy.

He pulled her close, rubbing his hands up and down her back. 'You literally got the wind knocked out of you. It's happened to me a few times, so I'm pretty sure that's all it was. Do you hurt anywhere? Do you think anything's broken?'

She shook her head, still clinging to him.

Summer was now beside them, speaking in a soothing voice. 'Casey—you sure gave us a fright. Are you okay?'

Casey leaned back away from Nick's chest, swallowing hard. 'I think so ... nothing hurts, but crikey that was not fun.'

Nick ran his hand down the side of her face, then cradled it in his palm for a moment. 'Take a few more deep breaths, letting the air out slowly, and you should begin to feel better.'

'What happened? It's all a blur,' Casey said, her voice still shaky as she looked back and forth from him to Summer.

Summer shook her head. 'I think a tree came down, not far from where we were. Scared the crap outta my horse and I hadn't gotten my foot in the off-side stirrup and didn't have a good hold on the reins. And the moment she went, Missy spun so fast—she's never done that when I'm riding her, but I've seen her do it in the paddock—and she was right beside us. Charity got the bit in her teeth, and there wasn't a thing I could do about it. If it weren't for Nick, we'd probably still be racing down the track full bore because it took all my effort just to stay on. I knew if I tried to turn her I'd lose my balance and come off, and possibly get trampled by Missy.'

Casey turned to Nick, her eyes filled with unspoken gratitude.

Max walked up, still holding his horse and Missy, who'd settled as if nothing had ever happened. 'You all right there, Casey?'

She nodded, giving him a weak smile.

'That was good riding, Nick. I knew you'd be right with Tom. He's a handy little horse. Suspect he knew exactly what you were trying to do. Keeps his head in most situations, not like these silly mares that get a bit stupid sometimes.'

Nick nodded to Max. 'Yeah, he didn't put a foot wrong.' Then he turned back to Casey. 'Do you think you can stand up now?'

When she nodded, he stood and held out his hands, helping her to her feet. She took a couple of deep breaths, and gave a tentative smile.

'I think I'm okay. Can't say I'd be in a hurry to experience that again, though.'

Finally, Nick could laugh—the sort of laugh you do when you're watching a movie and something scary happens, and you find yourself laughing afterwards. He bent down and picked up Casey's discarded helmet, again checking it for any damage. When he could see none, he handed it to her.

'I don't think you hit your head, but I'm glad you had this on. So, do you think you can ride back now?'

Her eyes filled with panic again, and she looked over to Missy and back to him, several times.

'We can walk if you prefer. I don't mind. But the chances of that happening again are pretty slim, don't you think, Max?'

Max turned to Casey. 'You know what these bloody gum trees are like—dropping branches all the time—but by the sound of it that was a whole tree that came down. I'd say for another tree to come down it'd be like getting bitten by a shark twice in one day. Missy's settled down, and so has that other silly mare. I think you'll be fine riding back. We can take it real slow.'

~~*~~

Casey didn't relax until they were out of the forest and riding along the side of the road. The good thing was nothing hurt. The bad thing was that she suspected tomorrow could be a completely different story.

When they got back to the house, Summer and Casey made their way to the verandah while Nick helped Max with the horses.

'Are you feeling okay now?' Summer asked. 'Do you want something cold to drink? Or a cup of hot tea, maybe?'

'No, I'm good. I'll probably take a long, relaxing bath when we get back to our cottage. I imagine I'll be a bit stiff tomorrow.'

Summer smothered a laugh. 'Sorry, it's not funny. I've had falls like that, and it isn't fun hitting the ground from that height. But I tell you, if it wasn't for Nick, I think we'd both have been in a bit of trouble.'

Casey's heart warmed, knowing that Nick had been there for her today. 'He's a good rider, that's for sure. Suspect Max would have done the same if he'd been on his own horse.'

'Probably, but it was quick thinking on Nick's part, not just good riding. And you should have seen his face when he saw you sprawled on the ground, not making a sound.'

A stronger burst of warmth raced through Casey. 'He looked worried, did he?'

Summer shrugged and pulled a face. 'Worried is an understatement. Petrified is more like it. I do think we all deserve a cup of tea after all that, and I made a vanilla slice yesterday. That should fix you right up.'

Summer disappeared into the house, and a few moments later, Nick appeared. 'How are you feeling?'

'Better. I suppose I should count my lucky stars that it wasn't anything more serious,' she said. 'Summer's gone in to make us tea, and she's made a vanilla slice. If you haven't had one before, you're in for a real treat.'

'Sounds good. The sugar will probably make you feel better. Suspect you're a bit flat—the aftermath of the adrenaline rush you had.'

When all the tea and been drunk and the vanilla slice was nothing more than crumbs on the plate, they said their goodbyes as they walked to Casey's car.

'Do you want me to drive back to town?' Nick asked.

Casey shook her head. 'I think I'm fine to drive. Unless you want to? I don't suppose you've ever driven on the left side of the road?'

Nick put his hand out, so she dropped the keys onto his palm. 'I drove in Ireland and the UK, so I think I can handle it,' he said, his voice dripping with sarcasm.

CHAPTER 30

Casey had forgotten there wasn't a bathtub at the cottage, but standing under the hot water as she took a luxuriously long shower did the trick. Donning the thick white cotton robe she'd found hanging in the wardrobe, she padded out to find Nick dozing on the small sofa in the corner of the room.

It had grown quite dark outside with the approaching storm, but the cottage was cosy, and she felt ever so safe as she gently dropped down onto the sofa beside Nick. His eyes opened slowly as she drew her knees up under her, and a smile touched his lips as he wrapped his arm around her shoulders and pulled her closer to him. Then he tucked a strand of hair behind her ear as he leaned toward her face, and whispered. 'You sure gave me a fright today, Miss Mason.'

She rested her head on his chest and listened to the soothing rhythm of his heartbeat. 'Yeah, I think I saw my life flash before my eyes. It all happened so fast and then hitting the ground and not being able to breathe. I did wonder if I was going to die,' Casey said, her face still tingling where Nick had touched her skin.

He took her hand, rubbing it gently. 'I wouldn't have let that happen. Never.'

She smiled, never feeling safer than she did right at this moment. 'When I heard your calm voice, I knew everything was going to be all right.'

He pulled her even closer, taking her hand with his free one, and cleared his throat. 'I've been thinking about something. I've been waiting for the right moment to bring this up ... to ask how you feel about my visit coming to an end, because it's not long until I leave, and really, I don't want to go.'

Casey sat upright, frowning, feeling both excited and nervous at the same time. They were finally discussing their future, and he'd been the one to bring it up. 'You don't?'

'No. I really don't want to go. Maybe I could look into getting residency or something?'

She looked up at him, a tentative smile touching her lips. 'But what about Devin? What about your job?'

He loosened his hold on her, shifted until his whole body faced hers, and then took both her hands in his. 'It scared me when I thought I might lose you up there on that mountain. I'd already been thinking about it, but that made me realise that I'd do anything to give us a chance, Casey. And if it means starting over with my career and begging your government to let me stay here, I'm willing to do that. I've got good skills. I'm sure I could find a job.'

Her thoughts raced round and round so quickly she couldn't get a handle on any of them. Was her lack of clarity something to do with the fall? This definitely wasn't the way she'd thought a conversation about their future would go. 'So ... you want to stay here? In Australia?'

He smiled and spoke slowly, his voice full of emotion. 'I want to be with you, Casey. In case you hadn't noticed, I'm hopelessly in love with you. If I have to stay here to be with you, so be it. Of course, if you'd like to come to California with me, I'd be happy with that too. I'd be over the moon, in fact. My place isn't a mansion or anything, but it's comfortable.'

A flash lit up the room briefly, and Casey turned to the window in time to see the second flash that followed it. The storm had arrived.

When she turned back to Nick, his face had changed, and there it was—that look she'd never seen a man give her. The same look she'd seen from time to time on Travis' face when he gazed at Alex. The look she'd dreamt would one day be directed toward her.

Love seemed to resonate from deep inside him, evident in the warmth of his smile and the glisten in his eyes. She swallowed hard, wondering how to stop the avalanche of emotions taking her voice away. He wanted her in his life. And he wanted her so much that he was prepared to quit his job and figure out how to stay in Australia.

'Casey? Did you hear what I said? I'm in love with you, and nothing would make me happier than being with you forever. Will you marry me? Because I honestly don't know if I can stand not having you in my life.'

Suddenly she felt nearly as breathless as she'd been when she'd fallen off the horse. She smiled and cleared her throat. 'Oh, Nick, I'm in love with you, too. And I do want to go with you to Sacramento. I've been thinking about it since you arrived.'

He leaned forward, kissing her gently. Then he pulled his hands away from hers and wrapped his arms around her, pulling her onto his lap. 'You make me so happy, Casey. I never knew love could feel like this.'

He kissed her again, removing the last shreds of doubt that had been clinging to her.

'I love you too, Nick, more than I could ever have imagined.'

He let out a sigh as relief lit up his face. 'So, is that a yes? You'll marry me?'

'Umm,' she replied hesitantly, watching as his smile faded, 'this is all happening so fast.'

His smile returned. 'It has been fast, hasn't it? But love can be like that, right? Creeping up with stealth, and then wham, it bashes you over the head. That's how it was for me anyway. But we don't have to get married if that's not what you want. Or maybe just not right away. We can talk about this again in a few months. How's that sound?'

She smiled and nodded, then loosened herself from his arms and turned to gaze out the small window again. 'When we first met, I thought you were quite arrogant, and *sooooo* not my type. But as I've gotten to know you, I've come to realise I've never had so much in common with anyone as I do with you. And yet, at the same time, we have some really different opinions on things.'

He snuggled up into her back and spoke softly into her ear. 'I've been thinking about that, too. While it always seemed a given that I'd have a big family one day, it's not as important as I thought it was. I mean, I always thought I'd be married by thirty, and starting a family right after, but I was a fool to think love could be micro-managed like one of my projects.'

She twisted so she could look at him again, warmth washing over her. 'I needed to hear that.'

When he smiled, and kissed her forehead, she continued. 'If having a big family is important, maybe we could adopt? Or we could become foster parents?' she said, trying to compromise. 'I don't want this to be a barrier between us.'

And then the memory of those little girls she'd seen at Yosemite drifted across her mind, and although she didn't say it out loud, she wondered if her attitude about having babies would change if she were to become pregnant with Nick's baby.

He placed his hands on each side of her face, rubbing her cheeks slowly with his thumbs as he gazed into her eyes. 'I don't want anything to be a barrier between us. I want you in my life, more than I've ever wanted anyone or anything.'

She felt her brow rise, almost involuntarily. 'More than the girl who inspired the song you wrote?'

He leaned back, joy erupting on his face as his eyes grew dark with passion. 'Oh, she doesn't even begin to compare to you, Casey Mason. You're exactly the woman I've been waiting to meet. And now that I've found you, I'm hanging on.' He pulled her close and kissed her again—a kiss mixed with passion and love. When he released her from the kiss, she slid off his lap and curled up next to him.

'We're going to be fine, Casey. We'll work through any differences. I promise you we'll be fine.'

Suddenly confidence replaced all her fear—confidence that they could work through anything, so long as they did it together.

CHAPTER 31

They arrived back at Casey's unit early the following afternoon. Casey stopped the car and turned to Nick.

'Would you mind if I run over to see Taylor for a half hour? I want to tell her what's happening, and I think it might be more comfortable for her if I go on my own. I won't be long.'

He leaned across and kissed her gently. 'Take as long as you need. I'll have a look at what sports are on and when you get back we can decide what you want to do for dinner. I want to take you somewhere nice to celebrate.'

Her heart nearly burst with joy. This was really happening. 'I'd love to. I won't be long.' She separated her keys, gave him the one to the front door, and then quickly rang to make sure Taylor was home before driving over to her place.

Taylor had a plate of shortbreads on the table, along with a pot of Casey's favourite tea.

'Sounded like you needed some girl-talk. Hope the weekend went okay?' Taylor asked, frowning.

Casey took a sip of her tea, trying to keep a straight face, but it was near impossible. Finally, she set the cup down and stopped trying to hide her smile. 'He asked me to marry him.'

'What? You're kidding, right? You're having a lend of me, aren't you?'

'No, I'm serious. He said he'd stay here if I wanted him to. Then he asked me to marry him.'

Taylor shook her head back and forth, but her eyes couldn't hide her joy. 'Oh. My. God. Did he get you a ring and everything? I want all the details.'

Casey explained about her fall off the horse and how the rest of the night had gone, while Taylor asked a million questions. At the end of it, Casey shrugged. 'It is wonderful, but there is one niggling little problem.'

Taylor tilted her head inquisitively. 'What's that?'

'You, of course. I'm going to miss you so much. I'll probably become a Platinum frequent flyer, with all trips back to see you.'

Taylor threw her hands up, waving them enthusiastically. 'Uh, no. I'll be there with you, silly.'

Casey felt her face scrunching up. 'You want to go back to California?'

'Uh, yeah, of course I do. When we were there at Christmas, I spotted these two vacant shops up the end of Main Street, just past the saloon. At the time, I'd thought either of them would make a great location for a bakery. I'd sort of put it out of my head, but when Nick arrived here to see you, I went online and have been watching them ever since. They're both still on the market.'

Casey shook her head, frowning with disbelief. 'Why didn't you tell me you wanted to stay when we were there?'

'I had that offer on the bakery at the time—you do know I'm still fuming over his counter-offer, right? I mean, what nerve, thinking he could come up with such an inflated price when I'm the one who built most of the goodwill in the business—anyway, things are different now, so if you're going, so am I.' Taylor raised a brow as her smile widened.

How hadn't she known this earlier? 'So, is this about Denver? Is he the reason you want to go back?'

Taylor shrugged coyly. 'Denver's part of it, for sure, but it's also the town itself. And Alex and Darleen, and all the ladies I met while working on the bake-sale. But there was no way I was going without you, so even when my offer for the bakery got knocked back, I couldn't see any point mentioning it.'

Casey shook her head, finding it hard to believe everything was falling into place so easily. 'So, should we ring Mum and tell her the good news?'

~~*~~

The following morning, Casey went to the flower shop and quickly got all the orders completed. She was anxious to get back to Nick, but there was one more person she had to talk to—Maree.

Sitting at an outdoor table at their favourite coffee spot, she broke the news gently.

Maree sipped her coffee slowly as she listened, then set the cup down and sighed. 'As much as I'm going to hate losing you, I think it's wonderful,' she said, warmth penetrating what was normally her businesslike façade. 'I'd do the same thing if I were in your shoes.'

'Really? You don't think I'm a fool for not jumping at the chance to buy into your business?'

'Honey, I need you much more than you need me. In fact, the way you've handled everything I've thrown at you, you'll have no trouble running your own business. I'd hoped tempting you with buying into mine might be enough for you, but I didn't pin much hope on that.'

'Oh, Maree. I think Nick is *the one*. I owe it to myself to see where our relationship goes.'

'Of course you do.' Maree picked up her spoon and scraped the froth from inside the cup. 'Like I said, I do understand. I certainly don't blame you for wanting to see how things work out.'

Casey let out a sigh of relief—encouraged by Maree's support. 'Thank you for understanding. It's important, because I really do appreciate everything you've done for me.'

Maree looked off into the distance, appearing deep in thought. 'It's been my pleasure having you here. And now, I wish you the best of luck, even though I've never had much luck with romance myself.'

Casey had always wondered about Maree, about why she wasn't married. She was certainly an attractive woman. 'Is that why you're still single?'

'Oh, honey, I'm not *still single*. I'm divorced—three times over. Each time I got divorced, I swore it would be the last time I'd fall for a man, and then I'd meet someone new and I'd give marriage another go. Thank God I didn't let any of them get their claws into this business of mine. That's something for you to keep in mind if you do end up buying your own shop. Try to keep your finances separate. But enough about that,' she said, slapping her hands onto the tops of her thighs. 'I think it's wonderful that you've met someone you're crazy about. Seriously, I wish you the best of luck with everything.'

Casey forced a smile onto her lips even though it saddened her to be leaving. 'I'm probably gonna need all the luck I can get. There are a number of things we don't see eye to eye on.'

Maree's face crinkled into a thousand laugh lines as she tried to hide her smirk. 'I find that hard to believe ... that you'd disagree with someone.' She rolled her eyes dramatically in a way that went well with the underlying sarcasm. 'Boy, I am going to miss you so much—you crack me up. But who knows, maybe I'll come over for a visit. If there was anywhere in the world I'd want to live besides Melbourne, I think it would be the San Francisco Bay Area.'

'Really? I'd love it if you came over to visit. You'd be welcome, any time.'

'I just might take you up on that.' Maree stood, pushing her chair back from the table. 'I know you'll be a success at whatever you decide to do, but if things don't work out the way you hope they will, know that as long as I own this business, you'll have a place back here.'

Casey stood and gave Maree a hug, and then they walked in silence as they made their way back to the shop.

When Casey pulled into her driveway a few hours later, her stomach growled as she thought about grabbing a pizza and heading to the beach again. All she'd had since breakfast was the coffee she'd had with Maree.

She opened the door and called out, 'Honey, I'm home,' just to be silly, but when she inhaled, she was met by the most beautiful aroma of warm spices. Had Nick been cooking? He didn't strike her as the type, and yet he lived alone so it made sense that he would know how to cook.

'Welcome home, honey-bun,' Nick said in the same jaunty voice she'd used. He was grinning, and carrying one of her big wooden spoons.

'What is that delicious aroma?' she asked, inhaling the scent again.

'Curry. I sure hope it tastes as good as it smells.'

'I didn't know you could cook curries,' she said, cocking her head, her grin erupting into a full-blown smile.

'It's something I picked up from Devin's mother. She's a fabulous cook, and last time I was there, I took photos of a couple of her recipes. This one calls for chicken, but I substituted cauliflower, and I think it should be okay.'

She threw her arms around him as he planted a kiss on her forehead, but as she pulled back she shook her head. 'You are full of surprises, Mr Gold, absolutely full of surprises. And I look forward to discovering each and every one of them.'

~*~ THANK YOU ~*~

Thank you for taking the time to read this second book in the *Romancing the Californian Cowboys* series. If you've enjoyed this book, please consider leaving a review on Amazon or Goodreads as this helps other readers to find the book.

If you are interested in hearing the song Casey wrote, and Nick sang, here is the link on YouTube: https://youtu.be/0zJ3YOPR_oM

I'm working on the next in the series, which is Taylor's story, but in the mean time you may also like to look at my other series, the *Copperhead Creek Australian Romance* series, which is set in the sleepy rural town of Willows, Australia.

The fictitious town of Willows is located in Victoria's Golden Triangle, the home of Australia's 1850s Gold Rush, and is inspired by small towns scattered throughout Victoria and South Australia. Each book can be read as a stand-alone featuring a new couple who find their own happy ending, but if you read the books in order you'll find characters from earlier books making reappearances as the lives of the small town residents overlap and tangle.

The books in the *Copperhead Creek Australian Romance* series are:

Taking a Chance (a FREE series prequel)
A Chance to Come True
A Chance to Get it Right
A Chance to Let Go
A Chance to Belong
A Chance for Snow
Murder at the Creek – A Copperhead Creek Mystery

~*~ ABOUT S M SPENCER ~*~

S M Spencer grew up in the San Francisco Bay Area where she rode horses along the beaches and across the tops of the rolling coastal hills of California. In the 1980s she was offered a job in Australia, which was the beginning of an adventure of which she has never tired. Still living in Australia, she writes from the semi-rural home she shares with her husband, horses, cats and dogs, as well as the kangaroos that pass through the paddocks from time to time.

You can find all of S M Spencer's books by visiting S M Spencer's Author Page at Amazon:
https://www.amazon.com/S-M-Spencer/e/B00PGE0G9U/

And never miss a new book, or a promotion, by following S M Spencer's blog: http://smspencer.online/blog/

www.ingramcontent.com/pod-product-compliance
Lightning Source LLC
LaVergne TN
LVHW091044080826
845145LV00002B/622

9781922270696